PLAYING WITH FIRE

PLAYING WITH FIRE

A Daniel Jacobus Mystery

Gerald Elias

severn
House

This first world edition published 2016
in Great Britain and the USA by
SEVERN HOUSE PUBLISHERS LTD of
19 Cedar Road, Sutton, Surrey, England, SM2 5DA.
Trade paperback edition first published
in Great Britain and the USA 2016 by
SEVERN HOUSE PUBLISHERS LTD

British Library Cataloguing in Publication Data
A CIP catalogue record for this title is available from the British Library.

ISBN-13: 978-0-7278-8614-9 (cased)
ISBN-13: 978-1-84751-715-9 (trade paper)
ISBN-13: 978-1-78010-776-9 (e-book)

All Severn House titles are printed on acid-free paper.

Severn House Publishers support the Forest Stewardship Council™ [FSC™],
the leading international forest certification organisation.
All our titles that are printed on FSC certified paper carry the FSC logo.

Typeset by Palimpsest Book Production Ltd.,
Falkirk, Stirlingshire, Scotland.
Printed and bound in Great Britain by
TJ International, Padstow, Cornwall.

To the Memory of Peter Prier, Violinmaker and friend

Shivering and frozen mid the frosty snow,
In biting stinging winds;
Running to and fro, stamping icy feet,
Teeth chattering in the bitter chill.

Resting contentedly beside the hearth
Whilst those outside are drenched by pouring rain.

We tread the icy path with greatest care for fear of slipping and
*   sliding.*
With a reckless turn we fall crashing to the ground and, rising,
Hasten across the ice lest it should crack.
We feel the chill north winds course through the home
Despite the locked and bolted doors . . .
This is winter, but still what joy it brings.

Sonnet by Antonio Vivaldi for his violin concerto,
'Winter,' from the Four Seasons
(Translation by David Cowley and Gerald Elias)

PART ONE

ONE

*T*he Largo from Winter of Vivaldi's Four Seasons floated from the living room into the cold December night. How it managed so effortlessly to permeate the window, which throbbed jelly-fish-like to the music's pulse, was perplexing, if miraculous. The music then ascended skyward, like gossamer, meeting the snow halfway. 'And a Merry Christmas to you!' Snow, on its way down, said to Music. Smiling, Music tipped his ear-flapped hat.

It seemed perfectly natural to Jacobus when the two new acquaintances then ingeniously transmuted into Glasnost and Perestroika, the legendary Russian pairs figure skating champions. Mounted on a smiling pig, they sped over the ice frictionless, as if flying, and their glossy costumes and long hair streamed behind them in the wind. They spun and leaped to the Vivaldi, defying gravity.

A jarring, threatening alarm interrupted their frolic. Glasnost, Perestroika, and the pig courageously maintained their smiles even as an immense cement wall, barring their path, suddenly loomed. 'Tear it down! Tear it down!' a determined yet comforting voice intoned, but it was too late. They slammed into the wall, and everything disintegrated into a cosmology of sparkling brilliance.

'Jake! Jake!' a new voice intruded.

'Don't shake me,' Jacobus said but feared his words were unintelligible. To his own ears it sounded like '*aahnngh.*' He curled up into fetal position on his threadbare couch, determined to avoid his own disintegration.

'Wake up, Jake.'

'Huh?' he replied.

'You were dreaming,' Yumi said. 'I hope it was a good one.'

'I wasn't sleeping,' Jacobus muttered. 'Just resting.'

The harsh ringing of his old rotary telephone, the culprit which had changed the course of his dream, finally stopped, but the Vivaldi continued. *A good recording*, Jacobus noted. *Excellent, in fact.*

Jacobus maneuvered into a more comfortable position. His big toe poking through the hole in his favorite pair of argyle socks, he stretched his cold feet over the edge of the couch and closer to the woodstove for warmth.

'Who was on the phone?' he asked.

'I don't know,' Yumi said. 'They hung up.'

'Who's playing the Vivaldi?' he asked.

'Me!' Yumi replied. 'Do you like it?'

Jacobus considered his response.

'It's no Paganini.'

'Well, Merry Christmas anyway!' Yumi laughed. 'That's my gift to you. Along with your very first CD player!'

'Christmas isn't until tomorrow,' Jacobus said. He turned his back to Yumi and acted as if he were going back to sleep.

'You can't fool me, Daniel Jacobus. When you're grumpy it means you're happy.'

'Then I must be very happy,' he said and put the pillow over his head.

In reality, it had been as pleasant a day as Jacobus could remember. *The rest of the world may be going to hell, but thank you, Vivaldi, for creating a few minutes of heaven on earth.* That was as close to the Christmas spirit as Jacobus was willing to venture.

The pork roast didn't tarnish his mood, either. Its succulent, rosemary-laden aroma beckoned enticingly and his empty stomach responded with an urgent rumble.

'Dinner ready yet?' he hollered.

'Any minute now,' Nathaniel called from the kitchen. 'Unless you need more rest time.'

They continued to listen to Yumi's recording while they ate. The four violin concertos Vivaldi ingeniously crafted were based upon sonnets Vivaldi, himself, had written. The music depicted the seasons of the year in the Italian countryside, replete with imitations of ice cracking, bird calls, drunken peasants, rainstorms, gunshots, and dying rabbits. Even as he filled his stomach with pork, potatoes, and Pommard, Jacobus listened approvingly, both to the music and to Yumi's performance. Nathaniel informed Jacobus – something which Yumi had asked him not to do – that the CD had recently won a Grammy.

If Jacobus worshiped any god it was music, and God forbid anyone took its name in vain. Violin lessons with Jacobus made even the most precocious student cringe under his unadulterated honesty. So-called child prodigies, and their ambitious parents and teachers, were a special target of his slings and arrows. He referred to them as 'human *foie gras*,' providing high cholesterol pleasure at the expense of being involuntarily force-fed by from the time they were hatched until their premature demise.

The stony path Jacobus offered, though, was lined with a garden of insight into the beauty of music and how to achieve it, richer than any Yumi had encountered before or since. She had been Jacobus's prize protégé, one of the few students able to not only withstand, but also to thrive under the intensity of his undiluted, piquant criticism.

Jacobus had challenged Yumi, when she began studying with him as a teen, to use her brains, her imagination, and most of all her heart, at a time when she believed that only the hands mattered to become a great violinist. But three years with Jacobus more than prepared her for the ultracritical world of classical music in which her star had risen to prominence above the international horizon.

What Yumi was never aware of, and what Jacobus would never tell her – he would hardly admit it to himself – was that her arrival from Japan at his doorstep long ago had yanked his life from the throes of an inexorable downward spiral. *If not for her*, he thought, and took another sip of wine.

After dinner they toasted the season with a bottle of seventeen-year-old Macallan that was Nathaniel's holiday gift to Jacobus. Trotsky, Jacobus's mammoth bulldog, lay indolently by the wood-stove as he gnawed contentedly on his own Christmas present, the shoulder bone of the pork roast.

Nathaniel lifted his glass once again.

'A toast,' he said. '*Here we will sit and let the sounds of music creep in our ears. Soft stillness and the night become touches of sweet harmony.*'

'*Twelfth Night*,' said Jacobus, draining his glass.

'*Merchant of Venice*, actually.'

'Whatever.'

Jacobus's phone rang again.

'Ignore it,' he said. 'I got something for you.' At length the ringing stopped.

Jacobus presented Nathaniel with a Size XXXL robe he'd bought in Great Barrington. He was confident Nathaniel would like the feel of the flannel, and the price was right, too. It was only when Nathaniel commented with the well-intentioned sincerity of a runner-up, 'My favorite colors. Green and pink stripes,' that Jacobus understood the reason for the fifty-percent markdown. *One advantage of blindness*, Jacobus thought. *It saves you a lot of money.*

'I guess I should give something to you, too,' he said to Yumi. He retreated to a corner of the living room where a pile of dust-covered LPs lay on the floor. Jacobus felt for the minuscule item he had stashed on top of the pile months ago, waiting for this moment.

'Here,' he said.

Yumi delicately opened the package that Jacobus had wrapped in a sheet of newspaper and carelessly bound with masking tape. It was an old score of Beethoven's String Quartet, Opus 130. Faded and brittle like Jacobus, it was the kind of thing that could sit unnoticed forever in an antique shop next to a collection of John Denver LPs.

For Jacobus, the Opus 130 was the greatest, most profound quartet in the entire repertoire. He had bought the score as a penniless student and took it to a Carnegie Hall performance by the Budapest String Quartet, his heroes. After the concert he brashly sneaked backstage, evading a battalion of wary security personnel. To reward his audacity each member of the quartet autographed the score. Other than his violin, that score was Jacobus's most valued possession and Yumi knew it. When she hugged him more tightly than she had planned, Jacobus said, 'Careful, you'll mess up my hair.'

'I don't think you've combed it since Thanksgiving,' Nathaniel said.

Yumi proposed that to add to the festivities they dive into their favorite Corelli trio sonatas before it got too late. As with almost all of their get-togethers, Yumi brought her violin and Nathaniel his cello. Jacobus, being blind, had of course memorized his part ages ago. His two sighted friends, meanwhile, precariously balanced their weighty music on flimsy folding music stands.

Both Yumi and Jacobus well knew that his former student had surpassed the teacher as a violinist. She was in the prime of her career as a concertmaster of the famed orchestra, Harmonium, and Jacobus was old and tired and couldn't be bothered to practice with any regularity. When he felt like playing, he played. When he didn't, his eighteenth-century Italian partner waited unceremoniously in its case for its next call-up. But even though Yumi and he understood their new status implicitly, Jacobus could still hear a nervous reticence when she played with him, the residual after-effects of their original relationship, as if she still needed his approval. It made him chuckle.

Nathaniel and Jacobus's friendship went back even further. They had been fellow students and professional trio colleagues, but over the years Nathaniel's passion for public performance waned, partly from stress and partly from being a black man in a white man's world. He rarely mentioned the race issue to Jacobus, to whom he was grateful for being color-blind even before he lost his sight. These days the demographics of the classical music world were substantially altered – a lot more women, a lot more Asians – but the number of African Americans were essentially the same: insignificant. So, more resigned than bitter, Nathaniel's interests gradually transitioned from music to musical instruments. He became an expert consultant in art and musical instrument fraud and theft, but continued to play cello when his mood dictated. This evening was one of those times.

Midway through the first Allegro of Corelli's A Major sonata, the phone rang for the third time, interrupting their music-making. Yumi offered to answer it but Jacobus said no, any disturbance on an otherwise memorable night could only be for the worse. After eight rings it stopped.

On into the winter night the music resounded, and when they finally played themselves out they put their instruments away. Jacobus nestled back into his dilapidated couch, whose old cushions conformed to the impression of his body, seeking a position to mollify his digestive tract. Jacobus asked Yumi to turn his new CD player back on and play a recording of Corelli's beloved *Christmas Concerto*. He could never get enough Corelli, even if one of these days he'd have to memorize where all the buttons on the newfangled gizmo were.

Nathaniel settled into the easy chair, and before long *The Merchant of Venice* slid from his hands. Rather than '*the sounds of music*,' the sounds of his snoring crept into Jacobus's ears. But on this night, even that didn't bother him. Yumi seated herself at a half-finished jigsaw puzzle of the Last Supper that Nathaniel had purchased for fifty cents at a Black Friday sale at the dollar store in Great Barrington. She had just found a piece that looked like it might be a part of the Passover tablecloth when, for the fourth time, the telephone rang. Its shrill G-sharp, ugly and discordant, clashed

with the sublime G major chord that ended the Pastorale of the
Christmas Concerto.

The phone startled Trotsky, who cradled his treasured bone in
his gaping maw and skulked off, seeking refuge in a far corner.

'Answer it,' Jacobus muttered to whomever.

'Are you sure?' Yumi asked.

'Yeah. It's driving me nuts. They just don't give up. And, Jesus
Christ, on Christmas Eve.'

Yumi let it ring ten times before she lifted the receiver.

'It's Amadeo Borlotti,' Yumi said to Jacobus, her hand over the
receiver.

Borlotti? Jacobus thought. The name was vaguely familiar. Yes,
it came back to him now. *A small-time violin repairman whose
reputation was untarnished by notable achievement.* Borlotti had
plied his trade not so far away in Egremont Falls, selling strings and
supplies and patching up student fiddles. Well, a living's a living.
There was never a shortage of fiddles dropped 'by accident' on the
gymnasium floor by passive aggressive adolescents after having
etched their initials on the instruments' backs with penknives. Jacobus
would never have trusted his precious Gagliano with someone like
Borlotti, who, as far as he knew, was little more than a hack.

*Why the hell's Amadeo Borlotti calling me on Christmas Eve,
and at this time of night?*

Jacobus rolled over on the creaking couch, his back to the rest
of the world.

'Tell him I don't need any rosin. When I do I'll call him. Should
be in about five years, more or less.'

'It's not that,' said Yumi. 'He wants to come see you.'

'Fine.' Jacobus heard Nathaniel stir. 'Nathaniel, are we doing
anything between now and New Year's Eve?'

'Nope. Free as birds.' Nathaniel yawned and made his way to
the jigsaw puzzle.

'What I thought. Yumi, invite Borlotti sometime next year. Shall
we say April? Maybe July?'

'He wants to come over tonight. He says it's urgent. Here, you
talk to him.'

Before Jacobus could protest further, Yumi pressed the phone
into his hand. He felt Yumi's weight, light though it was, settle on
to his hip. He held the receiver to his ear.

'Yeah.'

'Mr Jacobus,' said Borlotti. 'There is something I must tell you. It's very important. You are the only one who would understand. It's very important.'

'Third time's a charm,' Jacobus said.

'I don't understand.'

'You've already told me twice it's very important. One more time, maybe I'll believe you.'

Jacobus curled his legs to give Yumi more room, setting his stomach to growling again.

'It . . . it is a long story. I don't feel right talking over the phone. May I come to your home? Tonight? Now? It's only twenty minutes. I can be right there.'

'I don't want to be a party-pooper, Borlotti,' said Jacobus, 'but it's past my bedtime, and my elves have informed me my driveway's already covered with snow. If you killed yourself trying to navigate it at night my insurance company would raise my premium.'

'But—'

'Listen, Borlotti, tomorrow's Sunday. Christmas Day. Why don't you stop by in the morning? It should be plowed by then, and I tell you what? I'll have a pot of Christmas coffee going. We can eat figgy pudding and watch *Heidi* together.'

'Not tonight?'

'No dice.'

'How early tomorrow?'

'Whenever the cock crows, or nine o'clock, whichever is later.'

'All right, Mr Jacobus, if that is what it must be. Thank you.' He added, 'Merry Christmas.'

'And God bless us, every one,' Jacobus said and hung up.

'That was nice of you to invite him over,' Yumi said.

'My Christmas spirit. How could I say no? He was nervous as Trotsky getting a Parvo shot.'

'Why does he need to see you?'

'Beats me. The last time I went to his shop was years ago for an emergency repair. My student what's-her-face came for a lesson and her soundpost collapsed.'

'Poor kid,' said Yumi.

'Poor kid? Lucky me! She had a tone a chainsaw would envy.'

'I have a student who sounds like that.'

'Maybe it's her son.'

'Could be. I wish I had earplugs when he comes for a lesson.'

'What advice do you give him?'

'Switch to trombone.'

'Very sage.'

'I learned from the best.'

'Advice like that could put people like Borlotti out of business,' Nathaniel interjected, taking a moment from his concentration on the jigsaw puzzle.

'I went to Mr Borlotti's shop on my way back to the city once,' said Yumi, 'just to buy a set of strings. He was a very sweet man.'

'Ah, I like my women like I like my bagels!' Jacobus exclaimed.

'What do you mean?'

'Crusty on the outside, soft on the inside.'

'Like your head, with a hole in the middle.'

'How dare you talk to your elder like that?'

'As I said, I learned from the best.'

Yumi pinched Jacobus's bristly cheek, making him smile.

'Do you want me to tidy up the house for Mr Borlotti?' she asked.

'No, for God's sake!' Jacobus crooned croakingly, '*I've grown accustomed to this place.*'

'No doubt,' said Nathaniel. 'You've had the same junk for forty years.'

'Wall-to-wall clutter becomes you,' Yumi said to Jacobus.

'Thank you.'

'But when he's here Mr Borlotti might want to be able to walk in a straight line.'

'To quote my favorite hero,' Jacobus said, '"Bah! Humbug!"' Something clicked in his memory. 'And what was the name of Borlotti's shop? Something tacky. Like bad Dickens.'

'Ye Olde Violin Shoppe,' said Nathaniel.

'That's it! That's one reason I never went back. What's with this "ye" crap?' Jacobus lamented. 'It's bad enough they misspell words like "old" and "shop" when they put a damn "e" at the end of them, but "ye" doesn't even mean "the." It means "you"!'

'You sound like Andy Rooney,' said Yumi.

'Andy Rooney!' Jacobus barked. 'Andy Rooney's a curmudgeon!'

'Ho! Ho!' laughed Nathaniel. 'And what may you be, Daniel Jacobus?'

'Me?' he replied pensively. 'I am an analyst.'

The three lapsed back into their easy silence, eventually broken when Yumi volunteered to do the dishes. Jacobus mumbled that since she had washed them the night before, he'd take care of it.

He would have preferred waiting until morning, but if he did, the mice would make his house their winter mecca and crap all over the place. Ah, the hell with the mice. He'd do the dishes tomorrow.

'And why were you so damn reluctant to answer the phone just now?' he asked Yumi.

'Oh, just superstition,' she said.

'What superstition?'

'For Japanese, the number four is unlucky. It was the fourth time the phone rang.'

'What's so unlucky about it?'

'One of our words for the number four, *shi*, has another meaning.'

'It also means thirteen?' Jacobus said, pleased with his wit.

'No. It also means death.'

TWO

Christmas Day, Sunday, December 25

Contrary to predictions, the snow continued through the night. By Christmas morning, Yumi's fire engine red Camaro, which she had driven from New York City with Nathaniel, was locatable only by the antenna protruding like a periscope from a drifting sea of white.

Jacobus, in his pajamas, taking his turn at the puzzle table, was distracted from his intense concentration assembling Leonardo's masterpiece by touch alone when Nathaniel commented that the driveway hadn't been plowed.

'That's not good news,' Jacobus said.

Yumi shared Jacobus's misgivings.

'Do you think my baby will be OK?' she asked.

'The hell with your car,' Jacobus said. 'How's Borlotti going to get here? How are they going to deliver my *Sunday Times*? And what's a supposedly self-respecting young lady doing with a car like that, anyway?'

'Now that she's concertmaster of Harmonium,' Nathaniel retorted, 'a job, I might add, you helped her win, she can afford whatever car she wants.'

'I'd rather be in your '78 Rabbit.'

'That's because Nathaniel's Rabbit's just like you,' Yumi said. 'Zero to sixty in three hours.'

'*Et tu, Brute,*' Jacobus said. He returned to the jigsaw puzzle, but the aggressive patter of windblown snow rattling the house's windowpanes was an insistent reminder of the increasing improbability of Amadeo Borlotti's visit. With his driveway impassable, Jacobus called Borlotti to reschedule, dialing the numbers on his phone by feel. The ringing at the other end, higher pitched and faster than customary, suggested something might be amiss with the phone. Whatever the issue, Borlotti didn't answer and there was no answering machine. Perplexed, Jacobus finally hung up.

'You'd think he'd be inside,' he groused.

'Maybe he's on his way here,' Yumi suggested, ever the optimist.

'He'd have to be dumber than Trotsky to drive in this kind of weather.'

'Maybe he's at home and not at his shop,' said Nathaniel, ever the pragmatist.

'If I recollect, his shop, or shall I say "shoppe," is in his house. Old World style.'

'Well then, maybe the phone's out of order with this weather. Or he's out shoveling. Or at Mass.'

'Catholics.' Jacobus shook his head, taking a cue that Nathaniel did not intend. The very idea that Borlotti might have gone to church in a blizzard provided confirmation yet again – not that he sought it – of the absurdity of all religion, in Jacobus's unbiased view.

With no *Times* in the offing, so went the opportunity to indulge in the time-honored ritual of Nathaniel reading the news, Jacobus pontificating upon it, and Yumi rolling her eyes. The only newspaper on hand was a three-day-old *Shopper's Guide*, and for Jacobus there was but a single purpose for that free weekly advertiser: starting a fire.

He cautiously felt the air around the wood stove. Determining that the heat had dissipated sufficiently overnight, he gingerly gripped the still-warm handle, opened the door to the stove, and tossed in a few crumpled pages. Within seconds, he heard dormant embers begin to crackle.

'Let there be light,' Jacobus proclaimed with sacerdotal reverence when he heard them burst into flame. The heat quickly caressed his face and warmed the metal frames of his dark glasses. Retreating to his couch, he almost tripped over the great bulk of Trotsky, who had taken his proprietary, prone position next to the stove.

'Careful, Jake,' Yumi said.

'I know where I'm going.'

'Not that. A cinder popped out of the stove. I'll shovel it up. I wouldn't want you to catch on fire.'

'Now there's an idea,' said Jacobus.

'You want to catch on fire?' Nathaniel asked.

'Not me. Brünnhilde. Since there's no *Times*, how about a little immolation, at least until we find out if Borlotti'll show up? I haven't listened to Götterdämmerung since Birgit Nillson kicked the bucket. That ought to warm our Christmas cockles.'

Trotsky, with the acute sixth sense dogs possess, pawed at the front door to escape the five-hour Wagnerian marathon. Nathaniel opened the door and found a wall of new snow. Though as old as Jacobus, Nathaniel was a stronger, much larger man – horizontally so in recent years – and managed to shovel a small alley to give Trotsky a head start on his odyssey to his favorite tree. The dog, oblivious to the snow as he was to most things, tunneled into the drifts and disappeared.

Nathaniel closed the door and turned on the LP of Götterdämmerung, Hildegard Behrens singing Brünnhilde. Yumi made a pot of Jacobus's favorite coffee – percolated instant Folgers – and Jacobus resumed work on the puzzle.

Decades ago, Jacobus lost his sight literally overnight to foveo-macular dystrophy, in a single stroke ending his promising career as a concert violinist. With that drastic change in his life's path, he made an intensive effort to rally his other senses to compensate for his lost one. As a musician, his most precious commodity was hearing, so that came first. He dedicated a half hour a day listening to an encyclopedia of almost inaudible sounds that others wouldn't even have perceived, from floor creaks to melting icicles, composing an aural picture of the world around him. For smell, he 'memorized' the aroma of innumerable teas, coffees, cigarettes, and cigars. And even of perfumes and colognes, not that he would ever apply such odious concoctions to his own body, but simply to have a way to test himself against a labeled product.

Not the least of his long-term development projects had been to hone his tactile memory, already highly advanced as a professional musician. Jacobus took up the jigsaw challenge mainly because people told him he'd never be able to do it. Starting with an eight-piece wooden turtle, '*for Toddlers to Six Years*,' he gradually worked his way to five-hundred-piece puzzles. He could have gone to a thousand, he boasted, but he found them boring and repetitious.

His puzzle assembly method required the crucial, first step of feeling both sides of each piece with his fingertips, placing the shiny side face up. Then he felt the lobes and crannies of each and sorted them based upon similarity of shape. Corners and edges pieces he could do in his sleep. Finally, with an 'Aha!' of self-satisfaction, he found the correct piece and inserted it into a welcoming opening.

'I don't think it goes there, Jake,' Yumi said, placing a mug of coffee on the table with a calculated thud that enabled Jacobus to hear the mug's precise location.

'Of course it does. It fits perfectly.'

'Maybe not. I don't recall that Leonardo painted a pomegranate in the middle of Jesus' face.'

'Unless it was during his Magritte period,' Nathaniel added.

'Go to hell, both of you,' said Jacobus. 'But first give me the phone.'

He dialed Borlotti's number again with the same result as before. Trotsky, gleeful and covered with snow, barked to be let back into the house.

After Götterdämmerung's two-hour first act, Nathaniel donned his apron in Jacobus's oft-neglected kitchen. He conjured up his Kentucky grandmother's recipe for a savory stew of beef and root vegetables in a cast-iron pot, which simmered on the wood stove during the second and third acts. At the opera's climax, Brünnhilde rode her heroic steed, Grane, into the flames to join Sigfried, her lord and lover, for eternity. Thus the curtain fell on the Twilight of the Gods and dusk settled upon the Berkshires. The stew, its flavor enhanced by the pungent aroma of woodsmoke, was ready.

'Only a warped genius like Wagner could create ecstasy out of self-immolation,' Jacobus said, digging unceremoniously into a turnip.

'Don't you think there's a connection between pleasure and pain?' Yumi asked.

'What do you mean?'

'I never knew what they were singing about at the end there, but if you read the libretto: "*Radiant in the fire, there lies your lord,*

Siegfried, my blessed hero. Are you neighing for joy to follow your friend? Do the laughing flames lure you to him? Feel my bosom too, how it burns; a bright fire fastens on my heart to embrace him, enfolded in his arms, to be one with him in the intensity of love!"

'Couldn't one argue that the greater the pain, the greater the pleasure?'

Jacobus was about to agree, in theory at least, but then he considered the three pillars of pain on which his life had been based: his abuse as a youth at the hands of a judge at the Grimsley violin competition; the death of his parents in a German extermination camp; and the blindness which deprived him of a career as a concert artist.

'No,' he finally replied. 'No. You'd have to be a real sicko. Except for the part about feeling her bosom.'

After eating too much yet again, Jacobus collapsed on the couch and Nathaniel fell asleep in the old recliner. Jacobus tried calling Borlotti once more, but this time he couldn't even get a dial tone and roundly cursed the phone company for having allowed their wires to succumb to a measly blizzard.

Yumi tried calling on her mobile phone but the device searched unsuccessfully for a signal.

'Don't you get cell phone service here?' she asked Jacobus.

'How the hell would I know?'

Grumbling under his breath, Jacobus added a few logs to the woodstove to last through the night. Using the potholder that he kept on top of the woodpile next to the stove, he reached for the hot handle on the front, which he knew by design was directly above the single raised brick in the middle front of the hearth. After opening the door and adding the logs, he turned down the baffle handle on the left side of the stove, efficiently redirecting the heat that had been going straight up the chimney into a system of S-curves. Then, in the back of the stove, where there was a self-adjusting coil that attached by a chain to a metal flap that regulated how much heat the stove was producing, Jacobus closed the flap so that the fire would burn slowly all night. Finally, again on the left side of the stove, there was a one-inch hole, which, if closed by rotating a small panel over it, would essentially cut off the remaining air supply to the fire and slowly extinguish it. Jacobus carefully closed it halfway, so that in the morning the smoldering coals would be reduced to glowing, easily reignited embers. Usually a comfort to

Jacobus, on this occasion the chore evoked a troubling ennui, the origin of which he could not yet define.

Jacobus sat in front of the stove long after he had chased Nathaniel and Yumi away, all but ordering them to go to bed and leave him alone. From time to time a charred log inside the stove would collapse on itself and send a fresh wave of dry heat on to his face. As much as he tried to derive some insight from the heat – comfort, passion, epiphany – it aroused but a single sensation in response to Amadeo Borlotti's sudden, mysterious intrusion into his life. It was a sensation he struggled to dispel from his consciousness but which relentlessly insinuated its way back in, like the cold outside his window, demanding precedence over all others. It was fear.

THREE

Monday, December 26

Jacobus, who resisted sleep for its haunting dreams that persecuted him without warning, was as usual the first one to rise on Monday morning. It hadn't been the muffled whir of tires, informing him that snow-packed Route 41 was now navigable, that awoke him. Rather, it was the same pervasive, undefined unease tugging at the edge of his consciousness that had overcome him when he'd loaded the woodstove the night before.

The fire had burned down and it was cold in the living room. On his knees, he poked at the embers. He blew on them and little by little their liberated heat warmed his face, signaling him to ball up some sheets of old newspaper and place them on the eager coals. Upon hearing the whoosh of the paper's ignition he tossed in some kindling, then a log. The fire was restored.

Jacobus tried Borlotti yet again but the dial tone was still out and his apprehension mounted. He made a pot of coffee, a task at which he had become adept even in blindness. He always kept the can of coffee, the pot, the measuring spoon, the potholder, and the mugs in the same place. He knew how to jiggle the knob on the kitchen stove to boil the water faster, and how many seconds of pouring it would take to fill a mug.

Nathaniel, sporting his new robe, stumbled into the kitchen. Hearing Nathaniel's shuffling, Jacobus said, 'You've certainly perfected the art of burning the candle at neither end. Hibernation suits you.'

'I'll get the cream and sugar,' Nathaniel replied.

Halfway through their second cup, Roy Miller, the town's part-time police force, full-time plumber, and jack of all trades, arrived with his pickup to plow and sand Jacobus's quarter-mile, U-shaped gravel driveway. His customary tack was to barrel down the steep end and utilize the momentum to make a lightning pass back up to Route 41. But today Miller maneuvered very deliberately, backing and filling, backing and filling. Jacobus heard it all, gears grinding and blades scraping.

The noisy production awakened Yumi, who entered the kitchen with a loud yawn.

'Morning! Ooh, it's cold.'

'What time is it?' Jacobus asked Nathaniel.

'Quarter after nine. Why? Yumi not allowed to sleep in on a weekday?'

Jacobus didn't answer, but pensively sipped his boiled coffee. When he heard the truck's engine sputter to a stop, its door open and close, heavy footsteps approach the front of his house, and then the tamping of boots in his doorway, the cause of the distress that had crept insidiously into Jacobus's sleep suddenly came into clear focus.

'Damn,' he muttered to himself. He placed the mug gently on the kitchen table's worn Formica. 'Damn. Damn. Damn. We're too late.'

Yumi welcomed Miller and invited him in, quickly closing the door to keep out the bitter cold and blowing snow. Miller held a copy of the *Berkshire Eagle* in his gloved hand.

'Man, it smells good in here!' Miller said, who, like Nathaniel, had a nose for food, especially in large quantities. 'Been cooking lately?' He had little difficulty tracking down the pot of stew that was still sitting on the woodstove. He sniffed again. 'Jake, you burning pine again? You know you shouldn't be burning fresh pine.'

'Why the hell not?' Jacobus asked.

'Builds creosote. Especially when it's not seasoned. Your flue's too small as it is. You could end up with a chimney fire.'

'Is that a segue?' Jacobus asked.

'Come again?'

'You're here to tell me Amadeo Borlotti's house burned down Saturday night and he's missing, aren't you?'

'How the—?' Miller stammered. 'How did you—?'

'Don't sound so bewildered, Roy,' Jacobus said. He then related his brief but troubling conversation with Amadeo Borlotti on Christmas Eve, followed by the disrupted phone line.

'Sure you didn't read the story in today's *Eagle*?' Miller asked.

'What story?'

Miller handed Nathaniel the newspaper. Nathaniel read the front-page headline: 'Violin-Maker Missing, Home Burns.'

'So you talked to him,' Miller said, 'but that was before it all happened. How did you know there'd been a fire? That he's missing?'

'Give the man a cup of coffee,' Jacobus said to Yumi. 'Have a seat, Roy, and I will endeavor to explain.'

Miller balanced himself gingerly on a creaking kitchen counter stool, taking care that between its age and his weight it didn't collapse.

'Go ahead,' Miller said.

'It's nine-fifteen.'

Miller waited for more, but when none was forthcoming he asked, 'That's it? I must have missed something.'

With the sigh of a schoolteacher reviewing multiplication tables for the eighth time with a recalcitrant student, Jacobus continued. 'I'll start from the beginning, but it's the same reasoning as always. Just remember this: You start with a pattern. It's like Beethoven's Fifth. The entire piece is the inevitable consequence of the pattern set by the first four notes. When the pattern breaks you look for the reason; the stronger the pattern, the more significant the reason. It's really just putting two and two together. Do you understand what I'm talking about, Roy?'

'Haven't a clue, Jake,' Miller said. 'I'm more a Grateful Dead kind of guy.'

'Your loss.' Jacobus took a sip of coffee.

'There's a series of three strange events since Saturday night,' he continued. 'Number one: Borlotti's out-of-the-blue, agitated call, which I've told you about. Number two: yesterday when you did not come to plow. What's significant about that, Roy?'

'Well, is it that I usually plow right after the snow stops?'

'Usually! You're being modest. After all these years, yesterday was the very first time you missed plowing after a snowstorm, ever.'

'But yesterday was Christmas,' Miller responded.

'Yeah, just like it was two years ago when it snowed on Christmas. What happened then?'

'I plowed first thing so I could get to church with the family.'

'My point exactly. I figured there must've been a damn important reason to keep you away yesterday, especially from an extra paycheck to pay for all the Christmas presents. So I asked myself, why wouldn't you be here to plow? Odds were it was an emergency. But was it a plumbing emergency or was it a police emergency? Unlikely you'd disrupt Christmas with the family to fix a frozen pipe. So I'm thinking police emergency, and coming the morning after Borlotti's call, strange event number one, it was not unreasonable to guess there could be – might be – a link. And another unprecedented thing. You didn't even call to tell me you weren't coming.

'Then, when you didn't even show up by last night, that convinced me even more. You've always been the conscientious type. What, I asked myself, would make it so difficult for you to get here? I started with several simple, obvious possibilities, one of which was that you were too far away. Now, as the crow flies, no one could ever say that Egremont Falls, where Borlotti lives, is far away. It's usually only about a twenty-minute drive from here, but in the snowstorm, that twenty minutes could be two hours. Of course you could've been just about anywhere else, too, but after Borlotti's melodramatics, Egremont Falls was at least within the realm of possibility.

'Now for strange event number three: it's now nine fifteen. In the past, when you've cleared my driveway the morning after a night-time snowstorm, it's usually at the crack of dawn because I'm lucky enough to be the first stop on your plowing route, but when you showed up today, a Monday morning, it was already after nine. What could that mean? Knowing your considerate nature, it might have meant that for some reason you first plowed the customers who, unlike me, *had* to get to work. But what would prompt you, today only, to change the usual order? Why make me last and not first? Simple answer: To be able to spend more time here without worrying about angering your other customers by being late to their driveways. By keeping me last you'd have ample time to talk.'

'I did try calling you.'

'Obviously.'

'Obviously?'

'My damn phone line is down, which you wouldn't have known unless you had already tried calling. That's why you had to change the plowing order.

'If, then, the conversation couldn't wait for the phone company to do its usual magic, it would likely mean urgent business. And why in the world would you need to talk to little old me about police work? Answer: only if it related to my single, esoteric field of expertise. That would be fiddles. If Borlotti were in trouble – and by his phone call it sure sounded like trouble, you'd only need to talk to *me* if you couldn't talk to *him* – i.e. if he were dead, missing, or otherwise unavailable.

'So, I ask myself, what might cause you to think that he was missing and not just visiting his Aunt Sadie or unleashing his inner wanderlust? Certainly he wasn't missing when he called me, and nobody in his right mind was out and about Saturday night in the middle of a blizzard.

'Could he have suddenly gone on vacation? I don't think so! He was pretty anxious to want to see me yesterday morning, so it's highly unlikely he packed his Bermuda shorts and flew to Miami Beach for a spur-of-the-moment Christmas getaway. But even if he had, that wouldn't have been cause for concern because there would at least have been a paper trail for you to work with. Absent that, you must have had a heckuva reason to believe things weren't kosher. Something dramatic. Hell, you're not even the cop on his beat, so that means the Egremont Falls police had a special need for you.

'A burglary, maybe? Again, I don't think so. Let's say for the moment his shop had been broken into. If Borlotti had been there he would've called it in and you wouldn't be here this morning. So, it can only be that he *wasn't* there and you have no way of figuring out his whereabouts. What's a possible scenario, consistent with Borlotti's anxiety, that would prevent you from being able to find his metaphorical Bermuda shorts? A fire.'

'Or a kidnapping,' Nathaniel said.

'I considered that,' Jacobus replied. 'It's possible. But on a night like that getting away with it and not leaving any trace would have been a challenge. And since Roy here obviously hasn't heard from anyone with a ransom demand, I vote for fire.'

Jacobus paused for another sip, as did Miller. His mug, poised

in his hand since Jacobus had begun his explication, actually had
not yet made as far as his lips.

'But how do you know he's missing and not dead?' Miller asked,
pouring the now-cold coffee into the sink for a hot refill.

'That's self-evident, isn't it?' said Jacobus. 'If Borlotti had
died of natural causes you wouldn't have come here at all. By
the same token, if he'd been murdered you'd have had more
important business than to chitchat over coffee. But because you
don't know for certain he's alive, you want to find him before he
isn't, and you need my help to find him. And that's why the
Egremont Falls police wanted you on the scene, because of your
connection to me.'

'Well, maybe you're making sense, Jake. Maybe not. You've got
to admit it's just a theory.'

'Yeah, well Darwin had a theory, too.'

'And some people still doubt it.'

'That's because they haven't evolved yet.'

'Well, there *was* a fire. And Borlotti *is* missing . . . probably. But
we don't know yet if it was arson.'

'Don't worry. Everything will work out for the worst.'

FOUR

The outside temperature had dipped below zero, and only
Miller's promise of a free brunch at K&J's Diner pried
Jacobus, reclusive even in the best of times, from the snug
familiarity of his cottage for the frigid drive to Egremont Falls.
Yumi bundled Jacobus into two wool sweaters and helped him
on with his brown, corduroy jacket. She pulled a beaked hunter's
cap with wooly earflaps over his head, and protected his precious
hands with over-sized leather mittens lined with fake fleece. She
began to wrap his frayed tartan wool scarf around his neck.

Jacobus took off his dark glasses and put them in his pocket.

'Wrap it around my head,' he said.

'What?'

'I said wrap the scarf around my head. Eyes and all. Just leave
an air hole for me to breathe.'

'That freaks me out,' Yumi said. 'You'll look like the Mummy That Invaded Scotland.'

'That's your problem. I want to stay warm.'

As Nathaniel gave him a leg up into the front seat of Miller's eighteen-year-old Ford pickup, Jacobus said to Yumi, 'Stay here and keep the home fries burning.'

'Oh, no you don't!' she replied. 'If you think I'm going to stay here and let Trotsky slobber over me all day,' Yumi replied, 'you're even more senile than I thought.'

'What way is that to speak to a helpless old man?' Jacobus said, outwardly outraged, inwardly delighted. 'I thought they taught manners in Japan. Respect, obedience, and perhaps even filial piety.'

'Yes, they did,' said Yumi, blushing with embarrassment that Jacobus couldn't see. Had she gone over the line of informality? She decided not. 'But then I came here and studied with you.'

'Touché!' said Nathaniel.

'Ganging up on me again, are you? Well, if you insist on all three of us getting frostbite, that's your business. But don't think I need someone holding my hand.'

Nathaniel helped Yumi into the truck. She had to sit on Jacobus's lap to make room for Nathaniel.

'Isn't this fun?' Yumi said to Jacobus, who offered no response.

The acrid odor of Amadeo Borlotti's burnt house permeated the truck's cabin even before Miller opened the door. Jacobus, last in line, shuffled along a snow-packed path that had been improvised by the fire brigade to reach the perimeter of the accident scene. The path had become icy and Jacobus had to use his cane as a third limb in order to maintain his balance. With Yumi huddling against him, they hunched between the protective buffers of Nathaniel and Miller against the biting cold.

'We're like four penguins in Antarctica,' Yumi said.

'Only one difference,' Jacobus replied.

'What's that?'

'I'm fucking cold.'

The scene, too, could have been Antarctica, except for the obvious, disconcerting discrepancy: the smoldering, sodden rubble that had once been Amadeo Borlotti's home and shop. A stinging wind blew errant flakes of soot or snow – Jacobus couldn't tell which – on to a patch of exposed cheek, making his skin burn.

Awaiting the arrival of Sigurd Benson, the local fire chief, he stomped his feet to ward off numbness, leaning on his cane to maintain his balance.

Some things smell good when they burn. A steak. A good cigarette. Maple and oak and, yes, pine logs in his living-room wood-stove. Warm and inviting. So why was it that the smell of burnt wreckage made him sick to his stomach? Jacobus, inhaling the frozen air as deeply as his nicotine-coated lungs would allow, confirmed his ambivalent suspicions: To his relief, there was no trace of the stench of charred flesh. But on the other hand, where the hell was Borlotti? Jacobus asked himself yet again why he was there, freezing his ass off.

'It's so strange, Jake,' Yumi said. 'Everything is so pristine. So white. Except for the house. It's like a dark, ugly bruise surrounded by pale skin.'

That poetic information wasn't of much use to Jacobus, who shrugged. He had only a vague recollection of what white was, let alone a dark, ugly bruise. What a bruise felt like was much more important than what it looked like. Visual perception was a distant memory, and he hardly missed it anymore. There were even times when he felt that by losing his sight he had shed a burdensome encumbrance, like a caterpillar emerging from a cocoon, freeing his imagination to take wing. He didn't care that he might look more like a caterpillar than a butterfly.

'Where the hell's this Benson?' Jacobus asked. 'He gone missing, too?'

'He should be here any minute, Jake,' said Miller. 'Chilly?'

'Me chilly? Why do you say that? Can't be much less than twenty below. How'd you get roped into this anyway, Roy? This isn't your usual terrain.'

'As you said, Sigurd knows that I'm a friend of yours and wanted you to be here.'

'You could still have said no.'

'Sigurd's family and mine are from Rockdale, where I grew up. He was actually my scoutmaster when I was a kid and still acts like it sometimes, even though he's less than ten years older than I am. He can be a little on the dry side but we get along OK. He used to make us iron our Scout uniforms and we had to call him sir, and he called us mister. 'Mr Miller, you need to work on your taut-line hitch.' But he taught me how to start a fire without a match and got me out of hot water with my folks more than once. When he called yesterday for help with this situation it was hard to say no.'

'Not so hard,' Jacobus said. With his mitten, he wiped his nose that was running from the cold. 'Just takes a little practice. Watch me.'

'I didn't hear *you* say no to coming today, Jake,' Nathaniel said.

'That's because you were covering my mouth with your fat hand,' Jacobus said, his voice even more phlegmy from the ice in his lungs. 'And if I die of pneumonia, don't think you're getting any of my worldly goods.'

'Who'd want your stuff, anyway?' asked Nathaniel. 'The Goodwill?'

'Trotsky, my sole heir.'

'Didn't you tell me you hoped Trotsky would die so you wouldn't have to spend money on dog food?' Yumi asked.

'Morning, fellows,' a new voice called, accompanied by the sound of boots crunching quickly and lightly through the snow. 'Another beautiful day in the Berkshires.'

'Morning, sir,' said Miller, who did the introductions. Benson passed around a Thermos of hot, black coffee.

'This one was about the worst ever,' Benson said.

Jacobus opened enough space in his wrapped scarf to take a sip.

'I don't know about that,' he said. 'Tastes all right to me.'

Yumi gave him an elbow to his ribs, which would have been painful but for his staunch bulwark of clothing.

'I mean the fire,' Benson continued, taking Jacobus's comment at face value. 'Borlotti's house is so far off the beaten track, no one called it in until the fire was out of control, and then with the roads the way they were Saturday night, and his long, unplowed driveway . . . We did our best, but by the time we got here, it was pretty much a total loss. The bedroom's still standing – it was an add-on – but it can never be rebuilt.'

'Were there many violins?' Yumi asked.

'No way to know yet. But you can be sure they made Grade A kindling. And the flammables – glues, varnishes, oils, thinners. Shoot, even if we could've gotten here in one minute it would've been a dandy to put out. A perfect storm.'

'Is that where it started?' Nathaniel asked. 'In the shop with the instruments?'

'As far as we know at this point. And it burned so hot and so fast the roof collapsed under the weight of the snow before the heat could melt it. So even though most of the house is flat as a pancake, there are patches that hardly had time to burn at all.'

'What patches?' Jacobus asked.

'Bedroom, like I said. Basement.'

'Any cause yet, sir?' Miller asked.

'At this juncture it's too much of an ice-skating rink to determine one. The water from the hoses and the melted snow took all of two minutes to freeze after we put the fire out, so now we'll have to hack away at the ice to see what's underneath. As far as we can tell, it could have been just about anything from a cigarette to faulty wiring to a turpentine-soaked cloth on a radiator.'

'I've got a question, Mr Benson,' Nathaniel said. 'I live in New York City. We have fire hydrants on every block. But there's probably not one of those within ten miles of here. How do you get the water to put out the fire?'

'Not easy,' Benson replied. 'The way we try to do it is to find the nearest dry hydrant—'

'What's a dry hydrant?' Nathaniel asked.

'It's just a standpipe you hook the truck to. The pump on the truck pulls the draft. We actually have two standpipes within a half mile we usually could've drafted out of. One's by Denny's old garage down the road that way and one's in the other direction, by the bridge that goes over the Green River. But the problem was, we couldn't find them because we had whiteout conditions by the time we got here.

'So what we did was to drive one truck as close as we could get to the house and laid a five-inch supply line hose. That was our main attack truck. We put our second truck at the end of the driveway and hooked up to the supply line. We laid out two portable water tanks and had tanker shuttles from surrounding towns dump water in them. They got their water from our third truck stationed at Taconic Pond, about a half-mile from here. That's called the source pumper truck and it's got a high-power pump. Once we broke through the surface ice it pumped water into the shuttles.'

'What if there wasn't any pond nearby?'

'Nathaniel,' Jacobus said. 'Do you mind? I'm freezing my ass off.'

'I'll make it quick, Mr Williams,' Benson said. 'You've got foam and chemical apparatus as well, but nothing beats good old H-two-O. Unfortunately, none of it did any good in the end. As you can see.'

Jacobus was less concerned with the intricacies of rural fire-fighting than with the potential for frostbitten fingers.

'Maybe you just should've made s'mores and called it a day,' Jacobus said.

'No doubt,' Benson said, addressing Jacobus, 'you'd been wondering why I had to badger Mr Miller to bring you down here this morning.'

'Nah, that's perfectly clear. You want me to die of hypothermia.'

'Perish the thought. One reason was that with your expertise, we'd like you to examine any debris we come across that we can't identify. We're pretty good at determining accident or arson, but we always appreciate help from specialists.'

'Jake's an expert at debris!' Yumi said. 'His house is filled with it.'

This time it was Jacobus who returned the favor, pressing his cane into Yumi's boot and leaning on it.

'Could Borlotti have been smoking in bed?' Miller asked Benson.

'Don't think so. Hardly any fire damage in that part of the house. For sure the fire started in the shop. Besides, we talked to his best friend and asked the same question. Borlotti didn't smoke. It worries me, though, there's no sign of him.'

'Maybe he started it and ditched,' Miller said.

'It's possible,' said Benson, 'but his car's still in the garage, and the snow piled against the outside of the garage door was undisturbed. We checked the tires. They were dry and so was the garage floor, so I'm pretty sure the car was never used.'

'Maybe he left some other way, sir,' Miller pursued. To Jacobus, Miller's tone almost sounded patronizing. He wasn't used to that from him. Maybe it was because Benson seemed to have no imagination, whereas Miller was a seat of the pants problem solver.

'Have you come across any file cabinets, Mr Benson?' Nathaniel asked.

'None yet. But we still haven't gotten to the basement. Could be there. Why?'

'Tracing instrument and art fraud was my line of work. It's possible a small-scale businessman like Borlotti may have kept business records there. If it turns out the fire was set, we might find something in a file that could provide an explanation. If any valuable instruments were destroyed, there'll likely be some serious insurance claims. If it turned out that someone needed a lot of cash quickly it could be a possible motive.'

'Lots of ifs,' Benson said. 'Here's another. Let's just hope that if there are file cabinets, they didn't get crushed, burned, or drowned. Right now we're still treating the fire as an accident, but if it was a crime, we're hoping Mr Jacobus could tell us what other debris we should be looking for as evidence.'

'How about a dead body?' Jacobus said.

'Now, Jake,' said Yumi, 'be nice to Chief Benson. He doesn't know you well enough yet to appreciate your unique sense of humor.'

'And probably never will,' Nathaniel added.

Jacobus thought for a moment. 'In the absence of a dead body look for fine tuners.'

'Come again?' said Benson.

'Assuming the instruments were immolated and are now sounding celestial chords in violin heaven,' Jacobus continued, 'all that would be left here on the earthly realm would be the metal parts that didn't burn. Strings, maybe, but fine tuners are more solid, and I suppose less likely to melt.'

'What's a fine tuner look like?' Miller asked.

'Basically short brass screws with a round cap on a brass mounting. They're attached to the tailpiece of the instrument. They loosen or tighten the strings fractionally so you don't have to futz 'til the cows come home with the tuning pegs. Violins have a fine tuner on the E-string and most cellos have them on all strings.'

'What about violas?' asked Miller.

'Who cares about violas?' asked Jacobus.

Only Nathaniel and Yumi laughed, well aware of violists' inexplicable reputation as traditional whipping boys of the music world, where viola jokes abound. Benson and Miller, however, having no such insight, plodded on with their questioning.

'But what can tuners tell us about the fire?' Benson asked.

'Because once you find them, you might be able to piece together not only how many instruments and what kind of instruments were in the shop, but also where they were placed. Violins are generally laid sideways in cases or lined up on hooks against the walls, cellos likewise but on the floor, so you'd find the tuners distributed accordingly. If, on the other hand, you find a pile of tuners in a Boy Scout fire pit in the middle of the living room, you'd know there was some funny business going on.'

'See,' said Miller, like a proud father. 'I told you he knew his stuff.'

'Your endorsement means so much to me,' said Jacobus, covering his embarrassment. He had no difficulty handling insults, but nothing made him more ill at ease than undiluted praise.

'And the bows that go with the instruments,' Benson asked. 'Could they provide any clues?'

'I would expect they're total goners, but if you find a marshmallow at the end of one of them, that'll tell you something.'

'Maybe I take back my previous comment,' Miller said.

Jacobus had lost sensation in his nose from the cold air, and getting impatient with the banter, directed a question at Benson.

'You said my expertise was one reason you wanted me here. What's the other?'

'Tell me about your conversation with Amadeo Borlotti on Saturday night,' Benson said. 'The fire was likely set soon after.'

'May I be so bold as to ask, Sigurd, shouldn't I be talking to the police about that?'

'Rest easy, Mr Jacobus. I'm also the town police chief.'

'In that case, let's go for doughnuts at K&J's before I freeze my ass off.'

FIVE

'Hi, folks! I hope you're all having a joyous holiday season. I'm Scott and I'll be your server this morning. Coffee, everyone?'

'Extra hot,' Miller said, to which the others voiced unanimous assent. They also decided full breakfasts would take the chill off better than doughnuts.

Benson ordered hot oatmeal and fresh fruit, Yumi chose pancakes. Miller and Nathaniel drooled over the Trucker's Special.

'Bacon and eggs, over easy,' Jacobus said.

'Perfect! Would you care to see our bacon menu?'

'Bacon's bacon.'

'Not at K&J's! Today we have an heirloom no-nitrate bacon; a cob-smoked slab bacon, extra thick cut; and a local, organic apple-wood hickory bacon. That's my personal favorite. Or you can try our artisanal bacon sampler, which is one rasher of each, topped with our house-made seventy percent dark chocolate mole sauce for only six ninety-nine.'

No one ever described Jacobus as a patient man, and neither Scott the server nor the Johnny Mathis Christmas medley crooning in the background would do anything to alter that general perception. *Why the hell do restaurants need music in the first place?* he thought. And *Jingle Bell Rock* isn't even music. And it wasn't even Christmas anymore.

'The hell with the damn bacon. Just give me the eggs and an English muffin. And throw in an apple cider doughnut for the well-dressed little guy.'

'Jake, what's with you and doughnuts?' Nathaniel asked. 'You think the only thing police eat are doughnuts?'

'They dough nut?'

Jacobus took a sip of welcome, hot coffee as Scott the server departed.

'Have we met before, Mr Jacobus?' Benson said.

'No, you've never had the pleasure.'

'Then how did you know I'm a "well-dressed little guy"?'

'Pretty obvious,' said Jacobus. 'When we were walking to the cars your feet weren't sinking into the snow nearly as much as Roy and Nathaniel, who are big boys, and you were taking two steps for their every one. More like Yumi. Hell, I'd say you're even lighter than me, and I've hardly got any meat left on my bones.

'Also, when you handed me the Thermos, I could tell you were holding it with two hands even though it's not a particularly large one.'

'Maybe that was to keep my hands warm.'

'No way, Jose. You had mittens on when I shook your hand, and besides, since when is the outside of a Thermos hot?'

'But what about the way I dress?'

'Top of the line Thermos – the kind that has that little pouring gizmo on top, and the coffee was a Kona-Yirgacheffe blend. Not cheap. I had a flyfishing friend down in Florida who spent a fortune on creels and waders just to catch a goddamn eight-inch trout. Anyone who fusses about accouterments will fuss about the way he dresses.'

'Did you ever think about being a police detective?' Benson asked.

'Well, yes. As a matter of fact I did.'

'And?'

'And I decided I couldn't think of a less interesting way to make a living.'

Jacobus recounted his Christmas Eve conversation with Borlotti. With his acute memory, unimpaired by age, he recited it back to Benson almost verbatim, only leaving out the bit about figgy pudding. He also summarized his follow-up attempts to contact him on Sunday, all of which Nathaniel and Yumi corroborated.

'Any idea what might have been on his mind?' Benson asked.

By the pacing and inflection of Benson's question, Jacobus sensed there was inference behind the innocent inquiry.

'You're thinking Borlotti might have set the fire himself, aren't you?'

'Right now it's not much more than a hunch. But if it had been an accident, don't you think he would have called us at the fire department right away?'

'But,' Miller asked, 'for argument's sake, let's say he did start the fire. What could his motive have been?'

'The usual one is to collect insurance,' Nathaniel said.

'That's what I was thinking, too,' Miller replied. 'But wouldn't that be even more reason for him to call it in? He'd seem a lot less suspicious doing that.'

'I suppose, unless he had a different reason to make sure the place was destroyed totally,' Benson said. 'We'll probably find more as we dig, but for now it's just one possible theory.'

'But what about the car?' Miller asked. 'You said it was still in the garage. If he burned down his own house, how did he disappear?'

'Couldn't he have gone out of town,' Nathaniel suggested, 'by taking a cab to the airport? Maybe he was calling us from somewhere else.'

'From what Mr Jacobus said of his conversation with him,' Benson said, 'it definitely sounded like he called from home, or at least close by, since he wanted to see Mr Jacobus right away. And if he had gone out of town, don't you think someone would've known, or at least notified us by now?'

'You said it's *not much more* than a hunch,' said Jacobus. 'Is there a little bit of something you're not telling us?'

'There were some puzzling tracks in the snow.'

Scott arrived with their breakfasts, singing a traditional Christmas carol with his own lyrics.

'*Your food's here, merry gentlemen.*'

Jacobus slammed down his cup.

'First of all,' he said to Scott, 'even my dog could sing better in tune than you. And though it may be neither here nor there, the comma in "God rest ye merry, gentlemen" comes *after* merry. There are no merry gentlemen in the damn song or at this damn table. Especially now. So why don't you just give us our food and go a-caroling somewhere else. You know how to sing *Far, Far Away?*'

'You betcha!' said Scott, undaunted.

'Good. Now go do it.'

'Jake is an analyst,' Yumi explained to Miller and Benson.

'But before I go,' Scott continued, 'I checked with Chef Bob and he says he's willing to make you our traditional regular bacon.'

'He's willing, huh? OK.'

'How do you like it?'

Johnny Mathis began crooning, *'Si-ilent night. Ho-oly night . . .'*

'Burned to a crisp. And tell Chef Bob to turn that ear pollution off until next year.'

Jacobus couldn't see Scott wince as he left, but somehow he sensed it. He felt no regret.

'Now, tell me about the tracks in the snow,' Jacobus said to Benson, 'while I'm still in a good mood.'

'There were two sets when we got there,' said Benson. 'Of course we obliterated them – no choice – but those are the kind of things we take note of with a suspicious fire. One set went from the street to the back door of his house, or vice versa of course.'

'The back door,' said Jacobus.

'Exactly. The back door being the kitchen door. On a night like that you would think going in or out the front would have been more direct and much easier, since it's closer to the street.'

'Maybe someone didn't want to be seen coming and going,' said Nathaniel.

'Could be.'

Jacobus tore off a piece of English muffin, dipped it into an egg yolk, and popped it, dripping, into his mouth.

'But then it would be someone other than Borlotti,' said Jacobus. 'A man entering his own house wouldn't be worried about arousing suspicion.'

'Good point,' said Miller.

'What kind of tracks?' asked Jacobus. He wiped his chin with a napkin and not his sleeve, since he was in public. 'Footprints?'

'Yes, sir. Pretty deep in the snow, mostly within a narrow path, maybe made by a snow blower. Strange, though.'

'What was strange?' asked Nathaniel.

'It sounds like I'm arguing against myself, but it couldn't have been a snow blower. First, with a snow blower you get the snow piled up on one side of the path or the other where it's been blown off. Here the snow was untouched and level on both sides. There were no piles. Second, Borlotti had a snow shovel in his garage but there wasn't a snow blower anywhere.'

'Maybe a neighbor did it for him,' Yumi suggested. 'Mr Borlotti was an older gentleman.'

'We checked. Negatory. And don't forget the absence of a snow pile.'

'Maybe he just shoveled,' Nathaniel said, 'like Jake has me do.'

'I don't think so. The sides of the track were parallel all the way and the depth all along the path was just too even.'

'Sled,' said Jacobus.

'Yes!' said Nathaniel.

'Nice try, but that wasn't it, either,' said Benson. 'Sled blades would have left narrower tracks, and these parallel lines were much closer together and much deeper than any sled I've seen.'

'Did you check for treads in the footprints, sir?' Miller asked. 'See what kind of shoe or boot it was?'

'No time for that with the fire and with the snow still coming down. And by now the footprints are long gone. They were too deep in the snow, anyway, to get accurate tread readings. But the depth tells us one thing, anyway.'

'That whoever it was was there shortly before you arrived,' said Jacobus.

'Exactly. The new snow hadn't had time to fill them in.'

'Which would mean that the blaze went up really fast, suggesting it was started by that person.'

'Yes.'

'What was the second set of tracks you saw?' asked Jacobus.

'This was strange, too. East Grange Road, Borlotti's street, hadn't been plowed yet. Not too many people live on it and the road crews were up to their necks just keeping the main arteries open. But there was a set of tire tracks, from a truck.'

'How big a truck?' Miller asked.

'About the size of a delivery truck. FedEx or UPS.'

'Maybe Borlotti was getting a delivery?' Yumi suggested.

'I don't think so,' Benson said. 'First of all, it was late on Christmas Eve, and we checked with both FedEx and UPS. They both stopped delivering at seven p.m., and none of them had any record of sending a truck out to Borlotti's address at all during the day, anyway. Same with the local post office. Another curious thing is that the truck didn't park right in front of Borlotti's house. It had been parked just out of sight from Borlotti's house where there were some pine trees along the side of the road. Also, it was there for more than the few minutes it would have taken to make a delivery.'

'How do you know that?' Nathaniel asked.

'Where the truck stopped, the tires sank into the snow a lot deeper. And you could tell that the driver had a heckuva time trying to get it moving afterward. And you know that first set of parallel tracks with the footprints I was telling you about from the house? Those went out to the truck tracks.'

'So maybe if it wasn't a delivery, couldn't it have been that Borlotti was sending something?' Nathaniel added. 'Like a violin?'

'Possibly. But when the truck started up again, the tracks going away were deeper than the approaching ones. Even when you take into account that that would be the case anyway, because the approaching tracks would have had some time to fill with snow, I still think something pretty heavy must have been put in it. Heavier than a violin.'

'A lot of speculation,' Jacobus muttered. 'At this rate, they'll be playing *Summertime* and we'll still be sitting here.'

He found a spoon and stirred his coffee, not that there was milk or sugar in it, which was unthinkable, but to give himself time for the thinkable. This whole business reminded Jacobus of that most famous, most debated chord in music history at the beginning of Wagner's *Tristan und Isolde*. Until one mysterious layer after another was peeled away, no one could tell where it would finally resolve.

'Who's this best friend of Borlotti's you mentioned when we were out on the tundra?' Jacobus asked Benson.

'That would be Jimmy. Jimmy Ubriaco. Sixtyish, like Borlotti. Lives here in town. Directs the high-school band and orchestra. Plays string bass at parties and stuff to pick up some extra cash. You can imagine what the school pays the music teachers. Jimmy's a real do-it-yourselfer type.'

'How long have they been friends?'

'Since they were in knickers. Jimmy came down to the station yesterday morning.'

'On Christmas Day?'

'Believe it! He was fit to be tied when he heard about the fire and that Borlotti was missing.'

'How did he find out about it so quickly?' Nathaniel asked.

'Where do you live, Mr Williams?'

'New York City. Most of the time.'

'Well, in small towns like Egremont Falls, good news travels faster than the Internet, and bad news faster than the speed of light. We've already been offered a bushel of theories how the fire got started.'

'Were any of them constructive?' Yumi asked.

'One was that Borlotti burned his house down to cover up the fact that he had hidden his mad wife in the attic all these years and was really in love with his housekeeper.'

'And?'

'Borlotti never had a wife, housekeeper, or attic.'

'What a romantic story, though!' Yumi said. 'Someone should write a novel.'

'No one would ever believe it,' said Jacobus. 'You said this Ubriaco directs the band and orchestra and plays the bass. I gather since they're friends and in the same profession they've done business together also.'

'You bet they do,' said Benson. 'Borlotti fixes up all the school orchestra's string instruments. Poor Jimmy was beside himself because he had left most of them at the shop over the holiday vacation for Borlotti to do some maintenance work. The school had its big Winter Festival concert just before Christmas, and Jimmy says the instruments always get pretty beat up by the kids getting ready for that.'

'And now they're a pile of ash,' said Jacobus. 'Maybe you should have a follow-up with Jimmy. Maybe he knows where his good buddy might be.'

'I was actually hoping you'd do that, Jacobus,' Benson said. 'You know, one musician to another.'

Jacobus wanted nothing more to do with the situation beyond a free breakfast.

'He's not a musician,' Jacobus said. 'He's a band director. Have Scott the server talk to him.'

Benson ignored his remark.

'Let me know what you learn.'

'*Sleep in heavenly peace,*' Mathis sang.

This is not going to end well, Jacobus thought, but only grunted.

'*Sleep in heavenly peace.*'

SIX

R oy Miller dropped Jacobus, Nathaniel, and Yumi off at the curb in front of Jimmy Ubriaco's house and arranged to pick them up when their interview was finished. He then drove off on the snow-packed road to rejoin Sigurd Benson and the fire crew.

Jacobus probed with his cane. The paved walk leading to the front door had been shoveled clear. He poked holes in the snow on either side and determined that the path was wider than the one Benson had described to him that led from Borlotti's house to the unaccountable delivery truck. All that Jacobus discovered along Ubriaco's path was that he had no need to wipe snow off his shoes on Ubriaco's welcome mat. Jacobus rang the doorbell, which chimed the first five notes of Haydn's famous 'Surprise' Symphony melody. Jacobus had little tolerance for kitsch and took no pleasure from surprises, but even with his probing, analytic mind, he could not entirely discount omens.

'Come in! Come in! Door's unlocked!' Ubriaco hollered from somewhere in the house, interrupting an animated phone conversation.

'Eggnog in the kitchen. Help yourself.'

'He didn't even know we were coming,' Nathaniel said. 'That's very welcoming of him.'

'Only if you like eggnog,' Jacobus said.

Yumi helped Jacobus divest himself of his outermost layers of clothing.

'Doilies everywhere,' she whispered. 'A real old lady house.'

'I know,' said Jacobus. 'The Glade is making me wheeze.'

Nathaniel and Yumi escorted Jacobus to the kitchen counter where they found the carton of eggnog next to a bottle of rum and a tin of nutmeg. Nathaniel helped himself and served Yumi, but Jacobus, repulsed by the idea of diluting good rum in a colloidal concoction, took his straight.

They waited. Nathaniel was about to help himself to seconds when they heard Ubriaco talking to himself in another room.

'Christ Almighty, those insurance agents are a pain in the ass!'

'Holy mackerel!' Ubriaco said, changing his tune when he saw three strangers in his kitchen. 'Who are you folks? Jehovah's Witnesses?'

'We look that sanctimonious?' Jacobus replied.

'Well, I could tell right off the bat you weren't the three Magi kings because one of you is a girl, so I thought I'd go for my second choice.'

Nathaniel introduced the three of them and explained the reason for their impromptu visit.

'Have a seat,' Ubriaco said. And to Jacobus, 'May I help you to the couch, sir? People should be more considerate of the disabled.'

'Who's disabled?' Jacobus answered, and demonstrating virtuoso cane skills found a seat on his own, though narrowly avoiding knocking over the flocked Christmas tree next to it. 'Tell us about your pal, Borlotti.'

'I'm worried sick about Amadeo,' Ubriaco said. 'Him and me, we go way back. Jesus! Missing! I haven't had a minute of sleep!'

'How way back?' asked Jacobus.

'Our parents, they met on the boat to Ellis Island in 1919. Our papas were stonecutters and found work at the marble quarries around here. Amadeo and me, we went to grade school together. It wasn't like today where you have all these centralized schools, like factories. Egremont Falls still had a one-room schoolhouse. We had one teacher, Mrs Scagliotti, for six years! Boy, was she tough – but fair! I deserved all the detention she gave me, I'll tell you. But she started the school's first student orchestra and taught every instrument. Amadeo played violin and they gave me the bass because I was bigger. So Amadeo and me, we see plenty of each other. We're what you'd call bosom buddies. Hey, you want to hear a string bass joke?'

'Yes, please,' Yumi said, before Jacobus could decline.

'OK. There's this little kid and all he wants to do is learn to play the bass. The father says, "Why can't you learn a smaller instrument? A bass is too big to schlep around." But the kid cries and cries and finally the father says OK. So they get a bass and the father takes the kid into town for his first lesson. He picks him up after the first lesson and the kid says, "Dad, I learned to play with one finger." The father picks him up after the second lesson, and the kid says, "Dad, I learned to play with two fingers." The father picks him up after the third lesson, and the kid's not there! The father becomes frantic and looks everywhere but can't find him so he goes home and waits. The kid finally eases into the house at three in the morning, smelling like cigarettes and booze, and the father, asks, "Son, where the hell have you been?" And the kid, real nonchalant, says, "Oh, I had a gig."'

Ubriaco burst out laughing at his own joke. Yumi and Nathaniel joined him. Even Jacobus had to smile.

'You said you and Borlotti see plenty of each other. How recently?' Jacobus asked.

'Why, Saturday morning!'

'The day his house burned down and he disappeared?' Jacobus asked.

'Hey, friend, don't try to read anything into that.'

'Why not?'

'Because Amadeo and I see each other *every* morning. Six days a week at the café in town and Sunday at church. And when the weather's nice we play bocce and have a little homemade grappa together. I built my own court out back. Regulation size. If it wasn't covered with two feet of snow I'd show it to you.'

'I'll put it on my bucket list,' Jacobus said. 'What's the name of the café?'

'The Last Drop. Everyone goes there. It's the only place in town for real espresso. Actually, it's the only place in town, period. Why do you ask? You're going to check up on me?'

'Maybe. Maybe I just want coffee. Why were you so hot and bothered with the insurance agent on the phone?'

'Because at the same time I'm worried to death about Amadeo, I've got to file insurance claims for all the school instruments that were at his shop getting fixed up. There's no way they could have survived that fire. It's a disaster and not one of those son-of-a-guns will give me a straight answer.'

'Didn't the school insure them?' Nathaniel asked. By established practice, Jacobus let Nathaniel take over when his field of expertise entered the arena. For one, the intricacies of instrument insurance made Jacobus's eyes glaze over, sightless though they were. But more importantly, Nathaniel's calm, sympathetic questioning made interviewees more at ease after being badgered by Jacobus. Nathaniel was grateful for the paradox; that it was only when he was with his wizened, seemingly helpless, blind friend that white folks didn't feel intimidated by his blackness and large stature. Though Jacobus wasn't sure whether to accept that as a compliment or not, he didn't disagree with Nathaniel's assessment.

'Yeah, sort of,' Ubriaco answered, bringing Jacobus back to the present. 'But they're handing me this line that the fine print says the instruments are only covered within the physical limits of the school property.'

'But Borlotti must have had a policy, too,' Nathaniel delved. 'Instruments often automatically have temporary coverage under a shop's policy.'

'Don't you think I'm trying to find that out?' Ubriaco was almost shouting. 'His company is Concordia and the school's is Northeast Mutual. Amadeo's guys at Concordia won't even talk to me. They'll only talk to Amadeo, so until he gets back I'm stuck. Meanwhile, my guy gives me this mumbo jumbo about Bailee's agreements and mysterious disappearance, and—'

'Those are typical clauses,' Nathaniel said calmly. 'Bailee's agreements just determine who's responsible for left items. It's not restricted to musical instruments at a shop. It can be a shirt you leave at the dry cleaner or your car in a parking garage. It's pretty much your responsibility unless it's explicitly stated otherwise. "Mysterious disappearance" is a common exclusion in insurance policies. It's up to you to prove it, which isn't easy. You need to have a snap, crackle and pop case, or at least a smoking gun, metaphorically speaking.'

'Like I said, mumbo jumbo.'

'How many instruments are we talking about?' asked Jacobus. He was getting restless and the conversation didn't seem to be getting anywhere.

'Nine violins, one viola, two cellos, and four basses.'

'Only one viola and four basses? What does your orchestra play, "Asleep in the Deep"?'

'Well, you're a musician. You know. No one wants to play viola, but bass is cool, and like I said, you learn two notes on a bass and you think you're ready for stardom.'

'How much were the instruments insured for?' Nathaniel asked.

'That's another problem. The district has been having budget issues – surprise, surprise – and to make ends meet they raised the deductible to five hundred dollars per instrument, and most of them—'

'Aren't even worth that much,' Nathaniel surmised correctly. 'I see your problem. Even if they accepted your claims, which they might not, you'd only get back thirty, forty cents on the dollar. You'd end up netting a loss after paying the deductible, meaning it would make more sense to buy new instruments, even though they'd cost a lot more. But since the school doesn't have the money, you could end up losing the orchestra. Is that the problem, Mr Ubriaco?'

'You left out one thing,' he said. 'Without an orchestra I could end up losing my job, too! Not that it pays a helluva a lot, but at least it's a job, you know?'

'Anyone you know who *isn't* Borlotti's bosom buddy?' Jacobus asked. 'Someone who might want to do him harm?'

'Nah! Everybody loves Amadeo. He's got a gentle soul. He'd fix someone's fiddle and if he likes them – and he almost always does – he won't charge a dime. He fixes all the school's instruments for next to nothing, plus every year he donates to the orchestra scholarship fund. He's a sucker for charities.'

'That was the impression I had,' Yumi reflected. 'But I only met him once and that was a long time ago.'

'If it is determined that the fire was arson,' Jacobus pursued, 'and it's also true that Borlotti is universally beloved and no one would have a reason fix *his* fiddle, you tell me what logical conclusion there can be other than he torched it himself and took off?'

'That would never happen!' Ubriaco protested. 'Impossible! He'd have nowhere to go. Amadeo's not a wealthy man. And he'd never do that to his customers, with all those instruments there. Never! Would you burn your own house down, Mr Jacobus? For any reason?'

'Sounds like we're going around in circles,' said Nathaniel, interceding before Jacobus gave Ubriaco a handful of reasons he'd burn his own house down, not least of which was that in its present condition it could well fall down without much outside assistance.

'Jake, I think we should let Mr Ubriaco get back to his insurance situation.' Nathaniel gave Ubriaco his business card and offered to help him if he continued to make no progress.

'Thank you,' Ubriaco said. 'And I'll give you a heads-up when I hear from Amadeo. Jeez, I hope he's OK. And Christmastime, too. You folks want another eggnog? One for the road?'

'No, thanks,' said Jacobus. 'My doctor said I should try to stay away from poison.'

When they were outside, waiting for Miller to pick them up, Yumi said to Jacobus, 'When Mr Ubriaco made that comment about helping the disabled it was nice of you not to get angry.'

'Don't draw hasty conclusions.'

SEVEN

Miller drove them to the Egremont Falls town hall. The building had once been the local school before the county went to a centralized system. Benson chaperoned them to the combined police and fire department office, formerly the school principal's office. Jacobus, sitting in an uncomfortable, straight-backed, wooden school chair and getting woozy from the ineradicable residue of ancient mimeograph, felt transported back to his child-hood. It was as if he had once again gotten into hot water and was being sent to the office. Now, as then, he cringed at whatever punishment would be meted out. But he knew, one way or other, it was coming.

'This is what we have so far,' Benson said to his unlikely inner circle. 'Mind you, we haven't gotten to the basement yet, only the first floor, but so far there is no sign of a body.'

'Good news and bad news,' said Jacobus.

'Why do you say that, Jake?' Miller asked.

'Well, it raises some basic questions, doesn't it? Was it accident or was it arson? That leads to a whole train of other questions. If there's no body, and if the fire was an accident, why flee? And if he fled, how did he amscray? His car's still in the garage. Did someone in a delivery truck that just happened to be passing by in a blizzard stop to give him a lift? Or was it planned long in advance? And why no trace since?

'On the other hand, if he intentionally set the fire, why? And ditto, how and why did he leave without a trace? There's also the possibility that someone else set it. If that's the story, did they take Borlotti with them, and if so, was he a willing accomplice or did someone have to twist his arm? Or neck?'

'Exactly!' said Benson.

'Exactly what?' asked Jacobus.

'Those are exactly the questions we have to answer.'

'Well, thanks for the merit badge. I'm glad we're making so much progress. Is there anything else you haven't found that you'd like to tell us about?'

'Tuners,' said Benson. 'We found the remains of some of Borlotti's bigger tools – a router, I think, a band saw, sanders, table saw – but we didn't find a single one of those violin fine tuners you told us to look for.'

'You must be kidding!' Jacobus exclaimed. 'What are you, blind?'

'I'm perfectly serious. We even combed through the rubble with strainers because you said you thought it was important. We wasted a lot of man hours looking for those tuners.'

'No body. No tuners,' Jacobus said. 'That wasn't a waste of time.'

'What do you mean?' Yumi asked.

'It means there were no violins in the violin shop,' Nathaniel replied.

'That's right,' Jacobus said. 'So now we can add theft to arson and kidnapping.'

'We don't know if any of that's true, Mr Jacobus. The investigation is still in its preliminary stages.'

Yumi interjected.

'What about the school instruments Mr Ubriaco said were at the shop? Shouldn't there be traces of them?'

'There should. But as I said,' Benson replied, 'we haven't gotten to the basement layer yet. It's possible we'll find them there, and the rest of the instruments, though if we do I expect they'll be two dimensional.'

Jacobus was hardly assuaged.

'A violin repairman might store some fiddles in the basement, especially the crappier ones. I'll grant you that. But most likely that's where he'd store extra wood and materials. The shop itself is where most of the instruments should be, at least the good ones and the ones he's working on. There is something not kosher in Denmark.'

'Be that as it may,' Benson continued, 'it's not sound reasoning to base conclusions on the absence of evidence, so now that I've told you what we haven't found, I suspect you'll be interested to know what we *have* found, which might cause you to reconsider your conspiracy thoughts. For example, we found the source of the fire.'

'Based upon what?' Jacobus asked. Sitting in the old school chair he felt like Benson was talking down to him like his old school teacher, Dr Gunter, when he was a boy in Germany. Now, as then, he didn't like it. 'Daniel Jacobus, on what date did Martin Luther nail his ninety-five theses to the door of the Wittenberg Church?' When he didn't know the answer, Dr Gunter made him write out all the theses as punishment. It was one of the many reasons he'd become an atheist.

'Based upon where the fire burned hottest and the patterns of how it spread,' Benson answered. 'We traced the source to a Bunsen burner that must have tipped over and ignited an open can of spirit varnish, knocking it over and causing the varnish to flow over the worktable and floor. And as I noted before, there's probably no better fuel for a fire than a violin shop.'

'That's an inflammatory remark.'

'The smallest items we found were the metal parts of some of his hand tools – the wooden handles are long gone. Chisels, scrapers, knives, what have you.'

'That doesn't sound very interesting. All violin makers have that stuff.'

'Except that two of the knife blades were found apart from the rest of his tools. One was outside the house, near the kitchen door in the back, and the other was next to his bed. That particular one was a cleaver, and since the bedroom didn't burn, it still had the handle.'

'That *is* interesting,' said Jacobus. 'I'll bet you're thinking what I'm thinking.'

'No doubt,' said Benson, 'you're thinking that the cleaver next to the bed means Borlotti was worried about the possibility of an intruder, and the knife by the door means an intruder might have discarded it after paying a visit.'

'And you're *not* thinking that?' asked Jacobus. 'You're thinking that Borlotti used the cleaver to trim his toenails before bedtime?'

'I am not thinking of anything at this point,' Benson said. 'But I am having both knives tested for traces of anything that might be helpful.'

'In case he had a hangnail?' Jacobus mocked. 'In Ye Olde Shoppe of Horrors?'

'Any luck with file cabinets?' Nathaniel asked, changing the subject.

'Yes, but only bad,' Benson said. 'Total loss. They were old wooden ones. Burned, then flattened by the collapsing roof, then saturated from the hoses and snow, then frozen, then thawed.'

'Well, maybe not a total loss, sir,' Miller said.

'How so?' Benson asked stiffly, as if his competence had been questioned.

'Could make good mulch for the garden.'

'To grow lilies over Borlotti's grave,' Jacobus muttered.

'If it makes you feel any better,' Benson continued, unperturbed, 'we did find a Rolodex file by his bedside that's still relatively legible, though it's been damaged by water and smoke. I don't think I need to deputize you if you'd care to borrow it. Might give you some leads.'

'Thank you,' said Nathaniel.

'Is that it?' asked Jacobus. With all this talk of smoke he suddenly craved a cigarette.

'The only other thing of possible interest were some letters in a drawer in Borlotti's bedside table.'

'A cleaver, a Rolodex, and letters,' said Jacobus. 'Curious bedfellows. What's in the letters?'

'Sadly, we'll never know. Illegible beyond reconstruction.'

'Maybe someone on the Rolodex will know where Mr Borlotti is and we can find out what happened,' Yumi said.

'I doubt it. This story is no simple Dittersdorf ditty,' Jacobus said. 'For starters, take Benson's Bunsen. The burner might have started the fire, sure, but it didn't turn itself on. Someone lit it.'

'Yes,' Nathaniel agreed. 'And for the very reason that things are so combustible in a violin shop, the violinmakers I know keep their varnish at a safe distance from the flame in the unlikely event it would fall over.'

Miller added, 'And you also have to wonder if a little Bunsen burner falling could knock over a big can of varnish? Or did someone help it along?'

'And come to think of it,' Yumi said, 'if the Bunsen burner was on, it means Mr Borlotti was working. Why would he have been working late at night on Christmas Eve?'

Nathaniel chimed in. 'And why was it that not only *he* disappeared into thin air after the fire started, but all the violins as well?'

Miller added, 'And what's the deal with the knives?'

'I've got my own question,' Jacobus said. He rubbed his weary face, realized he hadn't shaved for a long time, and decided he didn't care. 'Why the hell did I not find out from Borlotti what the trouble was when I had the chance?' He inhaled the scent of the old schoolroom once more. 'Class dismissed.'

EIGHT

By the time they returned to Jacobus's poorly insulated house, the sun had gone down and the cold had seeped in. The thermostat in the living room had dipped to fifty-two and the woodstove was barely warm to the touch. Jacobus, exhausted, fell back on to his creaking couch and allowed his two friends to do one of the few chores that on all other occasions gave him pleasure – keeping the fire going. Nathaniel carried in an armload of logs from the shed where they kept dry, and dumped them into the woodstove. Jacobus heard Yumi tear pages from the Shopper's Guide for kindling. When she abruptly stopped he asked her why.

'Oh, nothing. I was just looking at some of these ads. I could have gotten you a kayak for Christmas instead of a CD player,' she said. 'Only eight hundred dollars. Like new, paddles included.'

'I'll give you a paddle,' he replied.

'You'd be up the creek without one,' she said. 'Then how about a three-hundred-gallon aquarium with free starter kit?'

'Sounds fishy.'

'Here's one: "Vintage gas wood-splitter. Needs loving home".'

'You're giving *me* gas.'

'Hey, how about . . .' Yumi stopped in midsentence.

'How about what? Cat got your tongue? Is someone offering lessons on "how to be a mime in one easy lesson"?'

'No. It's a wanted ad for violins.'

'Someone wants to buy a three-quarter-size Stradivarius?'

'I'm not sure. It says, "Top price for violins, old or new, regardless of condition." There's no name. Only a phone number.'

'I'm not planning on selling my violin anytime soon,' Jacobus said. 'Though if I don't start practicing a little, you'll wish I had.'

'It's not that. I think the phone number is the one you used to call Amadeo Borlotti. Could this mean he's holed up somewhere?'

Nathaniel stopped loading the woodstove, but Jacobus beat him to the obvious question.

'If the phone number he used to call us was the number at the house that burned down, why would this make you think he's holed up somewhere?'

'I'm not sure,' Yumi replied. 'Maybe he wasn't really calling from his house.'

Nathaniel quickly went into the kitchen and eventually found the white pages under a dusty pile of user manuals for kitchen appliances that had long since become inoperative.

'No,' he said. 'That phone number is listed under Borlotti's home address.'

'How old's that Shopper's Guide?' Jacobus asked.

'Current,' said Yumi.

'Puzzling. And why is it that someone who's been in business as long as he has is still trolling for crummy violins from Granny's attic?' he asked.

'Let's see if I can find out,' Nathaniel said. He found the number for the Shopper's Guide office and was connected to Astrid, the ad editor. Jacobus listened on his living room extension.

'I hope this is going to be quick,' Astrid said. 'I was supposed to be out of here a half hour ago. Everyone's trying to unload the junk they got for Christmas.'

Nathaniel assured her he would be brief. He referred to Borlotti's ad and asked how recently he had placed it.

'Sure, I know the ad,' Astrid said. 'It's been running a long time.'

'How long is long?' Nathaniel asked.

'Years. Ads like his get automatically renewed from month to month as long as the customer keeps paying for it, and I see that the Borlotti account is still active. Small businesses do it all the time. It's a very cheap way to advertise. Anything else?'

With no great expectations, Jacobus asked if they knew who might have responded to Borlotti's ad. He received the response he anticipated. Astrid told him the newspaper didn't keep records of any of that.

Yet another beguiling, unanswered question. Jacobus was about to hang up when Astrid added, 'But you might want to check with Arnold Westerhauser. He's a fancy-shmancy antiques dealer in Sheffield and runs quarter-page ads with us every once in a while. I think he's had violins from time to time.'

Nathaniel found the number for Westerhauser Fine Antiques in the Yellow Pages and called. There was no answer or even a recorded message to inform them when it would be open.

Jacobus had had enough sleuthing for one day and wanted to listen to some more Vivaldi and Corelli over several tall glasses of Macallan, but Yumi suggested, 'Why don't we divide the alphabet in three and call the names on the Rolodex?'

'Must we?' asked Jacobus.

'You have something more important to do, Jake?' Nathaniel asked as he relit the woodstove.

'Yeah. Take a crap. My physician ordered me to do my utmost to remain regular.'

'Jake, you haven't been regular since I've known you,' Nathaniel replied.

'What if we just give you W through Z?' Yumi suggested. 'There can't be many of those. I'll do A through L, and Nathaniel will do M through V. When it's your turn I'll tell you the names one by one with the phone numbers.'

'All right! All right! Since you insist on ganging up on a helpless, infirmed elder, what choice do I have? How unseemly of you both.'

'What should we ask when they answer the phone?' Yumi asked.

'How about, "Excuse me, but are you holding Amadeo Borlotti hostage?" When they say yes, problem solved.'

'Just for the sake of argument,' Nathaniel countered, 'Let's say they don't come right out and say they're holding him hostage. I'd suggest we ask about their relationship to Borlotti and the last time they saw him. If it was a business relationship, maybe we can find out what their dealings with him were. Maybe they'll know how to contact him. With violin dealers you never know what kind of shenanigans you'll come up with.'

As they were about to start dialing, Jacobus shouted, 'Saved in the Saint Nick of time!'

'What do you mean?' Yumi asked, but then heard what Jacobus had already heard, a car coming down the driveway.

'That'll be Roy Miller's truck,' he said.

Miller knocking on the door and stomping his feet to remove the snow almost obscured another noise that instantly aroused Jacobus's interest.

'Ah! Santa's brought us a post-Christmas present!' Jacobus said, reinvigorated before Miller was even fully into the house. 'I must've been a good boy this year. Yumi, pour the man a scotch. Double. We don't want to put *that* wood in the fire, do we? That wood's special, isn't it?'

'I confess,' Miller said. 'Tell me how you figured that one out.'

'Why, I asked myself, would Roy Miller be stopping by the woodstove on a snowy evening? Must have something to do with the investigation, of course. When you knocked on the door you dropped that box you're carrying, and I could hear there was wood rattling inside. But it wasn't the mundane clunk of logs from the woodshed. Too high-pitched. And well-pitched! More like the sound of planks. Dried planks. Considering the theme of the day, I'd have to say it's wood for making violins. So Benson was able to salvage something from the house after all?'

'Well, you got most of that right,' Miller said. 'But this wasn't in the house. It came in the mail for Borlotti. Today.'

'Someone who didn't know Borlotti was missing?' Nathaniel asked.

'Actually, it was sent it before he went missing,' Miller answered. He withdrew one of the planks from the box and handed it to Jacobus, who gauged by feel that it was about fifteen by twenty-four inches and about two inches thick.

'It's no big deal for a violinmaker to have wood shipped to him,' said Jacobus. 'But since you brought it here, you and Benson suspect something more. Is that right, Roy?'

'We do. It was shipped from Italy. Second, it looks pretty old. But that's all we know. We thought maybe you folks could help us out.'

'It does looks old,' said Nathaniel. 'Very old. It's quite lightweight so it's thoroughly dried. Maple. For the violin backs, ribs, and scroll. The edges are gray, but the face of it is fresh—'

'Meaning it's an old piece but was only sliced up recently,' Jacobus said.

'Yes, and the grain is really something, with a very striking flame,' Nathaniel said. 'You don't see much of this quality around anymore. It's got to be expensive.'

'So in other words we need to wonder what a hack like Borlotti would be doing with such A-1 merchandise,' Jacobus said. 'Who's the supplier?'

'There was no name on the package. No note on the inside. Not even a bill. Only an address. Cerretello Secondo, from a town called Cassalbuttano. We'll try to find out who it might be.'

Neither Jacobus, Nathaniel, nor Yumi had ever heard of the place.

'Just out of curiosity,' Jacobus said, 'how did Benson know the contents of the package?'

Miller seemed reticent.

'Marge, at the Egremont Falls post office, is also Sigurd's part-time secretary. She called Sigurd and told him a package for Borlotti had arrived, and seeing how he was missing and his house had burned down, she didn't know what to do with it – deliver it, hold it, or send it back. Sigurd said he'd pick it up and take care of it.'

'So far, so good. But isn't it against the law to open someone else's mail?'

Miller cleared his throat.

'I suppose. Sigurd said he left it in his office with his door unlocked, and when he went back somehow it had been opened.'

Miller downed his drink, hurriedly excused himself, and wished everyone a pleasant evening. Nathaniel, who after his Christmas vacation in the Berkshires would be returning to New York City, offered to take the wood to Boris Dedubian, the well-known international violin dealer, for further analysis.

Jacobus, who had known Dedubian for decades, said, 'Just make sure he signs a receipt for it, or it'll end up on his next violin.'

After Miller left, they returned to the Rolodex and started dialing phone numbers, holding out the general hope that someone on the list would give their investigation some direction.

'This is a conspiracy!' Jacobus declared, when he found out there were more names on the list between Watkins and Zera than between Alden and Levine.

After three hours of calling, they reconvened in the living room with what remained of the bottle of Macallan to compare notes. Some of the phone numbers either were no longer in service or had become marred by the effects of the fire, making dialing the correct number a roll of the dice. Those who answered the phone were indeed Borlotti's business contacts who had bought or had violins repaired by him, though some of them hadn't had any dealings with him for years. In general, they had been palpably, though understandably, reluctant to be forthcoming. Even a reasonable person might feel put upon when confronted out of the blue by such troubling events, especially in the aftermath of a holiday. After Yumi suggested they try beginning the conversation with, 'We'd like to wish you a happy holiday and only need a moment to ask you about . . .' the hang-ups diminished. Still, no one was particularly enthusiastic about discussing his or her relationship to Borlotti except to say he had gotten them good deals and they were absolutely content with the quality of his work. In response to their final question, the only question of consequence, really, the unanimous answer was, 'No, I have no idea where Borlotti might be.'

Nathaniel and Yumi chalked up the brusque responses to the unfortunate timing. Jacobus, who had a lower opinion of humanity than his friends, wasn't ready to be so accommodating. He thought they sounded like they were hiding something.

'Here's to humanity,' he said, and drained his scotch.

Jacobus decided to call it a night, whether or not his friends agreed with him. He went to load some logs into the stove for the night, when the phone rang. It had to have been after midnight. He lifted the receiver. Maybe it was one of Borlotti's customers who'd had a change of heart.

'Yeah,' Jacobus said.

'I know about Borlotti,' a woman said. The voice was like the Macallan. Smooth but potent. All business.

'Amadeo Borlotti?' Jacobus asked.

'You know another Borlotti?'

'What about him?'

'He's gotten me in trouble.'

'Who are you?'

'I can't tell you.'

'Well, I don't do anonymous accusations over the phone.'

After an indecisive silence, the caller hung up.

NINE

Tuesday, December 27

After breakfast they left Jacobus's house for the colonial town of Sheffield. Light flurries blew like dust in a brisk breeze. Nathaniel had packed his bags and the mysterious parcel of wood in the trunk of Yumi's car, because after their visit to the antique shop, Yumi would drive Nathaniel to the Metro

North train station at Wassaic for the two-hour commute to Grand Central.

It was hard to know which had come first, Sheffield or antique stores. Among the many that lined the town's main drag, Westerhauser Antiques stood out. With its white clapboard exterior and a pair of ferocious marble lions guarding its brick walkway, Westerhauser Antiques communicated am unmistakeable message: 'If you're not filthy rich, don't even bother coming in.'

Jacobus waited impatiently in Yumi's car, listening to a WAMC roundtable about the newest corruption scandal in the New York State legislature, while Nathaniel knocked on the store's front door and received the same response as he had from his phone call the day before. None. Yumi, tramping through snow, wiped frost off the showroom window with her parka sleeve, revealing a gaudy collection of furniture that appeared to have just been delivered from Versailles. But there was no sign of human activity inside.

A banging on the car window interrupted Jacobus's attention from the radio program.

'What?' Jacobus said. 'Can't I even listen to corruption in peace?'

'What are you people doing here?' a voice said. It was not a friendly voice.

'Shopping. My Louis Quatorze bidet is busted. What's it to you?' Jacobus replied.

'I'm security.'

Jacobus had trouble hearing the man's voice with the radio on and through the window. He turned off the radio but couldn't open the window without the key, which Yumi had with her, so he opened the door to the cold blast of winter.

'And I'm freezing my ass off,' Jacobus said, 'so tell me where we can find Arnold Westerhauser and we can all go home.'

'The store is closed for the season.'

'No kidding. Shall we play twenty questions?'

'Mr Westerhauser lives in New York City.'

'Care to narrow that down?'

'Sir, I am not at liberty to divulge his address.'

'How about his phone number?'

'Sir, I am not at liberty to divulge his private number.'

'Well, if I divulge to you my private number, which can only be found in an obscure little book called the White Pages, would you be at liberty to divulge to Prince Westerhauser that a certain Daniel Jacobus is seeking information in regard to a possible criminal investigation?'

Jacobus held a five-dollar bill at arm's length that flapped in the wind until it was plucked out of his hand.

'I'll see what I can do, sir.'

When Nathaniel and Yumi returned to the car, Nathaniel said, 'I'm afraid we've struck out, Jake.'

'Amateurs,' Jacobus said.

Nathaniel hugged Yumi goodbye at the train station.

'And thanks for being such a charming host, Jake,' he said. 'Best Christmas ever.'

'If I didn't know you better, I'd think you were telling the truth,' Jacobus replied.

Nathaniel promised to call as soon as he found out anything from Boris Dedubian about the beguiling planks of wood.

After the train left, Yumi drove them back to Jacobus's house. The sky had cleared and was a brilliant blue. The bright sun reflected off the snow, making it sparkle.

'And when do *you* have to go back to New York?' Jacobus asked her. 'I thought you worked for a living.'

'We're on our winter break. Not enough people are in the mood to go to symphony concerts right after the holidays. I guess they have to recover from all the partying before they can digest Brahms again. But I can't complain. I've got two more weeks of freedom.'

'Plans?'

'Other than to play duets with you?'

'OK, cut the BS.'

'I hoped I could spend the next few days here, and maybe do some shopping and antiquing –' Jacobus laughed at that – 'then go back to the city for New Year's weekend, and then, whatever. Is that all right?'

'Why not? Trotsky enjoys your company.'

Jacobus and Yumi returned to the Last Supper puzzle while listening to a Met performance of Handel's *Giulio Cesare* on the radio. A supposedly renowned mezzo who Jacobus had neither heard of nor wished to hear again sang the florid eponymous role, originally composed for a castrato. As impressed as Jacobus was with Handel's music, he had a hard time imagining that the real Julius Caesar could have had a voice in the same range as Tiny Tim.

'Too bad the ides of March didn't come sooner,' he said, which was the moment the phone rang. It was Arnold Westerhauser, who seemed to want to atone for the brusque treatment Jacobus had received from his security guard.

'This is the dead season for antiques in the Berkshires,' Westerhauser said. 'There's no sense keeping the store open when no one's around.'

'If I may be so bold as to ask,' Jacobus said, 'why does a fancy outfit like yours bother to advertise in a working-class rag like the Shopper's Guide?'

'I ask myself that very question sometimes. But you see, in addition to our store we also do estate sales, and when you buy an entire estate you don't always have consistent quality, so we have a lot of merchandise that we want to dispose of quickly. You know, some of the less expensive items like lamps, kitchenware, memorabilia. What my Jewish colleagues call schlock. You'd be surprised how many people respond to our ad in the Shopper's Guide.'

'Do those lesser expensive items include violins?' Jacobus asked.

'We don't actively seek them out, but we do get them from time to time with the estate merchandise.'

'Have you ever had any business dealings with a man named Amadeo Borlotti?'

Westerhauser chuckled.

'Funny sounding name, huh?' Jacobus said.

'No, it's not that,' Westerhauser replied. 'Yes, I've had dealings with Mr Borlotti. What I laugh at is that he only buys the lower end instruments that come our way. A few hundred dollars. Maybe a thousand, tops. It keeps spare change in our cash register. Though I'm no expert in this field by any means, I've offered to sell him a few better instruments at cost, but he always says it's out of his price range and only takes the bargain basement items.'

'Did you know that Borlotti is missing?'

'No.' Westerhauser sounded truly surprised. 'That's the first I've heard. But then again, he's outside my circle.'

'You have any idea where he might be?'

'Certainly not.'

He sounded truly offended.

TEN

A fter the call from Westerhauser, it was time for dinner. Yumi decided that she'd had enough pork roast and stew to last a few years, so she drove off to K&J's for a pizza. She asked what Jacobus wanted on it.

'Anything but pineapple or barbecued chicken,' he said. 'They'd throw up in Italy if they saw those things on a pizza.'

'You say so!' she laughed, closing the door behind her.

Jacobus called Benson to report on their progress, or lack thereof. Benson decided he might question Westerhauser himself to find out what he was doing the night Borlotti's house burned down, since Sheffield was just over the hill from Egremont Falls.

'Good luck getting his phone number,' Jacobus said.

Jacobus asked Benson if he had learned anything more from his scant evidence. Benson informed him that the cleaver next to Borlotti's bed was clean, but the knife by the kitchen door had traces of blood.

'That's not a big surprise, is it?' Jacobus said.

'Why not?'

'It's a kitchen.'

'Oh, I should have mentioned. It's human.'

'That's a big help. Chances are we could even narrow it down to North America.'

'We don't know Borlotti's blood type yet, but we sent it to the experts at the lab. They're working on it.' Benson's tone suggested that Jacobus lacked sufficient reverence for 'the experts.' It seemed he was capable of offending whole classes of people.

Jacobus asked about the one remaining item, or items, that were next to Borlotti's bed. The letters.

'As I said, they were illegible,' Benson said, somewhat testily, as if repeating himself was a waste of his time.

'Hey, Sigurd,' Jacobus said, 'Get something straight. I'm not doubting your competence. I'm just trying to help, and only because you asked me for my help. So take the stick out of your ass. There's more to a letter than what's written on it, or haven't you read your Sherlock Holmes manual? The paper, the envelope, the glue sealing it, the stamp, whether it's typed or handwritten. What can you tell me?'

'Hold on,' Benson said, his tone suggesting he grudgingly conceded the point. 'I'll get them.'

'OK,' he said when he returned to the phone. 'As I said, you can't read a word, but you can make out they were handwritten, and generally in pencil.'

'Can you tell whether it's a man's or woman's handwriting?'

'Sorry, too far gone. The envelopes are all the same kind; cheap, letter-sized, like the ones that come in a box of a hundred at Kmart. The paper is equally cheap-looking. In fact, some of them look like they were written on the backs of scraps of sales receipts or something. No way to tell.'

'So the author of the letters might have been working class or poor? Maybe writing from a workplace?' Jacobus theorized.

'Could be. The stamps are standard twenty-five-cents. That's all there is. What else can I tell you?'

'I assume the stamps have postmarks. Can you make out a date they were cancelled?'

'Too blurry.'

'How about *where* they were cancelled?'

'Hard to say. I can only make out a letter or two on some of them. Let me try to piece them together.'

'You do that,' Jacobus said. 'I'll just read *War and Peace* until you're finished.'

While he waited, he heard Yumi's car come down the driveway. When she entered the house, the aroma of sausage, peppers, and onions made his stomach start to churn in anticipation. Trotsky, who started barking, shared his sentiment.

'I think I've got it,' Benson said finally.

'Great. I only got up to chapter four.'

'It's either Sarasota . . . or Saratoga.'

Jacobus's antenna shot up, but before he acted on it he needed to act on his appetite.

'Let me chew on that, Benson. I've gotta go,' he said.

'But—'

'Sorry. The pizza's getting cold,' Jacobus said and hung up.

He ate quickly, partly the result of his hunger but more in his eagerness to make yet one more phone call prompted by Benson's disclosure. What they didn't finish, Yumi put in the fridge for Jacobus to salvage sometime within the next year. Then she dialed a phone number for him and went upstairs to practice – even though the ceiling was so low she had to sit down to play – so that she'd be out of Jacobus's hair.

'You said Borlotti isn't a wealthy man,' Jacobus said to Jimmy Ubriaco.

'Yes, that's what I said.'

'Yet,' Jacobus pursued, 'he does all these freebies and gives money away left and right.'

'Your point being?'

'How can a poor man afford to be so magnanimous?'

'I'm not sure that those two things are mutually exclusive. He always says, "What's money, after all? Just something to make you happy. And if you don't spend it, how can it make you happy?" He has simple tastes so he has enough to get by. And, he's got a generous soul.

'I'll give you a f'rinstance. One time he did a soundpost repair on a run-of-the-mill violin, but in writing out the bill he accidentally adds an extra zero and charges fifteen hundred dollars instead of one hundred and fifty, OK? He's like that sometimes. You know, head in the clouds.

'The violin's owner doesn't even look at the bill because she knows Amadeo's an honest guy and just sends it off to the insurance company, which pays the claim. You know, even with the mistake in the bill, it wasn't so much more than what the big New York City repairmen charge, which you and I both know is outrageous. A hundred fifty bucks! That's nothing for that kind of job. When the check comes, Amadeo immediately sees his error and wants to send the difference back to the insurance company. But he's not a rich man, and neither was she, so in the end I convince him to chalk one up to good luck. The two of them evenly split the thirteen hundred and fifty dollar mistake and Amadeo donated his half to the school music program.'

While Jacobus was listening to Ubriaco's story he also heard Yumi practicing the first movement of the famous Mozart Sonata in E minor for violin and piano. It was hard for him to concentrate on one line of thought without losing the other thread, but did he sense there was a connection between the two? He listened to Yumi a little more before responding to Ubriaco.

'So let me understand,' he said. 'Now you're telling me Amadeo's got a generous soul to go with the gentle soul you told us about the last time we talked to you. Anything else he's got in his soul?'

'What do you mean?'

'You see, so far I've got this image of the Little Old Violinmaker, Me, all by his lonesome, chiseling wood in his little elf shop, sipping nostalgic espressos at The Last Drop, and toddling off for Sunday Hail Marys. A piece of the puzzle is missing. What else is in the picture? What's Borlotti saying in confession, Jimmy, that he doesn't want the vast unwashed to hear? What's spicing up his life other than bocce on the green? Is wood the only thing he's chiseling?'

'You're making something out of nothing.'

'Hey, who's blind here? Someone turned generous Amadeo's house and livelihood into a pile of stinking, smoldering ash! Someone made gentle Amadeo vanish in the night like the ghost of Christmas Yet to Come!'

'I've told you everything I know!'

'Really? Tell me about Saratoga, Jimmy.'

An abrupt silence. An answer in itself.

'Ah, so it does ring a bell! Could it be Saint Amadeo has some less than savory associates at the racetrack?'

'No doubt you'll read too much into this, Mr Jacobus, which is why I hadn't mentioned it, but, yes, Amadeo loves to go to the track. Maybe he's even in Saratoga this very moment.'

'Now? Watching the horses pull sleds?'

'No, I suppose not. He mostly goes in the summer. During the season.'

'A big-time gambler then? Hit the jackpot for a while, but then his luck ran out?'

'He doesn't bet.'

'How do you know that?'

'That's what he says.'

'That's what he says? You mean you don't you go with him, his bosom buddy from the old country who he sees every day?'

'No, I've never gone with him. He says he loves to watch the animals run and wants to be all by himself.'

'That reminds me of the constipated horse that came in last.'

'What do you mean?'

'Lame horse shit.'

'He's never lied to me. Yet . . .'

'Go ahead. I'm on pins and needles.'

'I've offered to go with him, you know, just for the hell of it, but he always refuses. And whenever I've asked him about it, he says it costs him a lot of money to go to the track. Then he gives me a little smile – kind of a sad smile – and says he puts all his money on his flower child.'

'How touching. So he goes to the track and loses money on his flower child, but doesn't bet.'

'That's what he says.'

'Jimmy, has it ever occurred to you that My Flower Child might be the name of a horse?'

'You don't know what you're talking about, Mr Jacobus. Gambling has nothing to do with this. And I resent the way you talk about my closest friend.'

'Well, get this, Jimmy. Your pal is missing along with a lot of violins. His house is burned down, and ulterior motives are multiplying like rabbits. Somewhere there's a reason and it seems to me like money might be a good place to start.'

'Actually,' said Ubriaco, 'it's a good place to finish.'

Ubriaco hung up on him, not unexpectedly. Jacobus was fully aware of his penchant for unpleasantness but felt justified when people stonewalled him. There were times, though, when he felt his inner rage about to explode, righteous though it may be. The dizziness, the pressure inside his head. The inability to exhibit restraint. So it was a sense of relief more than anything else when Ubriaco terminated their conversation.

He slumped back into his couch, breathing deeply to bring himself back down to his normal crustiness. Yumi was still practicing the Mozart. Focusing on the music helped him. He paid special attention to how she varied the nuance each time she played the plaintive melody. Though Mozart wrote the same melody four times during the movement in identical fashion for the violin – five if you count when it's in B-Minor – the piano accompaniment is different every time, changing the atmospheric conditions and suggesting different meanings, different emotions, different directions. Yumi, practicing those eight measures over and over again, coloring them this way and that so they were never exactly the same twice in a row, pulled it off so effectively that Jacobus could intuit the underlying changing harmonies, even though there was no piano to be heard.

But, as impressed and proud as he was of Yumi's musicianship, it was the music itself that gave him unexpected insight. All the more haunting for its utter simplicity, the melody was hardly more than an upward arpeggio that gradually settled back down again to where it began. So modest, so unassuming, so unpretentious. It was Amadeo Borlotti, at least the Borlotti that Ubriaco was trying to portray. Yet the undercurrent in the piano was unpredictable and brooding. The first time it was in precise unison with the violin. Then, each ensuing time, it became more and more conflicted. It was like a calm sea with sharks below the surface. Even though the violin melody tried to retain its dark serenity, it inevitably showed its tragic face from behind its mask.

The playing stopped. Jacobus heard Yumi's stockinged footsteps enter the living room.

'How did it sound?' she asked.

'Not bad.'

She kissed him on the cheek.

'I'm going to load the woodstove,' she said. 'Then I'm going to get into bed, pull up the covers, and read for a while. What better way to spend a winter night in the Berkshires?'

'What are you reading?'

'A really creepy mystery. Do you want me to tell you what it's about?'

'Mystery? Can't be bothered.'

She gave him another peck, and soon Jacobus was alone.

Jacobus called Benson and reported the result of his conversation with Ubriaco and suggested they check two records: Borlotti's bank records and the track record of a thoroughbred named My Flower Child.

'Those might be profitable leads, Mr Jacobus,' Benson said. 'They're certainly creative. I don't think we'll have much trouble tracking down where he banked his money, and I'll get hold of the Saratoga authorities and have them talk to the track people there. I'm sure they're familiar with the whole lot of ne'er-do-wells in that line of work. Maybe you and your friends could go there as well. Check out some of the music stores. Nose around the track. Who knows what you might turn up? It's the middle of winter but maybe someone will enlighten us as to how Borlotti lost money without betting the horses.'

'Keep an eye on Ubriaco, too,' Jacobus said. 'His bluster's covering up something unpleasant just like his air freshener.'

'Don't you worry. And FYI, we've put out a missing persons

alert for Borlotti, covering all the standard bases. Bus stations, train stations, airports. We're beating all the bushes.'

'Any leads?'

'Not a trace.'

Jacobus was about to turn in for the night when the phone rang again. Someday, he thought, there will be a way to turn the damn things off.

It was Boris Dedubian, calling after hours at Nathaniel's urging.

'Your phone's been busy,' he said.

'Call me Mr Popularity.'

'Mr Williams was very insistent I ring you,' Dedubian said, as if calling at nine at night was the most inconvenient thing he'd ever done. 'That wood he showed me was, I must say, interesting. Very interesting.'

'Are you at liberty to divulge what's interesting?' Jacobus asked.

'Why, of course!' Dedubian replied, sounding surprised. 'After all, that's why I'm calling.'

'Never mind. Family joke. Tell me what's interesting.'

'Jake, the selection of wood used to make and repair fine violins – maple and spruce – is a crucial step in the process. Perhaps the most important consideration of all. You can have the finest crafts-manship, but if the wood is pedestrian, the violin will never sound good. I'm sure that much you know very well.

'You can get those woods almost anywhere, but great quality is hard to find. I always keep my eyes open for when the old European luthiers retire. As soon as I hear they plan to fold up shop, I bid for their wood. You see, this wood Mr Williams brought me is very old. It has been cut from the tree three, maybe four hundred years ago. To me it appears this is not American wood. It is wood, I believe, that comes from the forests of northern Italy and western Yugoslavia.'

'How do you know this?' Jacobus asked. 'Is it labeled, "*fatto in Italia*"?'

'That's funny, Jake,' Dedubian said. 'You are a very funny man. Of course, I don't know this one hundred percent sure, but I am fairly certain, because it is in many ways similar to the wood on some of the great Cremonese instruments.'

'How is it similar?'

'That is a very good question. I have recently received a study from Cornell University, sponsored by the American Luthier Society, of the dendrochronology of the maple and spruce from two dozen famous Stradivaris, Guarneris, and Amatis. It is amazing what has been learned about wood and their ability to trace its origins. This wood that Mr Williams brought me, I believe, comes from those same forests. That is why he wanted me to call you.'

'Everyone's still trying to discover the "secret" of Stradivarius, huh?'

'Yes. They do the chemical analysis of the varnish. They do the CT scans of the instruments so they can see the cross-section at any point. They do all the measurements down to the micro-millimeter.' Dedubian chuckled. 'And you know what? They overlook what is perfectly obvious to everybody.'

'And what is that?'

'Antonio Stradivari was a superior, uniquely gifted craftsman. No one can beat him.'

'Not that I disagree, but don't you have a few Strads in your shop that you're itching to sell and haven't been moving?'

'Well . . .'

'What's holding them up?'

'I'm not sure,' Dedubian said. 'They've got pedigree provenance with all the right certificates. Hill, Wurlitzer, Beare. They're in excellent shape. They're from his Golden Period.'

'How much are you asking?'

'Between three and five million.'

'I wonder if that might have something to do with it.'

'It might,' Dedubian said, not at all put off, 'but in the twenty-first century that will be considered a bargain. Believe me.'

'No doubt,' said Jacobus. 'If we ever live that long. Boris, let me ask you about something else. Are there fluids in violinmaking that are particularly flammable?'

'Jake, you know, you are a very funny man.'

'Yes, you've told me that. I'm a million laughs. But can you answer my question?'

'Jake, if the other tenants in my building knew the compounds I use, they would shut down my business.'

'Could you be a little more specific?'

'I'd be happy to. We use pure alcohol for touch-up work, turpentine for making varnish, zylene and acetone for cleaning, and nitric acid to color boxwood.

'Nitric acid does not itself burn, but it oxidizes organic matter and makes it highly flammable. We also use anhydrous ammonia, which is explosive under certain conditions. It's not, on its own, very flammable, but if the chemical were to leak, it can ignite when it becomes about sixteen to twenty-five percent of the air – a huge, usually detectable concentration – and reaches temperatures of at least one-thousand-two-hundred degrees Fahrenheit. Since it takes so much heat to ignite, it's not usually the source of a fire, although it could ignite if a fire was caused by something else. Does that answer your question?'

'Consider me enlightened. Thanks for calling, Boris. I owe you one.'

Jacobus sat alone in the dark. Accident or arson? He wasn't sure now. His restless mind was never able to compartmentalize ideas or disciplines. Everything was interconnected. Inseparable. Thinking about the fire took him back to the Mozart sonata. Most composers would have been content to stick to standard expectations and finish the movement in a cheery major key. But nothing Mozart ever did was standard. Despite occasional glimpses of sunshine, he finished the movement as he began it, in ill-omened E-Minor. Yes, the story came to a conclusion, but without affirmation, leaving the listener uneasy, with more questions than answers. It was tragic. Or was it? Without understanding how he'd gotten there, Jacobus found himself coming back to wondering what use a modest violin repairman might have for three-hundred-year-old Italian wood.

ELEVEN

Wednesday, December 28

Jacobus fed Trotsky his daily breakfast of liverwurst and a can of baked beans, and had stuck a few more parts of the apostles into the jigsaw puzzle when Nathaniel called. He was exasperated. *A rare occurrence, especially first thing in the morning*, Jacobus thought. Nathaniel had just spoken to the friendly folks at Concordia Insurance, 'where integrity isn't a word. It's who we are.'

'Jimmy Ubriaco might not be the most forthcoming person on the block,' Nathaniel said, 'but he was right about Concordia.'

'You went to their office?'

'No. Phone.'

'Might it have been better to talk to them in person?'

'In Fort Lauderdale?'

'Well, it *is* warmer there.'

'If it is, it would be nice if some of that warmth had rubbed off on their office manager, Sean Larson. After I identified myself, I told him all I wanted to know was whether any recent claims had been filed by Borlotti, who, I understood, was one of their clients. Larson said he was not at liberty to divulge that information—'

'Obfuscation 101. Where is it they teach that course?' Jacobus hollered.

'My sentiments exactly, Jake,' Nathaniel said, 'but that was only the beginning. I asked whether he had even heard about the fire at Borlotti's. He seemed very surprised and admitted he hadn't, but said if that were so, they would undoubtedly be hearing from Borlotti soon. I told him that Borlotti has been missing since the fire—'

'Let me guess. At which point your new friend, Sean, told you in that case they would have to wait for him to return and verify the loss before they could go any further with processing claims.'

'You hit the nail on the head. He said, "Sorry, we don't have an exception in his policy for that. We must hear from Mr Borlotti first. Anything else would be unethical."'

Jacobus barked a laugh.

'But I didn't give up, even then,' Nathaniel continued. 'I mentioned some of the names on the Rolodex who we'd called and asked if any of them were Concordia clients.'

'Stonewall?'

'Reinforced concrete.'

'Don't forget, my dear friend, integrity is who they are. So that was the end of it?'

'Almost. By this point I was getting a little frustrated –' Jacobus laughed again – 'so I asked to speak with Borlotti's agent. Larson hemmed and hawed, and so I demanded—'

'Bravo!'

'And Larson told me that his agent, a gal named Minerva Forsythe, was unreachable at this time.'

'She was in the ladies' room?'

'"She has taken an unexpected, indefinite leave."'

'Where did she go?'

'Larson said Hawaii.'

'Someone from Fort Lauderdale going to Hawaii? Likely story. I still bet on ladies' room.'

'Well, that was it. I know insurance companies can give you the runaround, but that one made me dizzy.'

'Then why not try some of the others?' Jacobus asked.

'What do you mean?'

'Borlotti's company is Concordia, and probably a few of his customers. But there must be other companies that specialize in instrument insurance, where you have established contacts. Why don't you call them? Do an end run?'

Williams sighed.

'Later, maybe. I was thinking of coming back up today. What's for dinner?'

'Liverwurst and baked beans.'

'I'll take a rain check.'

With Nathaniel girding his loins for a grueling morning with the insurance companies and Yumi practicing for a recital, Jacobus felt the guilt of a wastrel if he didn't do something productive. So he called Roy Miller and suggested breakfast at K&J's.

'I've got a repair on tap this morning, but it's someone's vacation home and the owner lives somewhere in Redondo Beach. It can wait.'

They both ordered the morning's special, buckwheat pancakes with 'artisan, ethically raised, house-crafted sausage patties' and locally grown, organic blueberries.

'What's the repair?' Jacobus asked.

'Guy's pipes burst overnight from the cold weather. His security service let him know and I got the call. If some of these out-of-town summer folks only knew what winters in the Berkshires were like, they could easily prevent stuff like that from happening,' Miller forked down half a pancake. 'But then when disaster strikes, they expect me to fix the problem yesterday, like all I do in life is wait by the phone for their call. Then they want me to clean things up so that it looks like new, and get all uppity when I send them a bill.'

'Charge them extra for their whining.'

'Don't worry. I do. They should just count their blessings their security service called them. If the water sat there until summer, the house would've been a total loss.'

'How did the security service know the pipes had burst?' Jacobus asked.

'The house has a thermostat that's wired directly to their office. If the house temperature drops below a certain level, they automatically get an alert. During the storm on Christmas Eve their electricity went out, so the furnace couldn't ignite, yada, yada, yada. By the time they called me and I got to the house the pipes had burst, but I was able to shut off the water so the damage wasn't too bad. Sometimes accidents do happen, but if those morons had drained the pipes there never would've been a problem.'

'You think Borlotti's house burning down was an accident?' Jacobus asked.

'If he weren't missing, I'd say for sure,' Miller replied. 'There's nothing to suggest it wasn't.'

'What about the security alarm that didn't ring?'

'What do you mean?'

'I assume that with these security gizmos, just like with the thermostat, if a fire starts, the temperature of the house goes up so much that the security firm immediately gets a signal and comes running. Isn't that how it works?'

'Yes,' said Miller. 'Or the fire department. Sometimes they're wired directly there. But you're assuming Borlotti had a security system.'

'Of course I am. What violin shop doesn't?'

'How do we find out for sure?' Miller asked. 'All his records were destroyed. You want to ask his friend, Jimmy what's-his-face?'

Jacobus laughed. 'I think I need to let Jimmy cool off for a while after the last time I spoke to him. But there can't be too many security firms out here. You think you can give some a call and find out if any of them serviced Borlotti's house? Only after you're done with the plumbing, of course.'

There was too much food for Jacobus to finish so he asked Scott the server for a box to take home.

'Sure thing!' Scott said. 'Savin' up for lunch?'

'No. My dog, Trotsky,' he said.

'Trotsky likes pancakes?' Scott asked.

'Just the blueberries.'

When Miller dropped Jacobus back home, Yumi was gone. She left a note on the door so that Miller would see it and let Jacobus know that she had gone to the outlet mall in Lee for post-Christmas sales.

With nothing better to do, he took out his violin and began to practice. Not that he had anything to practice for. With few exceptions, he hadn't performed publicly in decades and frankly had no desire to. For him, connecting with the music, holding the violin and feeling his fingers touch the strings and create this complex sequence of vibrations that found a gateway to one's every emotion was all the reward he desired. Most of the music he now played he had memorized before he had gone blind. That was the big benefit of memorizing, difficult as it may be. Once tucked away in the brain, it was always there somewhere. After his blindness, learning new music became more of a challenge. He had to learn by ear, listening to the same music over and over again. And of course in those days, they didn't have all these CDs that you could stop and start. They didn't even have cassette tapes! So he had had to memorize vast swaths of music at a time, and though no one believed him when he asserted that's how he learned the Alban Berg violin concerto, it was true.

Today, though, his muse gravitated toward the twelve Corelli violin sonatas, music not nearly as complex or dramatic as Berg, but whose clarity of form and melody helped clear his mind of all the tangled loose ends Borlotti's disappearance had created. The perfect synthesis of intellect and heart, whenever Jacobus finished practicing Corelli he could think better and felt a greater understanding of humanity and the world.

He had just finished the fugue of the C Major sonata when Nathaniel called.

'Finally done!' he said. 'You want to hear what I've found out?'

'Later,' Jacobus said and hung up. He continued on to the Adagio.

He put his violin away when his arms tired after playing through the first six sonatas. Then he lay down on his couch to take a nap, Trotsky thumping on the floor by his side.

He was awakened by Nathaniel's call.

'You have some interesting news,' Jacobus said.

'How do you know that, O, omniscient one?' Williams replied.

'Because you woke me up from my nap, so you better.'

Nathaniel had approached his carefully cultivated personal channels at FreedomWide, Alliance, and Northeast Mutual, the company Jimmy Ubriaco had said insured his school's instruments. Nathaniel told them he was looking for claims Borlotti had filed himself or Borlotti's customers had filed, which would be apparent because Borlotti's name would be on the repair invoice.

'Two things seem curious,' Nathaniel said. 'It looks like there's a pattern over the years that started with small, inexpensive claims for repairs, then gradually increased into several thousand dollars for some instruments. The second interesting thing was that a good number of his customers owned high quality eighteenth- and nineteenth-century Italian makers of some renown, like Testore, Ventapane, Carcassi, Scarampella – instruments that fetched high five-figures and low six-figures, which they had bought from Borlotti.'

'So, two new questions,' Jacobus said. 'First: Why so many people would take valuable instruments to a repairman with such a modest reputation, even though they might have bought them from him.'

'I had the same question,' Nathaniel said. 'You don't necessarily want to have your vintage Mercedes serviced by the used car dealer you bought it from. So I called the owners. They weren't any happier to hear from me the second time than the first. But I did get the impression they were pleased with Borlotti's work and that he charged much less than it would have cost to have the repairs done in New York.'

'That makes sense,' Jacobus said. 'Second question: If that guy Weimaraner—'

'You mean Westerhauser?'

'Whatever. If Weimaraner said that Borlotti only bought the bottom of the barrel from his estate sales, what was he doing transacting big instruments?'

'Good question. And Borlotti trolling in *Shopper's Guide*. Same.'

And still Jacobus's inner Corelli was troubled. 'And what about Ubriaco? Did you ask about the school instruments?'

'Northeast corroborated what Ubriaco told us. His claim is absolutely in order. They just won't do anything about it until they hear from Borlotti's insurance company, Concordia. So I think our friend Jimmy is cleared on that one, though he may be out of a job.'

'My heart breaks for him. One more question. Did any of the owners say their valuable instruments were in Borlotti's shop when it burned down?'

'Yes, about a half dozen of them.'

'Were they alarmed that they might have gone up in smoke?'

'You'd think. Surprisingly, some weren't.'

'Did you inform them at as far as we can tell the shop had mysteriously been cleared of violins?'

'No. I didn't. Seemed premature.'

'Wait a minute!' What was bothering Jacobus about Nathaniel's report suddenly bubbled to the surface. 'Something isn't kosher. How can they say he charged so little when the claims they filed were high?'

'Jake, why did you have to say that?' Nathaniel wailed.

'Why not?'

'Because now I'm going to have to call all of them back again.'

Jacobus heard a car drive up. It wasn't the engine of Yumi's car, though. He would have heard that a mile away.

'Hang in there,' he told Nathaniel, and hung up.

Sigurd Benson was at the door.

'What do you have for me, Sigurd?' Jacobus asked.

'How do you know I have anything for you?'

'By gracing my humble abode in person instead of calling,' Jacobus said. 'And I'm pretty sure you don't want me to make you lunch.'

'You're right. I have something to give you. And something to tell you.'

Benson remained hesitantly in the doorway.

'Well, come on in and spit it out, Sigurd!' Jacobus said.

Jacobus offered him a cup of Folgers instant. Benson politely declined.

Benson made his way to the easy chair in the living room. Jacobus returned to the couch.

'We found two-hundred-thirty-thousand dollars in a strong box in Borlotti's basement,' Benson said.

'Two-hundred-thirty!' Jacobus said. 'Now, that's interesting! What could poor, old Amadeo be doing with that amount of change stashed away? What took you so long to find it?'

'We had to jackhammer through the collapsed floor to get to the basement. There was a safe under a lot of rubble. Based upon the layering, it had been upstairs in his shop. With its weight, it no doubt contributed to the floor collapsing.'

'Yet more questions! If Borlotti committed arson, why did he leave the money? If someone else torched the place but didn't take the money, what would be the motive?'

'To steal the violins?'

'Then why burn the place?' Jacobus was getting dizzy going around in circles. 'Any other major discoveries?'

'I don't know if I'd call it major,' Benson said, 'but we tracked down Borlotti's savings and checking accounts. Lee Bank. Nothing unusual. He had enough coming in to cover his mortgage and the usual living expenses. No splurging. No big trips. The checks he wrote were the boring ones everyone else writes. We called his credit card companies. The usual monthly checks. Occasional lapsed balances but nothing to sound any alarms. We even called the IRS and his returns were as routine as we would want ours to be.'

'All of which makes the two-hundred grand in the safe even more interesting.'

'Yes, it does. We also found Ubriaco's instruments, by the way. Or what was left of them. In the basement. They were two dimensional, but just like he said, we counted nine violins, one viola, two cellos, and four basses.'

Jacobus heard something in Benson's voice.

'You're leaving something out.'

'Well, I'm not sure if I am and I'm not sure if I'm not. But it was just something curious.'

'Come on, Sigurd. Let's have it. You're doing such a great job unburdening yourself.'

'We also counted the remains of nine violin cases, one viola case, and two cello cases, but only three bass cases. It's possible one bass case is missing, though it's also very possible that it had been upstairs and got incinerated. Or we just missed it in the wreckage.'

'I suppose,' Jacobus said, though he wasn't convinced.

'One of the bass cases still had its wheels intact. I measured the distance between them and it was about the same as my recollection of the tracks in the snow. The ones that went from Borlotti's house to the truck.'

'So you think he was sending that special someone an empty string bass case?'

'Possible,' Benson said.

'At ten o'clock on Christmas Eve?'

'Less possible.'

'Any fine tuners?' Jacobus asked.

'Just the ones by Ubriaco's instruments.'

'All right. Keep me up-to-date. Good work, Benson. You've restored my faith in human nature.'

'Seriously?'

'No, but good work anyway.'

'Just one more thing, Mr Jacobus. We've heard back from our

colleagues in Saratoga. They did find a mucker at the track who recognized Borlotti's description and confirmed that he had come from time to time to watch the horses run. And, you were right, there was indeed a racehorse named Flower Child.'

Pay dirt!

'He ran one race, finished eighth in a nine-horse field, and then was put out to stud. That was in 1968. One of the co-owners was Sonny Bono. That must have been how the horse got its name. Frankly, I thought your idea was very creative, but I don't think it's going to get us anywhere. Hope I haven't burst your bubble.'

Jacobus recalled the Abbott and Costello routine where the street-smart Abbott tried to explain the intricacies of the track to Costello. Much to the naïve Costello's horror and chagrin, Abbott insisted that 'the mudder ate the fodder.' Now Jacobus had something to eat, too. Crow.

'I guess I've been kicking a dead horse,' he said.

'Not at all,' Benson replied. 'It was a long shot. But we're still waiting to hear about other possible connections Borlotti might have had with the track. I've brought you a bunch of copies of the latest photo of Amadeo Borlotti we could find. That's mainly why I drove over here. I thought maybe you wouldn't mind going to Saratoga and spreading it around. It's from a four-year-old *Berkshire Eagle*. Borlotti was honored for subsidizing the Egremont Falls high school orchestra's trip to a national orchestra convention in Atlanta.

'Ubriaco go with them?'

'Seems so. The article says, "Though the orchestra did not win a prize, orchestra leader James Ubriaco was upbeat. 'We're just so proud of them. It was an experience our youngsters will never forget.' " '

Jacobus imagined hundreds of small town, hormone-driven teenagers at liberty in Atlanta for a week, and thought, *damn straight they'll never forget it.*

As Benson was leaving, Yumi returned with three new pairs of shoes for herself and leather gloves for Jacobus for when he went outside to collect firewood. While trying them on, Jacobus told her about his conversations with Nathaniel and Benson.

'Isn't flower child what hippies called each other back in the 1960s?' Yumi asked.

'Back in the 1960s? You make it sound like the Dark Ages. Why?'

'Just that maybe flower child is a person.'

'You really think a codger like Borlotti is regaling a teenage honey with love beads?'

'Maybe when they were both teenagers. Maybe she was a lost love and he just found her and they ran off together.'

'And you think a fairytale like that is more likely than him gambling away his money at the track?'

'I just think it's sweet.'

TWELVE

B y noon the temperature had risen a few degrees, which should have been cause for optimism, but the thick blanket of ground fog it spawned only made the scene more depressing. Jacobus felt the chill, dismal gray in his bones. It matched his mood and frustration over his failure to discover anything of value for the investigation. The reasons for Borlotti's disappearance and his house being burned down were still a total mystery, and Jacobus felt as if he were being teased with new pieces tossed into the jigsaw puzzle box while his back was turned. Pieces that might not even fit. But once he had a bit in his mouth Jacobus was determined not to give it up, and there was still time in the day to pursue the racetrack connection.

Traffic was light on I-90 as he and Yumi drove northward past Albany, but visibility and road conditions were miserable. Yumi, who found the new adventure exhilarating, had to rein in her speed.

'I'm fine going to the racetrack with you,' she said to Jacobus. 'I've never been to one before and I'm really excited, but those letters don't have anything to do with horses.'

'Why not?' Jacobus asked. 'Borlotti seems to have lost a lot of money and won a lot of money. With Saratoga postmarks, what more likely way than at the racetrack?'

'Jake,' Yumi replied. 'Do you remember when I was studying the Brahms concerto with you and you scolded me during a lesson for overlooking the obvious?'

Jacobus remembered as if it were yesterday, but said, 'How the hell do you expect me to remember every lesson?'

'Well, let me remind you. I was trying to be a real virtuoso, to discover something in the music that no one else had ever seen. To find the true Brahms! So I was pushing and pulling the tempos and overdoing everything and just twisting the whole thing into one big pretzel. You said, "Yumi, do me a favor. You'd make life much more pleasant for me if you just play what Brahms actually wrote instead of trying to guess what he had for dinner." '

'Your point is?'

'Jake, what kind of letters does a man put next to his bed? Not betting forms. Not IOUs. They had to be love letters.'

'You think "my flower child" is his girlfriend?'

'Yes, I do.'

'How the hell am I going to find her, then?'

'I don't know. But you will. You always do.'

They started out at the track, anyway. Abandoned in winter, the bleakness of the Saratoga racetrack was palpable. During the racing season, the massive, antique grandstand and the grounds around it swarmed with highlife and lowlife alike; eating, drinking, schmoozing, and of course, betting. Now, all the vitality, all the hubbub, all the color, all the horses, their jockeys, their entourages, and the rest of the human support system that exists for the sole purpose of making money off the animals had long since departed for the winter racing season at Hialeah and Santa Anita, taking the sun with them. The forlorn, wooden grandstand, overlooking the silent track and sculpted garden infield, now all snow-covered, was almost lifeless. The only personnel to be found milling about were an electrician performing off-season maintenance, a trucker delivering hoses, and a skeleton crew of security people who, with little hesitation, escorted Jacobus and Yumi off the premises. Before the gate was unceremoniously clanked shut behind them, Yumi did manage to ask whether anyone knew Borlotti and to pass out copies of his photo, but no one gave the slightest indication of knowing or caring who he was.

Yumi, enjoying the change of pace the adventure provided and not yet discouraged, drove the two of them into town to ask around whether anyone had ever heard of Amadeo Borlotti. Their first stop was at Lemansky's Music Company, whose window display boasted the store to be the 'top seller of musical instruments to schools in the greater capital region since 1954.' Jacobus's pipe dream was to find Borlotti there at the store, repairing violins with old Italian wood while his adoring hippie girlfriend looked on, and then go home.

But it was not to be. Ray Lemansky, store manager and son of its founder, Walter Lemansky, had heard of Borlotti but was certain they had never done any business with him. He borrowed a photo from Yumi and passed it around to the employees in case Borlotti might have come to the store without purchasing anything, but no one recognized him. When Yumi mentioned that Borlotti worked in Egremont Falls, Lemansky said, 'That's Jimmy Ubriaco's turf, isn't it?'

'How do you know that?' Jacobus asked.

'We sold instruments, music, stands, cases – you name it – for his school orchestra and band years ago. Those instruments have got to be pretty beaten up by now. I expect Jimmy will be back sometime soon.'

'Don't bet on it,' said Jacobus.

He and Yumi left the store and skidded along the sidewalk in the damp cold, arm in arm, from one business to the next, inquiring and handing out Borlotti's photo with great persistence but little hope. Jacobus began to feel like someone whose cat was missing. Maybe, he half jested, they should pin flyers with the photo on telephone poles with a note saying, 'Cute and affectionate. Sometimes responds to Amadeo. Reward. No questions asked.' And attach little phone number tags at the bottom. The cold hastened their decision to take a hiatus from their search, and after striking out yet again at a new computer software store called Giddy App, decided to seek refuge from the elements, their disappointment, and the penchant of local businesses to capitalize on the horseracing theme.

'There are a few cafés and bakeries across the street,' Yumi said. 'Want to try Thorough Bread?'

'Nix.'

'Tea Biscuit? Change of Pacers?'

'Double nix.

'There's a luncheonette on the corner. Sloppy Joe's.'

'Yix!'

'You sure? It looks like a real dive.'

'What's a little heartburn between friends?'

They entered the luncheonette and sat at a corner table. Jacobus, as was his custom in a new setting, explored it with his hands to gain his bearings. There was a lot he could ascertain – the type of table covering, napkins, silverware, plates, salt and pepper shakers, and condiments. The shape of a ketchup container could speak volumes. Even the absence of those things gave him a good idea of what the establishment held in store.

On this occasion his hands stuck to the plastic tablecloth. So far so good – just the kind of place he liked. Expanding his range, he felt some coins with his right hand and began to shunt them to the side of the table.

'Hey! Get your slimy hands off my tip!' said a low, raspy voice. Jacobus's instantaneous impression: a bitter young lady who clawed for every cent; who, like him, had self-destructive tendencies, ruining her chances for the very tips that seemed to mean so much to her. Her voice, an octave too low, bore the same wear and tear of smoking too much as his. Indications of a tough life. Well, life wasn't fair, was it?

'Don't worry, honey,' Jacobus said. 'I left my tin cup at home. Just give us the menu.' This she did, slapping it down on to the table, grabbing her change, and departing.

'Nice,' said Jacobus. 'I like her.'

'This is interesting,' said Yumi, changing the subject. 'The Sloppy Joe story. It's on the back of the menu. Did you know that Sloppy Joe was one of the most famous horses here in Saratoga? On August 7, 1963, he beat Red Herring in a stakes match for the biggest purse ever up to that time. Did you know that?'

'Nah, I must've been playing polo that day.'

'Red Herring was favored but Sloppy Joe won by a nose.'

'Of course,' Jacobus said.

'What do you mean, "of course"?'

'Herrings don't have noses.'

The waitress returned to take their orders.

'What kind of meat do you put in your sloppy joes?' Jacobus asked. 'Sloppy Joe?'

'Only for special customers.'

'And who might they be?'

'The ones that don't make that same stupid joke every day.'

'In that case, I'll have a sloppy joe.'

'You want the sloppy joe special?' she recited as if for the thousandth time, which it might have been. 'Sloppy joe and cuppa joe. Same price.'

'How can I refuse such an enticing offer,' Jacobus said.

When she left, Yumi asked, 'Why do you have to taunt everyone, Jake?'

'What do you mean? I like her!'

'And how's a blind man going to eat a sloppy joe?' Yumi asked.

'Just watch me,' said Jacobus.

'I'd rather not. You only brought two sleeves.'

While they ate, Jacobus and Yumi agreed not to dwell upon their non-starting investigation. They talked about what an awful winter it had been, which led to them discussing how accurately Vivaldi's 'Winter' portrayed it, even though it had been composed almost three hundred years earlier and thousands of miles away.

'Let's hope it's not a metaphor,' Jacobus said.

'Meaning?'

'Vivaldi's sonnet. *"We tread the icy path with greatest care for fear of slipping and sliding. With a reckless turn we fall crashing to the ground and, rising, hasten across the ice lest it should crack."* We've been slipping and sliding. I'm not looking forward to crashing to the ground.'

Yumi put her hand on his cheek.

'You're just being your usual, sweet, pessimistic self. It'll all work out.'

While Yumi made a trip to the ladies' room, the waitress came to the table to give them their bill.

'What's your name, honey?' Jacobus asked.

'It's on my name tag.'

'As you can plainly see, young lady, I can't.'

'Not my problem, is it?'

'Well, I suppose it is. I want to know the name of the person who I'm thinking of giving a big tip to, that's all.'

'In that case, it's Dahlia.'

Jacobus heard the quiet clatter of cheap ceramic as she cleared their dishes and stacked them in her arms. He made a quick intake of breath.

'My little flower child,' he said.

Jacobus had no difficulty hearing the dishes crash to the floor.

THIRTEEN

J acobus provided Dahlia with sufficient financial incentive to pay for the broken dishes and persuade her to talk further. The luncheonette closed at three o'clock. She agreed to meet them elsewhere after work.

'There's a bar two-and-a-half blocks from here on the left,' she said. 'Nasty Brews. Wait for me there.'

An hour later Jacobus was about to conclude she had given him and Yumi the slip when he heard the front door of the bar open. Since there had been few afternoon customers in the place that reeked of piss, beer, and cigarettes, he guessed it was Dahlia, and he was right.

'Got a cigarette?' she asked, sitting down at their table in the corner.

'Sorry. Doctor's orders,' Jacobus said.

'Your loss. Enough chitchat. That bastard promised not to tell anyone where to find me. It was supposed to be "our little secret,"' she said.

'He didn't. We found you all by ourselves. We were hoping you could tell us where *he* is.'

'What are you talking about?' Her voice was fast and clipped.

'Borlotti's been missing since Saturday and his house was burned down.'

'Missing! He's missing? I need a drink. Or your doctor make you give that up, too?'

'I switched doctors for that.'

'I'll get you something,' Yumi said, and went to the bar.

'We're a little in the dark here,' Jacobus said. 'You and he have a relationship. That much we figured out. Give us the backstory.'

Yumi returned with a Canadian Club and water and gave it to Dahlia. Jacobus heard her drain it then put the glass down heavily on the table.

'Why should I?' Her defensiveness was as thick as her voice.

'We're trying to find him. Clearly he means something to you and his disappearance is a surprise. I'm assuming you'd like to see him found, too.'

'Why are you after him?'

Jacobus gave Dahlia enough background to justify their presence, but intuitively avoided mention of working with the police. Instead, he talked about his common interest in violins with Borlotti. It was enough to convince her.

'I met him at the track, maybe six, seven years ago. I don't know. I was waiting tables at the Club Terrace. I did the breakfast buffet shift for the diehards who came at dawn to get their rocks off watching the horses work out. He came all the time. He always sat in the same place in the dining room, off to the side by himself. He never talked to anyone.'

'Except you.'

'Except me. Yeah, except me. At first, he would only say stuff like, "nice eggs" or "may I have another cup of coffee, please?" He always says "may I" and "please" and "thank you." At first I never said anything back because he was such a loser. Made me feel guilty, so one day I said, "So, you win a lot of money on the horses?" It's what you say to everyone there, like "How are you?" And he said, no, he never bet on races. He just thought it was beautiful to watch them run in the morning.

'Do you have a cigarette?'

'No. Just like last time.'

'I thought, what a jerk, but at least he wasn't the sleaze or those richies who grab your ass and think they're entitled. He kept coming to the track for breakfast and he started getting more comfortable talking. He was a nice man. He was harmless.

'One day I bring him an extra grape jelly for his toast, and he tells me he's got something for me. It was a watch. I say, "What the hell's this for?" and he tells me he noticed I didn't have one. He thought I'd like it. He was sweating like a pig, so I had to laugh and that kind of broke the ice. After that we began to meet for lunch or we'd take a walk between my morning shift and night job.'

'What job was that?' Yumi asked.

'There's a spa in town called Back Stretch. The usual: massage, hair, manicure, make-up. For people who could afford it, you know? I did cosmetics. It was a good job.'

'You don't have it anymore?' Jacobus asked.

'No, I don't.' Her tone of voice strongly suggested that conversation was a nonstarter.

'So did you and Borlotti begin a relationship?' Yumi asked.

'Hell, no!'

'What else would you call it?' Jacobus asked.

'It depends on who you ask. He'd say it was, but he never really asked me what I thought.'

'He gave you the watch. When you accepted it don't you think he had good reason to conclude that?'

'He can think whatever he wants. Who am I to stop him?'

'Is the watch the only present he's given you?' Jacobus asked.

'He gives me a present every time he comes. He sends me money. What am I supposed to do, give it back?'

'How much money? Overall?' Jacobus asked.

'I need another drink.'

'First tell us.'

'I don't really keep track. Maybe a hundred thousand. Maybe more. Maybe less. I don't know. A lot.'

'And gifts? What kind of gifts?'

There was silence.

'I asked, what about the gifts?'

'She shrugged, Jake,' Yumi said.

'Sorry, darlin', I can't hear shrugs.'

'Lots of gifts. Jewelry. A purse. Flowers. Those kinds of things.'

'Are you sleeping with him?' Jacobus asked.

'Are you sleeping with Tokyo Rose here?' Dahlia shouted. Even with a near empty bar, it was suddenly quieter.

'No, he is not!' Yumi whispered. Jacobus laughed.

'I only ask,' Jacobus continued, 'because you nearly had cardiac arrest when I first mentioned Borlotti's name and almost passed out when I told you he was missing. I think that was a fair question.'

She laughed a laugh that was bitter and tinged with embarrassment.

'If you want to know the truth, I offered. Yeah, I offered. I figured what the hell, I owed him one. Guess what? He turned me down.'

'Really? Is he homosexual?'

'Worse. Old-fashioned. He won't sleep with me until I marry him. He won't even let me come to his house. He says it's not "proper."'

'Has he gotten down on one knee and proposed?' Jacobus asked.

'You're a sarcastic bastard, you know that? But since you asked, yes, that's exactly what he did. A month ago.'

'And you said no. Is that right?'

'I said I'd think about it. And then he sent me another letter, putting his proposal in writing, along with some money. A lot of money. He said I could keep it even if my answer was no.'

'Twenty thousand dollars?' Jacobus asked.

'No. Ten thousand. Why?'

'Long story. And how did you respond to his little pre-nup Christmas present?'

'I wrote him back. It wasn't the first time, either. I told him yes, I cared for him, but no, I wasn't the marrying type. And I kept the money, in case you were wondering.'

Before Jacobus could ask the next question he heard Dahlia make a strange, choking noise. It took him a moment to understand she was making an effort not to cry.

Yumi said, 'It's OK. We'll find him.'

'You've just answered my next question,' he said. 'Since you wrote that letter turning him down, you haven't heard from him and thought he'd finally given up on you. That you'd lost him for good and you'd never hear his name again. That's why it threw you when I mentioned his name.'

'Except now he's really lost. Son of a bitch. I need another drink.'

'Soon,' Jacobus said.

'You mentioned that he sent you "another letter,"' Yumi said. 'Was there a previous one? Does he write you often?'

'Almost everyday. That's why when I didn't hear from him after that last letter, I thought that was it. He likes to write poetry in his letters. He writes poems. Stupid love poems. With little kid rhymes, or the first letter of each line would spell out 'I love you.' Dumb stuff like that.'

'Do you think we could borrow them?' Yumi asked.

'Why?' Alarm in her voice.

'Maybe they could help us figure out where he is, Dahlia. Sometimes those poems are like little puzzles, and no one's better than Jake solving puzzles. He'll tell you that himself. If you'd like, I'll read them privately first. If they get too personal I won't read them to Jake.'

'Wait here,' she said.

'We can come with you,' Yumi offered.

'No!'

She stood up abruptly, almost knocking her chair over. Jacobus heard the door of the bar close loudly.

As soon as she was gone, Yumi put her hand on Jacobus's arm and asked, 'Jake, is Dahlia the woman who called you and hung up?'

'Not unless she's had a tracheotomy since then. No, it was someone else.'

'Do you want a drink while we wait?' Yumi asked.

'I better have some coffee at this point.'

Yumi returned with one for each of them. It tasted even worse than his coffee at home.

'How did you know about the ten thousand dollars?' Yumi asked.

'Just a hunch. There were two-hundred-thirty-thousand in Borlotti's strongbox. A strange number, so I figured it started as a quarter million with twenty-thousand spent. But if I'm right and she only got ten, where's the other ten?'

'Do you think he had another flower child?' Yumi asked.

'An Iris, Rose, Daisy, Camellia, or Lily?' Jacobus said. 'Maybe he had a whole garden for all I know, but it sounds like he was too smitten with Dahlia to pollinate anyone else.'

'I think she's a drug addict,' Yumi said.

'I was thinking about that, too. Hyper. Fidgety. What else?'

'Her sleeves were rolled all the way down.'

'It is winter, after all.'

'Yes, but she's also skinny as a rail. Almost emaciated. She can't be much older than me but she looks haggard, and has too much make-up on. Her hands never stopped moving. She just has that look. I see it all the time in the city.'

'That's a pretty blanket statement.'

'When I have time, I volunteer at a drug treatment center. It's surprising how many addicts don't look any different than anyone else. But when they do have that look, it's hard to imagine they don't have a problem.'

'Was Dahlia wearing the watch Borlotti gave her?' Jacobus asked.

'No!' Yumi said. 'She wasn't! Maybe she's pawned that and all the other presents, too.'

'Maybe that's another reason she was peeved he hasn't written back. Her cash cow's teat has run dry. You think she loves him?'

'Not sure. He at least loves *her*. He's no matinee idol.'

'You've got his mug shot. Tell me what he looks like.'

'Short, chubby. Gray hair. Not much of that and combed straight back. Looks like he needs to shave twice a day. He's trying to smile but he's got two sad eyes and one sad eyebrow. And he must be at least twenty-five, thirty years older than she is. She'd be pretty if she were healthy.'

'Benson needs to find out why she left her job at Back Stretch.'

'And if she still works at the Club Terrace in the summer, or whether she might have left that also.'

Dahlia returned twenty minutes later, just as they were again about to conclude she wouldn't.

'Here,' she said. 'These are all of them. I've gotta go.'

'What's your phone number?' Jacobus asked.

'I don't have one.'

'Then what's your address?'

'I don't have one of those, either.'

'Then how do we contact you?'

'You know where to find me, right? I've gotta go.'

After she left, Yumi said, 'And we didn't even get her last name.'

'And I thought I had a brilliant student!' Jacobus said. 'Where did I go wrong?'

'What do you mean?'

'Try looking on one of the envelopes.'

'Of course. I was just about to,' Yumi said, covering up. 'Her name is Dahlia Maggette.'

'Maggot?'

Yumi spelled it for him and pronounced it more carefully.

'And is there not an address under Ms. Maggette's name?'

'Yes, Mr Holmes. And it's written in a beautiful, flowing hand in blue ink with an old-fashioned fountain pen.'

'And what does the address say, Dr. Watsonette?'

'It says, "Care of Sloppy Joe's".'

FOURTEEN

Thursday, December 29

Jacobus fidgeted for two hours and three cups of coffee before calling Benson at eight o'clock in the morning.

'So now we know where Borlotti's money went,' he said in conclusion.

'Yes, but we still don't know where he got it,' Benson replied, 'or where he is, or why his house was torched.'

'Burning questions,' Jacobus said. 'But I'd bet Borlotti was in the dark that his money, wherever he got it from, was supporting his sweetie's drug habit. From what she said, she never let him anywhere near where she lived, wherever that is, and it sounds like if he had known she was an addict, he would have been too old-fashioned to have tolerated it.'

'We'll do a background check,' said Benson. 'I wouldn't put it past someone like that to be extorting him somehow. Maybe he really *was* homosexual but didn't want anyone to know.'

'Maybe, but I don't think so. Yumi read the letters Borlotti wrote to her. Six years' worth. He was clearly smitten, and in his flowery, old-world way made it quite clear he was ready to tie the knot.'

'Well, we'll see. Drug addicts are devious people, capable of fooling anyone in their quest for a fix.'

'Thanks for the seminar,' Jacobus said, prepared to terminate the call.

'I've got some information for you, Jacobus. Number one: Ubriaco has a shaky alibi for Christmas Eve. He was at an annual Knights of Columbus holiday party. There were about fifty knights that can vouch for him being there. But the festivities might have ended before Borlotti's house was torched.

'Another thing is, Westerhauser has an airtight alibi. Not that he was ever a suspect. He was at a big fundraising gala at MASS MoCA in North Adams.'

'Anything else?'

'Maybe. We traced the address of that wood from Italy.'

'What was the name again? Castle something?'

'Cassalbuttano. It's a suburb of a city called Cremona. Ever hear of it?'

Jacobus almost dropped the phone. Cremona, Jacobus informed Benson, just happened to be to violins what Jerusalem was to religion. It was the home of Stradivari, and the Amati and Guarneri families, and of an untold number of violinmakers since. Today alone there were currently well over a hundred professional makers in Cremona.

'If Borlotti had a Cremona connection,' Jacobus said, 'there's something going on other than patching up school instruments.'

Jacobus heard Yumi shuffle into the kitchen.

He was stumped what to do next, he told Benson, but would give it some thought. Maybe contacting someone in Italy. But he didn't know anyone in Italy. And what would he ask them to do? He said he would get back.

'Uch, the weather's awful today,' Yumi said. 'It's like sleet. Jake, I think I'm starting to get cabin fever.'

'Back to the Last Supper puzzle?'

'I think the Last Supper is giving me heartburn. Would you mind if I went back to the city?'

Jacobus heard her pour herself a cup of coffee.

'Whatever.'

'I've got some friends in Soho who are having a New Year's party this weekend.'

'It's only the twenty-ninth,' Jacobus said.

'They like to celebrate.'

If Yumi left, Jacobus would only have Trotsky to converse with for the foreseeable future. With that depressing prospect in mind, he told Yumi about Benson's discovery regarding the parcel of violin wood.

'Jake, let's go to Cremona!' Yumi said.

'No thanks.'

'Why not?'

'Money, for one. Two, neither of us speaks Italian. What are we going to do, walk around the piazza, point to Borlotti's mug shot and say: 'Wood. Wood'?'

'Very funny. It just so happens I have a very nice violin made by a Cremonese maker. It's only ten years old. Have you heard of Marcello Bertoldo?'

Jacobus shook his head. 'Olive oil?'

Yumi ignored him.

'He's won some big international prizes,' she continued. 'I've never met someone who's made one of my violins.'

'That's because not too many violinmakers live to be over two hundred years old.'

'It would be so exciting!' she said, ignoring his jest. 'We could meet him and he'll translate for us. Who better to ask about violin wood than a violinmaker?'

'How do you know he speaks English?' Jacobus argued.

'I'll call him and we'll find out. If he starts singing *Funiculi Funicula* I'll hang up. And don't worry about the money. I've got plenty of miles on my credit card.'

Jacobus objected strenuously. Not only was he a skinflint, the idea of Yumi paying his way was humiliating.

'I understand how you feel, Jake. But don't forget, without your help I'd never be making all the money I am now.'

'How do you know this Bertoldo will be willing to help?'

'He's like Borlotti!'

'A violinmaker?'

'No! He's an Italian male.'

By day's end, Yumi had arranged it all. First thing the next morning they would drive to JFK Airport, where Yumi would leave her car. They had confirmed reservations to Milan, the closest major international airport to Cremona. Roy Miller agreed to take care of Trotsky while they were gone, which wouldn't be more than a few days. Benson expressed relief that the trip wouldn't incur any expenses upon the strapped resources of the EFPD, and wished them luck.

Finally, Yumi called Marcello Bertoldo. Not only was he fluent in English, he was a Dante scholar working on a new English translation of 'The Divine Comedy,' which, he laughingly admitted, he expected he would never finish. He was delighted to have received a call from the owner of one of his violins, and graciously agreed to help find the unknowns who had sent the mysterious wood to Borlotti and to be their interpreter. He eagerly awaited her arrival and of her esteemed teacher. He even offered to find hotel rooms for them, which Yumi had neglected to do.

'Leave it to me,' he said.

After hanging up, Yumi said to Jacobus, 'I turned on the old charm,' Yumi said, 'and told him how much I love his violin. I've got him eating out of the palm of my hand.'

Or vice versa, Jacobus thought.

FIFTEEN

Friday, December 30

Nathaniel, jealous he wouldn't be going with them, met them at the gate to wish them bon voyage. When it was time to board, a customer service representative helped Jacobus on to the plane, the first 747 he had ever been on. Yumi, carrying her violin case, followed them. The co-pilot greeted the passengers as they entered the cabin.

'What's that you've got in that case, young lady?' he asked. 'A machine gun?'

'Anti-aircraft,' Jacobus said, and everyone laughed heartily.

They were served breakfast shortly after take-off. After the food was cleared a flight attendant announced, 'We will now begin our movie service for the flight to Milan. Our feature film today will be 'Scent of a Woman,' featuring Al Pacino.'

'Is that the one where Pacino tries to act like a blind guy?' Jacobus asked.

'It is,' Yumi replied. 'It just came out. They say he does a great job. I don't imagine you want headphones.'

'Wake me when it's over,' Jacobus said and was soon snoring loudly.

After the movie, an early dinner was served. Jacobus had the pot roast, Yumi the teriyaki chicken. Both said it was OK, but bemoaned the good old days when airlines offered steak and lobster.

'I'll bet someday they might even make you pay for meals on planes,' Yumi joked.

'Never happen,' Jacobus said, and went back to sleep.

It was late Friday night when they arrived in Milan, the combined result of the eight-hour flight and the six-hour time difference. They quickly cleared immigration and customs control, whose disinterested agents waved cigarettes in the air as they heatedly debated a contested goal in the 1956 soccer match between Juventus and Bologna. Once through, Jacobus and Yumi were greeted by Marcello Bertoldo, who apologized profusely that the airport bureaucrats wouldn't let him go all the way to the gate to meet his distinguished guests. He embraced Jacobus so emphatically his glasses almost fell off.

'And is it possible my poor violin could ever be as beautiful as its owner?' he asked. He kissed Yumi on both cheeks. 'No, it is not.'

'What do you think of pineapple on pizza?' Jacobus asked.

'It is an abomination!' Bertoldo said. 'Why do you ask?'

'Just wondering. Let's go.'

Bertholdo drove his Alfa Romeo convertible a hundred miles an hour on the Autostrade, arriving miraculously intact at the Albergo Mariani, a three-story, fifteenth-century stone building on Cremona's Piazza del Duomo. He commanded the bellhop to take their bags, light as they were, up the stairs to their rooms on the second floor, and make sure every courtesy was extended to *il dottore* and *la signorina*. Then he wished them both a *buona notte*, kissing Yumi on both cheeks once again.

'*A domani*,' he said. 'Until tomorrow. I meet you here.'

After Bertoldo left, Jacobus said to Yumi, 'Let me guess. He's good-looking, too.'

'Yes. He is.'

SIXTEEN

New Year's Eve, Saturday, December 31

B ertoldo met them at the hotel bar for morning coffee. They sat in wrought iron chairs around a small, round, marble table facing a window with a view of the brick and stone piazza and the cathedral that dominated it. Though it was almost thirty degrees warmer than in the Berkshires, it was still too cold for them to sit outside. Since the view was of no import to Jacobus, that was fine with him.

'*Signori*,' the waiter said indifferently, approaching them from behind. He placed the *prima collazione*, pastries and espresso, on the table.

'*Madama Butterfly*!' he exclaimed when he caught sight of Yumi's reflection in the window.

'I think you're mistaking me for someone else,' Yumi replied, but not testily.

'No, that is not possible! You are the . . . the vision of *la Madama* herself. If I am wrong, it is only because you are more beautiful than . . . than . . . I cannot find the words. *Signorina,* you must help me with my English so I will have the words. Will you teach me? I wish to learn. My name is Carlo. Tonight, perhaps?'

Bertoldo said something in Italian to the waiter – something brusque – who argued for a moment and then left.

Jacobus took a sip of espresso. *Even better than my Folgers at home*, he thought. *If only the cup were bigger than a thimble.*

'What did you say to the waiter?' Jacobus asked Bertoldo.

'I know him. His English is good enough. I told him not to bother innocent young ladies.'

Yumi chuckled.

'You found him amusing?' Bertoldo asked.

'And good-looking.'

'More than me?' Bertoldo asked. Jacobus couldn't tell whether or not Bertoldo's disbelief was sincere, but it was certainly convincing.

'He had a nice smile,' Yumi said.

'His smile? But his teeth were not as white as mine.'

'Nor as straight, now that you mention it. But Carlo does have nice lips.'

'But not as full as mine.'

'Maybe not. But I liked his dark eyes.'

'They were dead. When I smile, my eyes dance.'

'I liked his wavy hair.'

'Girl's hair! Do you not prefer mine?'

'Short curls? Perhaps. The Roman senator look? Maybe. But Carlo did have a nice physique. I liked the way he moved.'

'You think so? He had no muscle. If we were on a *calcio* pitch I would run him over.'

'What's a *calcio* pitch?' Jacobus interjected. He was enjoying the free entertainment and wanted to be sure of the details.

'A football field. Soccer.'

'Oh,' Jacobus said. 'Say, could you order me another coffee from Carlo?'

'Not here. We go somewhere else.'

Pigeons flapped around them as they strolled to another bar on the opposite side of the piazza. If Bertoldo's description of himself was to be believed, Jacobus conjured up an image of Michelangelo's David. Not that there was any way to know if the model for the white marble statue had dancing eyes, black hair, or who even smiled. Curiously, Jacobus simultaneously thought about Amadeo Borlotti and the stark contrasts with Bertoldo. It aroused his sympathy that circumstances out of Borlotti's control – like physical appearance and, to some extent, personality – had conspired to make his existence almost invisible.

Bertoldo found them a table where they sat facing away from the previous bar.

'The coffee here is much better,' he said. 'And the waitresses provide much better service.'

'Yes, I'm sure,' Jacobus said.

'I hope your rooms were to your satisfaction,' Bertoldo said, the charm in his voice returning.

Jacobus had no complaints. He appreciated the room's spareness. No fancy gizmos that required a Masters in electronics. No extra furniture to trip over. One ancient wooden armoire, weighing a ton and smelling of mothballs; thick, velvet curtains that kept out the cold, and a bed with a mattress even softer than the one he had at home. His explorative hand did pass over something initially unrecognizable, with a smooth and hard surface, screwed to the wall above the bed . It took him a few moments to process the information as the plaster legs of Christ on a crucifix, but Jacobus considered it a minor price to pay for a comfortable room.

'Slept like a baby,' Jacobus said.

Bertoldo laughed boisterously.

'Like a baby!' he repeated. '*Un scherzo!* A joke! And you, *signorina*, did you, too, sleep like a baby?' he asked, with an inflection quite distinct from the way he addressed Jacobus.

'Actually, no,' she said.

'No? I will get you a better room!'

'The room is perfect, Marcello.'

'Then what is the problem?'

'It's just that I was too excited about being in Italy to sleep.'

'Ah!' Bertoldo sighed. 'In that case . . .'

Bertoldo told them that since it was New Year's Eve he would make plans for them. They would celebrate late into the night after visiting these mysterious violin people, so they would eat lightly and try to get as much rest as possible during the day. *Would that be satisfactory?* He would take care of everything, but first could they explain more what needed to be done?

Jacobus summarized Borlotti's shop burning down and his ensuing disappearance, the arrival of the violin wood, and tracing the address to the outskirts of Cremona.

'But that's crazy! First of all, it is not legal to ship such wood out of Italy,' Bertoldo said, with his accent in which every word ended in a vowel and the word 'wood' sounded more like 'woooda.' 'I don't know where they could have gotten this wood. We all try to get old wood. Otherwise it takes years to dry properly and who has such time? But we usually find it at shops of makers who are retiring. Sometimes they've had it in the family for generations. We are like the ants at a picnic. As soon as our little antennas sense the sweet dessert we all swarm to it. So, if these friends of Borlotti wanted to sell this wood, there are so many makers here that would buy it, no questions asked. And a good price, too.'

'We thought Mr Borlotti was just a repairman,' Yumi said. 'Have you seen instruments that he's made?'

'I have never heard of him. And I thought I had heard of everyone.'

Jacobus sat in the back seat of Bertoldo's sports car, which was comfortable if a bit cramped, until they reached the center of prosperous Cassalbuttano, a mere stone's throw from Cremona. But when Bertoldo took the winding roads in the suddenly rural landscape as a cue to speed up, Jacobus was buffeted from one side of the car to the other. Bertoldo laughed each time the car swerved, and so did Yumi, but Jacobus could detect the nervousness in hers.

'Aren't you afraid?' Bertoldo asked her at one point after a particularly enervating curve.

'I'm fine,' she replied. 'You can let go of my hand now.'

As easy as Cassalbuttano was to find, locating Cerretello Secondo was a different story entirely. Not even knowing the name of the party they sought made finding the address particularly difficult. In between wrong turns they stopped and discussed what their strategy would be once they found where they were going.

'What type of person would be shipping violin wood to Mr Borlotti?' Yumi asked. 'Another violinmaker?'

'I don't think so, *princessa*,' Bertoldo said. 'No violinmaker would part with the precious wood you describe. No matter how much he could sell it for, it would be worth much more when it finally became a violin. It must be a broker of some sort. Or a wealthy businessman with connections. Someone who can find such an obscure maker as Borlotti to sell wood to must know the world market profoundly.'

Jacobus laughed in the backseat.

'You disagree, *dottore*?'

'As far as we know,' Jacobus said, 'it can be anyone out trying to make a buck. It could be a carpenter who had some extra lumber. It could be a grandma on a pension who was cleaning out her attic. It could be a wholesale violin supply store. Or if you're real lucky, Bertoldo, it'll be a beautiful woman.'

outside, even with the fire burning. Not the same kind of wood as in his own stove, Jacobus thought, judging from the scent, but it reminded him of home, nevertheless. They were escorted to a large wooden table in a room Jacobus quickly gathered was the kitchen. Sounds were brittle and echoey, indicators of hard surfaces and open spaces. Smells of food were abundant. He was seated in an old wooden chair that scraped on a stone floor. The room was acoustically alive, amplifying the *sotto voce* conversation of the handful of the men and women surrounding them. Though Jacobus could not understand the words, the undertone was crystal clear. Extended silences between clipped comments. Sentences ending in questions. Sudden bursts. He had the feeling that they were being scrutinized with suspicion even though the gurgle of wine being poured into glasses sounded friendly enough.

Bertoldo engaged the Vassaris in lengthy conversation. They spoke so quickly and with such passion, sometimes all of them simultaneously, that Jacobus's years of listening to Verdi and Puccini were no help at all. One individual in particular – he had the strong voice of a young man – seemed to be the family leader. Unable to withhold his curiosity any longer, Jacobus asked Bertoldo what he had found out about the wood.

'Not yet, *dottore*. Not yet,' Bertoldo said. 'We are still talking about the wine. They make it from their own grapes. It is good, don't you think?'

'Yeah, it's great, but tell them we can't stay more than a week.'

'First we gain their trust,' Bertoldo said, 'then we find out about the wood. These things take time. *Pian piano*. Little by little. There is for certain something they are very afraid about.'

Plates were set in front of them with the surly plunk of obligatory hospitality. They were served a peasant-style lunch, sausages and pig liver roasted in the fireplace, served with cheese, pasta with wild greens, and freshly baked bread. Wine continued to be poured. Though the food was better than at any Italian restaurant Jacobus had ever been to in the U.S., they had not been made to feel welcome in any other way. Every once in a while, someone would ask him, 'You like?' with little conviction. No one had attempted to engage him or Yumi in conversation or even ask them a question.

At one point Bertoldo leaned over to Jacobus and said in a quiet voice, 'I am making progress.'

'What's the story?' Jacobus asked.

'But I am already so lucky in that regard, *dottore*,' Ber
'Aren't I, *princessa*?'

Yumi didn't answer that question, but asked another.

'Not knowing who we're going to meet, how will w
their connection to Mr Borlotti?'

'Simple,' Jacobus said. 'We'll ask them.'

Finally, after stopping a half dozen times to ask direc
getting conflicting advice from strangers who felt it imp
also discuss government corruption and how their neighl
cheating them, they turned off the correct dirt road and
dusty drive that ended at a rustic farmhouse. As they got (
car, a brood of hens began to cluck anxiously from a p(
pair of old hounds trotted up to them, sniffed at their pant
then wandered off. Painted on the stuccoed stone wall of 1
was a sign: *Cerretello Secondo. Famiglia Vassari.*

No one responded to Bertoldo's knock on the door. He
again, more insistently, with no better result.

'That's funny,' Jacobus said. 'I'm sure I smell smoke com
a chimney.'

'I suppose they could have left a fire burning,' Yumi s
there are also cars parked in front of the house.'

'We will try a little trick,' Bertoldo whispered to them.

Knowing very well Jacobus and Yumi didn't know the l{
in a loud voice he said to them in Italian, 'There is no o:
We will wait until they return! In the meantime, let's get
wine and sit in their doorway!'

Shortly thereafter, there was some rustling from within.

'*Chi parla?*' came a nervous whisper from behind the d

'He wants to know who we are,' Bertoldo said.

Bertoldo identified himself as Cremonese and if they
necessary to confirm that, he shouted out his phone numb
two people with him were wealthy Americans who wantec
the real Italy.

Five minutes later the door opened. Bertoldo told Jacot
Yumi to follow his lead.

'*Prego*,' said the young man holding the door.

'He's inviting us in. Just do as I do.'

'*Permeso*,' said Bertoldo, which Jacobus and Yumi repe{
they entered.

The inside of the farmhouse was not much warmer th

'The loud one, he is named Ansaldo Vassari. Both of our grand-fathers fought in the Resistance.'

'They were friends?' Yumi asked.

'No. They didn't know each other. But if they had, perhaps they would have been.'

'Excellent progress,' Jacobus said.

'Thank you.'

As the day progressed, the house warmed marginally, more from the sun than from the fireplace, but not enough for Jacobus to feel comfortable taking off his coat. He and Yumi conversed with each other, but otherwise kept quiet in their effort to decipher the verbal hieroglyphics.

As a rule, Jacobus preferred when people made no mention of his blindness, but being totally ignored was beginning to get under his skin. Whether it was the language barrier or something more, he wasn't sure, though he suspected it was something more.

It was easy for Jacobus to tell that the ongoing conversation between Bertoldo and the Vassaris was becoming more animated as the meal progressed, but at the same time it continued to sound contentious.

'These people are very stubborn,' Bertoldo told Jacobus and Yumi as plates were cleared from the table. 'They are telling very little. Perhaps we should come back another day.'

'*Pian piano?*'

'Exactly.'

'I have a better idea,' Jacobus whispered.

'Yes?'

Jacobus barked out, 'Egremonta! Egremonta Fallsa! Egremonta Fallsa!'

The women cried and invoked the protection of their respective patron saints and fled from the room. The men uttered loud and confused protestations.

'I think you've made an impression,' Yumi whispered to Jacobus.

'Now we're getting somewhere,' Jacobus replied. 'Get me this Ansaldo fellow,' he said to Bertoldo. 'I've got some questions.'

Bertoldo, sounding apologetic, asked Ansaldo Vassari, who had left the kitchen, to sit across from them at the table. By following Vassari's trail of '*Si, Signore. Si signore,*' Jacobus could hear his request was taken seriously.

'Ask him how they know Amadeo Borlotti.'

After a rapid exchange, Bertoldo said, 'Ansaldo Vassari is Borlotti's nephew. The others are all relations of one sort or another.'

'Wonderful,' Jacobus said. 'Ask him about their Christmas present to Uncle Amadeo.'

Additional crying and praying ensued when Bertoldo translated into Italian. The response was extensive. To Jacobus it sounded like a mass confession.

'For several years the family has been supporting Borlotti's violin-making by sending old wood to him,' Bertoldo translated. 'They have gotten this wood from old sites all around Lombardy, the region in which Cremona is found.'

'What kind of sites?' Jacobus asked.

'Construction sites. All the time now, old farmhouses like this one are being torn down and rebuilt for *agriturismo*. This is the new economy. You feel how cold this house is? There is no insulation, just thick walls. But once a house like this is cold, it keeps in the cold like a refrigerator. And the only heat is the fireplace, but it is inefficient and all the heat goes up the chimney. The tourists want more comfort when they come for the Italian experience, *si*? So they tear down the inside walls of these houses and put in new electricity, new windows, new kitchens, new bathrooms, new swimming pools. All for the rustic Italian experience! It is an irony, *no*? In the process, a lot of the old wood gets thrown away.'

'It sounds like a better idea to me,' Jacobus said, 'to make new fiddles with the old wood than to haul it off to the dump.'

'Yes, but is it legal? For these people to take the wood?' Yumi asked quietly.

'No. It is against the law,' Bertoldo replied. 'It is stealing. Because it is not only wood. We don't want people tearing down old houses just to get the valuable parts. We have the laws against these activities, but this is Italy, after all. The Vassari either obtain the wood when someone's back is turned, or when they pay someone to look the other way. When they find the best wood, they saw it into planks and ship it to this Borlotti, who has paid them well for their efforts.'

'So when we showed up today,' Jacobus interjected, 'they thought we were the authorities here to arrest them?'

'That is precisely what I think.'

'But we don't look like authorities. Do we?' Yumi asked.

'You look *different*,' Bertoldo said. 'Both of you. And for people like these, who are not used to strangers, anyone different they view with suspicion. For them, even someone from Umbria or Naples is considered foreign. That is why, as *Dottore* Jacobus guessed, being arrested is exactly what they are afraid of.

'As you might have surmised, the Vassari are not a rich family. They work hard with the vines and the farm, but around here if you do things the old way the struggle becomes greater and greater. Everything now is for the tourists. Stealing the wood and then smuggling it was their way of making ends meet. Now they have lost that and will probably have to pay a much bigger price for breaking our laws.'

'And that's why they're all so upset?' Yumi asked.

'Yes, I think so,' said Bertoldo. 'We Italians are a very emotional people.'

'Yes, I've noticed that,' Yumi replied.

'Well, I feel bad for them, but that's not really why we're here, is it?' Jacobus said. 'Borlotti must have been a bad boy for his house to have been turned into a lump of coal for Christmas. Ask Vassari what they know about that and where Borlotti is right now.'

Vassari responded with a slew of imprecations punctuated repeatedly with passionate appeals to the Madonna.

'Vassari swears this is the first he has heard about Borlotti's house burning down,' Bertoldo said. 'And Borlotti's disappearance appears to upset him deeply. But he says they can't help us. They say there is nothing they can tell us, but they begged us to leave them in peace.'

SEVENTEEN

The drive back to Cremona was much faster and much quieter. They arrived at the Mariani in early evening. Bertoldo told them to rest up, because he had made a reservation at Da Elio, his favorite restaurant, for a traditional New Year's Eve dinner.

'After today, I'm not sure I'm going to be in the mood to celebrate,' Yumi said.

'But, *princessa*, life must go on! There is much to celebrate. If not for these tragic circumstances, we would never have met each other. It is like Dante, don't you think?'

'What time's dinner?' Jacobus asked.

'The reservation is for eleven o'clock.'

'That's a strange time to eat, don't you think?'

'If you would prefer, I can make it later.'

Jacobus and Yumi returned to their rooms. Jacobus spent an hour pushing buttons on his room phone trying to figure out how to access an international operator who spoke English. He finally got through to Benson's line in Egremont Falls, where it was still only around noon. Marge, his part-time secretary answered, 'Oh, he's just about to go out to shovel snow. We had at least six inches last night and—'

Jacobus, picturing the dollar signs spinning for the phone call as if on a gasoline pump, didn't wait for the end of the sentence.

'Just put him on,' he said.

When Benson got to the phone, Jacobus gave him a full report, hastily recounted.

'Well, we're making progress anyway,' Benson said.

'Are we?' Jacobus asked. He had traveled a long and expensive way to deal with a peripheral issue that shed scant insight into their main objective.

Jacobus decided to shower to help stay awake for the night ahead. The shower was fitted with a hand-held device with which he was unfamiliar, and could only manage to direct the stream of water either to his chest or to the toilet on the other side of the bathroom. He gave up and washed his face in the sink.

Boisterous revelers filling the piazza overflowed into Da Elio and into every other bar and ristorante with an air of frenetic expectancy, not so much for what the next year would bring, because everyone knew it was too much to expect peace and prosperity, but rather for a night of celebration of food, wine, and camaraderie.

Yumi sat between Jacobus and Bertoldo, their backs against the restaurant's inner stone wall. The general din, punctuated by spontaneous group song and a poet who demanded to be heard above all others, was too loud to enable them to converse in a normal voice, making it easier for them to avoid discussing Borlotti. Instead they talked, or rather shouted, about violins. With all the ambient noise, Jacobus couldn't hear half of what Bertoldo was saying but noticed that Yumi was leaning away from him and toward Bertoldo. It might have been so she could hear him better, but Jacobus thought otherwise, partly because he also noticed she wore a fragrance he had never smelled on her before.

A bottle of local wine was plunked down without being ordered.

'A fine violin is like a beautiful woman,' Bertoldo proclaimed, pouring three glasses. 'The elegant neck, the round shoulders, the narrow waist, the—'

'Expense,' Jacobus said. *This is going to be a long night*, he thought.

Their *cena* began with an antipasto of cured meats, cheeses, and olives, followed by cannellini bean soup with shavings of black truffle. Then there was a *prima* of homemade tagliatelle with porcini mushrooms and another of broiled asparagus topped with eggs, Parmesan cheese, and more truffles. As he did with violins, Bertoldo somehow managed to compare food to a beautiful woman. More bottles, and with each bottle Bertoldo's paean centered more and more on Yumi.

A waiter brought the *seconda, zampone e lenticchie,* a dish of savory, stewed lentils served with a sliced, boiled pig foreleg.

'A pig's foot is like a woman,' Jacobus proclaimed, but was cut off under the table by a kick in his shin from Yumi.

'*Zampone e lenticchie* is our traditional New Year's Eve dish,' Bertoldo said. 'They say it is good luck for the new year. That it will bring us money.'

'They should say it will bring us heartburn,' Jacobus said. 'That way they might be right.' It wasn't long before he poked his fork into his plate and was disappointed to discover there was nothing left.

For dessert they ate *torrone*, a nougat-like confection with almonds and honey, along with espresso, and the meal finally ended with housemade grappa.

'*Buon anno*,' Bertoldo said, lifting his glass.

'*Buon anno*,' Yumi replied.

'And may all our mysteries be solved,' Jacobus said, draining his glass. 'And thanks for dinner, Bertoldo. It beats liverwurst and beans.'

They made their way out of the restaurant and into the piazza, where the crowd was only starting to dissipate. Horns and singing swirled around him, and if not for Bertoldo guiding him by the arm, Jacobus would have been hopelessly spun in circles.

'And is it true that you will return to your country tomorrow?' Bertoldo asked. 'Must it be so soon? Surely the *polizia* there can finish this case.'

'What do you think, Jake?' Yumi asked. 'What do you say we stay another day or two?'

'Sorry.'

'But I so wanted to show you my new violins!' Bertoldo said. 'I need musicians like you, with an excellent ear, to tell me how to set them up with perfection.'

Jacobus knew the game. He would play the innocent with great sincerity.

'I'm sure you do,' he said to Bertoldo. 'But Yumi here has two excellent ears. You don't need me.' And then to her, 'Why don't you stick around for a couple days. I'll go home and walk the dog.'

'I couldn't let you go home alone,' Yumi said.

'Don't worry about me,' he said. 'I'll be fine. Nathaniel can pick me up at JFK. I'll be fine.'

Bertoldo escorted them to the Mariani lobby. It was about two in the morning and Jacobus was eager to collapse into his soft mattress.

'Marcello asked me to play the violin he made for me so he can compare it to his new ones,' Yumi said. 'I think he and I'll go over to his shop for a while.'

'Just be sure you get me to the airport on time,' Jacobus said.

'No worries, *dottore*,' Bertoldo said. 'No worries. *Buon anno*, my friend.'

Yumi kissed Jacobus on the cheek and whispered, 'Thank you,' in his ear.

'Bertoldo! Signore Bertoldo!' came a shout. The voice sounded familiar, but desperate. Agitated.

'It's Ansaldo Vassari,' Yumi said. 'He looks like a wreck, Jake.'

'Vassari!' Bertoldo said. '*Cosa fai qui?*'

What the hell was going on? Jacobus wondered. Vassari certainly didn't sound like he was about to toast them *buon anno*.

The four of them went to the bar in the hotel, where they had been what seemed days ago but had only been the previous morning. Bertoldo sat everyone down, ordered four grappas, and talked in soothing tones.

'*Calma*, Vassari. *Calma. Piano. Piano.*'

But Vassari didn't seem capable of heeding Bertoldo's advice, and his rapid fire monologue did little to hide the despair underneath.

The two men spent the better part of an hour talking. Jacobus, beside himself not knowing what was going on, refrained from interrupting. Finally, chairs moved. The two men stood up. Jacobus was coarsely embraced, and it wasn't by Bertoldo. Vassari patted Jacobus on the back as he hugged him, and Jacobus felt Vassari's tears on his own cheek. Then Vassari said '*Addio*,' and fled, his footsteps echoing in the empty, cobbled piazza.

'*Madonna*!' Bertoldo said under his breath.

'The cops gave them a raw deal for smuggling the wood?' Jacobus asked.

'If it were only that,' Bertoldo said, with a sad laugh, 'they would have been relieved. No, the situation is worse than that. Much worse. I will try to remember the whole story the way Vassari just told me it.

'Yesterday, Vassari received a call from a shipping company, telling him a parcel from America had arrived for him at Fiumicino Airport in Rome. They provided him with an invoice number and told him he had to pick it up within twenty-four hours or it would be returned. Sold on the black market, more likely. Vassari had not been expecting a package, and had only recently sent his own shipment to Signore Borlotti in America. He wondered whether it had for some reason been returned. That had never happened before – he had always taken careful precautions. He asked the dispatcher what the package was. "How the hell do I know?" he said. "It's not my package."

'Vassari hates going to Rome. In our region some people say that the Romans are dirty and they smell. They say the food in Rome is unpalatable, and as for the wine – they would rather drink their own piss. I don't say this, of course. I am only telling you what others say. Vassari says Cremona, home of Stradivari and Guarneri, is Italy's most civilized city. You may know that no less than the great opera composer Giacomo Puccini once lived in Cassalbuttano. And so now Vassari had to leave, long before dawn, for the five-hundred-kilometer drive south to that cesspool Rome. He complained his Fiat was no match for the Mercedes and Volvos that sped by him on the Autostrada, and the cost of *benzina* is ridiculous – God forbid the government will ever do something about it – though it tasted better than the coffee he drank at the Autogrille on the way. At least that is what he has said to me.'

'And he didn't really know why he was making this trip?' Yumi asked.

'No. After getting turned around in circles for an extra hour between Rome and the airport, by midday Vassari finally found his way to the cargo terminal. Once there, he was surprised how indifferent the security was, even by Italian standards.'

'The airport in Milan was certainly busy,' Jacobus said.

'Yes, but compared to the passenger terminal, the cargo area has not so much of the hustle and the bustle. It is more like a huge airplane hangar. And the Carabinieri, who always seem to like intimidating the tourists with their *fasciti* uniforms and their machine guns, were not to be found in the cargo terminal.

'Vassari searched for the international cargo desk, but the signs pointed him to every which way and he got lost all over again. Finally he managed to find the desk. He presented his credentials, the invoice number, and a ten-thousand lire bribe to the attendant – that's about seven American dollars – who gladly escorted him to the entrance of the warehouse where his parcel was stored. The attendant then graciously accepted another five thousand to guide Vassari through a maze of aisles, which were lined floor to ceiling with cargo of every shape and size.

'Vassari was amazed to find that his package was not a package, but an enormous plywood box. A crate, I think you call it. It had five or six heavy-duty, metal clasps that were snapped shut. For its safety, or so Vassari presumed, all the seams had been sealed with thick tape, and it was further secured with bunky chords.'

'I think you mean bungee chords,' Yumi said.

'*Grazie, princessa*,' Bertoldo replied.

'While Vassari pondered what to do with the enormous crate,' he continued, 'the attendant suggested that he would be happy to assist Vassari carry the parcel to his car for only twenty-thousand lire.

'"*Vaffanculo!*" Vassari cursed at the attendant. I am sorry to use such a coarse word but this is what he told me. The attendant reciprocated with the corresponding hand gesture and disappeared immediately thereafter, leaving Vassari to manage himself.

'As you can imagine, it took Vassari half an hour just to drag the enormous crate to his Fiat and then another half hour to fit it inside. That he was able to manage it at all was miraculous, as no matter how he arranged it, part of it always protruded from one window or another. He put those bungee chords to good use, not only to hold the crate in place, but also to make sure the door stayed shut for the return trip.

'It was already dark when he returned to Lombardy. You cannot tell now, in winter when the plains are fallow, but most of the year they are dark and rich. When he passed between the rows of pines that lined the approach to his farmhouse, Vassari was very happy to finally be back in the home that his family has lived in for centuries. You can imagine how relieved he was after such an exhausting day.

'After he parked his car, his sister-in-law Fiamina called him from the doorstep. She told him to hurry because they were just sitting down to eggs and truffles for dinner.

'Vassari wasted no time. He hadn't eaten all day and was very happy to abandon his cargo for his favorite supper. His family all clapped him on the back and praised him for his endurance, and – after they took a look at the car – for his magnificent feat of engineering. Leonardo the Second, they called him. He accepted the jest in good humor and joked it would take an even greater feat getting the case out than it was getting it in.

'After supper was over, his brother and cousins helped him with the task. They extracted the crate from the car and pretended it was a casket. They carried it into the kitchen with solemnity, like pall-bearers at the funeral of a national hero – though I can't remember any recent ones – and set it on its back on the same kitchen table at which we took our lunch.

'Vassari's younger brother, Paolo, peeled the heavy tape from the seams of the crate. He said, "Bringing a string instrument to Cremona? It's like what the English say: bringing the Newcastle to the coal."

'His cousin Emilio, who undid the metal clasps, said another joke. "Yes, and I think they have filled the crate with a ton of that coal."

'Lifting the wooden lid, Vassari discovered a case fitting snugly inside, a string bass case held in place with Styrofoam battens. It was the quality of case used by student musicians, of lighter weight and constructed with reasonable strength. I have some such cases in my shop I can show you, but you know what I mean.

'Paolo asked, "I wonder why *zio* Amadeo would send an instrument to us?"

'"We shall see," Vassari said, who had to open yet another set of clasps and yet another lid. "Maybe he's smuggled us a shipment of those Hebrew National hotdogs he's always talking about".'

'The family's levity began to leave them when they noticed a smell. Their concern increased when they found that the inner case contained not an instrument, but a large, black plastic garbage bag. Then they opened the bag. It wasn't coal inside, and it wasn't hot dogs, and assuredly it wasn't a string bass. No. It was a decomposing body with a bullet in his forehead, and carved into his chest were long, slender f's, like the f-holes on a string instrument. Yes, I am sure you have guessed by now. It was the body of their Uncle Amadeo. Amadeo Borlotti.'

'That, my dear friends, and not smuggled wood, is the true reason why the Vassari family was reluctant to open their door for us today. At the farm, Yumi said she didn't think we looked like authorities, and she was right. The Vassari family was terrified not because they thought we were there to arrest them, but to kill them.'

PART TWO

EIGHTEEN

New Year's Day, Sunday, January 1

The festivity of the evening, like the remaining crowds, had vanished into darkness. Yumi and Bertoldo were in no mood to make music together at his shop. After much discussion, though, Bertoldo convinced her to stay in Cremona for a few more days.

Jacobus called Benson back to inform him of the gory postscript to the wood-smuggling story. Benson's secretary, Marge, answered the phone.

'Do you have any idea what time it is here, Mr Jacobus?' she asked.

'Give me a hint.'

'It's past dinner time!'

'Well, sweetheart, where I am it's almost breakfast time, so if you wouldn't mind rousting the good man from his beauty sleep I'd be much obliged.'

'That changes everything,' Benson said when Jacobus told him the details. 'I'll make you a confession, Mr Jacobus. In all my years I've never worked a murder case. We'll need to deal with the Italian authorities, no doubt.' He sounded shaken, but Jacobus couldn't tell whether it was more from the former or latter statement.

'Never mind,' Benson continued, summoning his inner Scout. 'We'll sort it out. Good work, sir. Good work. And a happy New Year to you.'

It was almost dawn and Jacobus worried that if he fell asleep he'd miss his flight, so he stayed up for what little remained of the night. Since day and night were indistinguishable to him, he relied on his biological clock to inform him. But the flight to Milan and the time difference had gotten that so out of kilter he had lost track of how he was supposed to feel. And so he fretted until Bertoldo arrived at the hotel, precisely at 6:45, to take Jacobus to the airport. Yumi joined them for the drive. Bertoldo had already called the Vassaris to commiserate and to offer some advice. He reported to

Jacobus that the conversation with them had been productive, now that the family knew the whole story from the American side.

The Vassaris had been paralyzed with indecision since discovering their uncle's body and almost welcomed Bertoldo's strong recommendation that they surrender to the local authorities. He convinced them that if they made a clean breast of things and admitted to the wood smuggling, and if by their cooperation the police were able to discover who killed their uncle and for what reason, there was a good chance they would be exonerated of their seeming complicity in the far more egregious crime, the murder of Amadeo Borlotti. And, Bertoldo assured the Vassaris in a deft aside, if everything worked out for the best he would be happy to buy wood from them in the future. No questions asked.

Bertoldo and Yumi embraced Jacobus when his flight to JFK was announced.

'*Ciao!*' Yumi called out as he boarded the plane.

'Yeah, *arrivederci*,' Jacobus said, and took his seat. He put on his seatbelt and slept the whole way back.

Nathaniel met Jacobus at his arrival gate at JFK. Because of the time change it was only two hours later than when he'd departed Milan.

'Hail the celebrity!' Nathaniel said in greeting.

'What the hail are you talking about?' Jacobus said. 'You've been drinking too much eggnog.'

'The news about Borlotti's body. It's already on the airwaves.'

'How's that possible? We just found out ourselves last night.'

'News travels faster than planes, Jake. An anonymous source leaked it. The Carabinieri didn't deny it. WCBS mispronounced your name, though. They called you Daniel Jacobs.'

'I'll sue.'

'It'll be in all the papers by tomorrow.'

'Anonymous source?' Jacobus asked.

'That's what it said.'

Bertoldo? No. Why would he do that? Who else? Jacobus thought. He decided he might have a private chat with Marge, Benson's receptionist. Or not. He was finished. Spent. He had done his job and had handed it over to Benson. Let him figure out the who's and the why's. Now he could return to real life: listen to music and play the violin. Finish the jigsaw puzzle.

New Year's Day traffic was light into Manhattan as America slept off its collective hangover and prepared for football bowl games. Nathaniel offered to put Jacobus up in his apartment, but after the exhausting weekend he declined. He just wanted to go home and rest. So Nathaniel dropped him off at Grand Central Station, where Jacobus boarded a Metro North train to Wassaic Station, which was about an hour from his house. Roy Miller met him there and offered to stop by at his own house to pick up Trotsky. Again Jacobus opted to go straight home and asked Miller to bring Trotsky the next day.

Back in his living room, Jacobus collapsed on to his couch. He had no idea what time it was, only that it was late. The house, having been unoccupied for four days, was freezing, but he didn't even care. He was exhausted.

'Pour me a drink,' he said to Miller. 'And help yourself. And may the New Year be less of a pain in the ass than the old one.'

For the next half hour, while starting the fire in the woodstove, Miller took vicarious delight recounting the blow-by-blow of the sensational Borlotti story, as if it were the first time Jacobus had heard it. Egremont Falls hadn't been in the news since an article about organic hay farming two years earlier. Now the place would be crawling with local sleuths and Benson was no doubt in his situation room designing a strategy to deal with it all. Too tired to object, Jacobus let Miller spew.

'*His* problem,' Jacobus said, smacking his lips after finishing his scotch. '*His* problem.' Jacobus's only loose end was a visit to Dahlia Maggette.

'Yep, glad it's not mine, either,' said Miller. 'Well, I better be going. I'll turn the lights out on my way out.'

'Thanks for nothing,' Jacobus said, with a laugh.

After Miller left, Jacobus put a few more logs on the fire and sat on his living room couch, listening to Yumi's recording of the Four Seasons. He closed his eyes and smiled.

Jacobus woke with a snort. The scratches of Yumi's LP had roused him. He shook the cobwebs from his head. Something was not right. *Yumi's recording isn't an LP. It's a CD. There shouldn't be scratches.* Even more, there was no music.

The scratching was icy snow crunching under the tires of a car coming down his driveway. It wasn't Yumi's car. It wasn't Miller's or Benson's, either. It was somebody who wanted his arrival to be unheard. The car coasted slowly, engine off. *Maybe the car's head-lights are dashed as well*, Jacobus thought.

He made an instantaneous decision. In his own house he had the advantage as long as it remained dark. He stole through the living room and kitchen, sidestepping the floorboards he knew creaked, and opened the door to the basement. On the wall was the circuit box. He felt for the main breaker and pulled it down, shutting off everything. Below the box was where he kept his cane. He clutched it tightly and positioned himself next to the kitchen door, praying the intruder would enter without a flashlight and would turn on the light switch.

The car door opened and was pressed closed with delicacy. Cautious footsteps made their way to his front door. Jacobus breathed as silently as he could, through his mouth. The door swung open slowly and Jacobus took a step back. Cold air and the skittering of dry leaves in the night's breeze swept in. Jacobus waited. Whoever it was stood still inside his house. Waiting? For what? Move, damnit! Jacobus couldn't be sure where the person was until he moved. They were both waiting. Then he heard a hand fumble along the wall for a switch, and finding it, turn it on. Jacobus heard the click. Then, the lights not going on, several more desperate clicks followed in quick succession.

Jacobus now knew exactly where the intruder stood. He swung.

'Shit! My shoulder!' the intruder screamed.

A woman!

Jacobus was surprised for a moment. But only for a moment.

'Ah! Ms Forsythe. May I call you Minerva?'

'How did you know?' Forsythe said, through gritted teeth.

He had heard the voice once before. The midnight caller who'd hung up.

She had not identified herself then – at least not explicitly – but in reality she had. He just had to mentally rearrange a little chronology. Jacobus's ear, memory, and mental discipline – three ineradicable benefits of his early musical training – enabled him to identify this unexpected guest. And why she was here. This was a new piece of what was beginning to finally resemble an organized jigsaw puzzle. He just hoped he wasn't mistaking another pomegranate for Jesus's face.

'I'll tell you what I know, and you tell me what you know,' Jacobus said. 'Fair enough?'

There was silence.

'I asked you, fair enough?'

'I nodded,' she said.

'I don't do nods. I do yes or no.'

'Yes,' she said.

'Good start,' Jacobus said. 'Stay there a minute, I'll switch the lights on for you and get you an ice pack. Like a drink?'

They were soon seated in the living room. Forsythe didn't think her arm was broken but willingly accepted the ice bag and three aspirin, which she downed with a scotch on the rocks.

'May I smoke?' she asked.

'Be my guest. Secondhand smoke is one of my few remaining pleasures.'

To his surprise, the tobacco he smelled was from a pipe. Mac Baren, he thought. Expensive. Just like the perfume she was wearing. He inhaled as deeply as he could. The intoxicating combination of the tobacco and the pine in his woodstove was as pleasurable as a good dinner, though he could have done without the perfume or the several aromatic products she had sprayed or rubbed on to her body.

He exhaled and began.

'This is what I know. When my companion, Nathaniel Williams, recently contacted various insurance companies to track down claims involving a violinmaker named Amadeo Borlotti, they hemmed and hawed, as insurance companies are wont to do. The loudest hem came from Concordia, which clearly did not want to discuss the matter. But when friendly manager Sean Larson finally fessed up that Borlotti's agent, one Minerva Forsythe, was, to put it bluntly, on the lam just around the time that Borlotti's house gets burned down and Borlotti himself goes missing, that raised a red flag. Your turn. Tell me about you and Borlotti.'

'Yes, I was his agent. He got me in a lot of trouble.'

She stopped.

Jacobus said, 'That's not exactly even-steven, honey. Tell me more. How did he get you in trouble?'

'I showed him a violin. He convinced me it was a genuine Stradivarius and wrote a certificate for it. He stood to make a lot of money for writing that document. You see, when a dealer writes a certificate, he can charge a percentage of the value of the instrument.'

'Don't treat me like a babe in the woods, honey. I'm familiar with the ins and outs.'

'I'm sorry. I just wanted to be clear. And then, because of Mr

Borlotti's authentication, I was able to sell the violin to someone and paid Mr Borlotti a big commission.'

'Except it wasn't a Stradivarius? Was that the trouble?'

'I didn't know that at the time. But the person I sold it to found out and now he's very angry. That's why I had to sneak in like this. I'm afraid someone's been trying to follow me.'

Jacobus scratched his head. He put a thought in his back pocket.

'And the sales price of that violin was two-and-a-half million dollars?' he asked.

She gasped.

'How did you know?'

'That's immaterial for now. I want to know more about your relationship with Borlotti. He's dead, you know.'

'Yes. I heard. It's very sad, but there's really not much to say. From our business dealings, everything had always seemed on the up and up.'

'Such as?'

'Such as his appraisals, certificates of authentication, claims for repairs. Our reimbursements to him and his customers were consistent with the industry. I had no reason to doubt his integrity. You can check my track record. I was with Concordia for seventeen years and made them a lot of money. You mention red flags. I could spot them before my esteemed colleagues even saw flags.'

She tapped her pipe on his ashtray, pressed in some more tobacco, and puffed on it aggressively, its pungent aroma embraced by Jacobus's nasal cavity. For her, it was a pause in her narrative. For Jacobus, it was a red flag.

'Clearly,' she continued, 'when I read that someone had burned down his house I became very distressed. It seemed evident that someone wanted to do him harm.'

'Why did you jump to the conclusion that it had anything to do with the Stradivarius? After all, up to that point, weren't you still under the impression it was genuine?'

'In the insurance industry we have a term called risk-benefit analysis. I knew there was a likelihood the whole sordid business might have nothing to do with the violin, but I was unprepared to take the risk if it did.'

'Here's another question? You just said you were distressed when you read someone burned down Borlotti's house.'

'Of course I was. Who wouldn't be?'

'Indeed. But at that point in time when you first called me, no one had said someone burned it down, because no one knew that. All the media said was that it burned down. Why did you think otherwise?'

'Can I have another scotch?'

'Help yourself.'

'Well, maybe I did jump to conclusions, but it certainly seemed like arson. Especially when he went missing. Wouldn't you agree?'

Jacobus muttered something that could have been taken for yes or no, depending on what one wanted to hear.

Forsythe said, 'You've told me how you gathered I was incognito, but you still haven't told me how you knew it was me who called you and hung up. I didn't give you my name.'

'It's very obvious. The day after it's on the front page that poor Amadeo's house burned down, I get a call. I asked myself, who would be in a position to have such a keen interest in Borlotti's situation to be able to say "I know about Borlotti? He got me in trouble." There aren't all that many likely possibilities. Could be a customer. Could be a violin dealer. Could be a business person. Sometimes a few words paint a thousand pictures. The voice didn't have the inflection of a violin player or a violin dealer, but it did sound a helluva lot like a business person! And when Nathaniel later determined that one Minerva Forsythe, who had been Borlotti's agent, had created some discomfort with her colleagues at Concordia . . . Well, it seemed pretty self-evident.

'And now with the news he's been murdered, it became much more urgent to contact me. Whatever 'it' is. Which explains your presence tonight. Right?'

'I'm nodding,' she said.

'Good. Now explain to me why, if you're afraid you're being followed and of being harmed, you're telling me this all hush-hush and not going straight to the police?'

'That's a very reasonable question,' Forsythe said.

'Frankly, Ms. Forsythe, whether you think it's reasonable or unreasonable is immaterial to me, but it is a question and what you've given me is not an answer.'

'I'm afraid that . . .' she started. 'I'm concerned that the police will think that I was involved in the deception. Conspiring with Mr Borlotti to defraud.'

'It's convenient that Borlotti's not around any more to contest that, don't you think?'

'That did occur to me, yes. The authorities might even have the preposterous idea that I was involved with his murder.'

'So your risk-benefit analysis of the situation directed you to me.'

'Exactly. I knew they had asked you to help them investigate.'

'How did you know?'

'Through some contacts who Mr Williams had been calling at the agencies. The connection to you was clear. Williams said as much. I felt it was my duty to tell you what Borlotti was trying to get away with. I don't even need to get the money back that I gave him. I just want to help you.'

'You can,' Jacobus said. 'All you have to do is tell me who you sold the violin to.'

'That's the problem. I can't,' Forsythe said.

'And why not?'

'If you knew him, you would know why not. It would put both of us in too much danger. He can be a dangerous man. You have to believe me.'

'Have you tried giving him his money back?'

'It wouldn't help. He thinks I betrayed his trust. Humiliated him. The money's not as important as that. There's no going back.'

Jacobus put that one in his back pocket, also. It was running out of space.

He said, 'No matter. It won't be too hard for Mr Williams to find out who insured a two-and-a-half-million-dollar Strad, even if it's a fake one.'

'Yes, it will.'

'And why is that? He's very good at what he does.'

'Because it's uninsured.'

Unlike almost all reasonable musicians, Jacobus had never insured his violin, primarily because it rarely left his house. Though its value was only a fraction of a Strad, it was worth well into the six figures. But a Strad was a different order of magnitude entirely, and for someone to fork out two-and-a-half million dollars, to an insurance agent yet, and then not insure the violin was beyond credulity. Before Jake could express disbelief, she continued.

'I know what you're thinking. That I'm making up fairytales. But it's the truth. It wasn't that he was being reckless. And he wouldn't blink at paying the fifty-thousand-dollar annual premium. It's just that he's very private. He collects very valuable art from very private sources, so for him his privacy is worth more than the violin. As an insurance professional of course I tried to persuade him to insure it, but, you know some people are very quirky like that.'

'Yes, they are,' Jacobus said. Forsythe had a pat answer to all of his questions, as if she had rehearsed every possibility beforehand. As she said, a true insurance professional. He sensed that he would get nothing more from her.

'What's your phone number?' he asked.

'I can't give it to you,' she said. 'But I'll be in touch if I find out anything.'

Jacobus shrugged.

'Suit yourself.'

He heard Forsythe rise from her chair and begin to walk away. Then she stopped.

'You never did explain how you knew the violin sold for two-and-a-half million.'

'It's inconsequential. The police found two-hundred-thirty-thousand dollars in Borlotti's cookie jar. To me, two-hundred-thirty-thousand is a strange number of cookies. I figured some of them had been munched on, so I rounded it up to an even quarter-million. I'm thinking if we're talking 'a lot of money' for a Strad, and ten percent as a standard payoff for Borlotti's certificate, then the asking price for the Strad must have been two-and-a-half million. Just an educated guess. The kind of actuarial assumptions you insurance people work with all the time.'

Jacobus escorted Forsythe to the door.

'Drive carefully,' he said.

He listened to her pull out of the driveway and head south. Then he immediately dialed Roy Miller's number.

'Yes, I know it's the middle of the night,' Jacobus said. 'There's a car heading down Route 41. No, I don't know what kind, but at this time of night how many are there going to be? You can catch up to her before she gets to Great Barrington. Just get the license plate number for now. Call me.'

Fifteen minutes later the phone rang.

'Got it,' Miller said. 'Plus the make and model. I'm pretty sure it's a rental, but that'll make it even easier to get whatever information we need to keep tabs on her. I'm tailing her now, and I called Benson. He wasn't too happy about having his eight hours interrupted, but he'll take over once she's south of Barrington.'

Jacobus went upstairs and lay in his cold bed, pulling a heavy wool blanket over him. He could understand Forsythe sneaking to his house for fear of being followed. That much made some sense. *But once here, why not knock on the door if she wanted to talk to me? Why the cat burglar act? Unless she was hoping to find something. Had she been aware that Nathaniel and Yumi were gone? And Trotsky, too, who would at least have raised an alarm and at worst bitten an intruder's leg off? Maybe, since all the lights had been out, she thought I was out of the house, too.*

And why had she said that knowledge of the violin buyer's identity would put both of them in danger? Tired as he was, Jacobus didn't get much sleep.

NINETEEN

Monday, January 2

M iller, whose business was closed on Mondays, dropped Trotsky off first thing in the morning. Jacobus, hearing the high-pitched whimper even before Miller opened the front door, gathered the strength to brace himself. Trotsky was on top of him, slathering his face with ecstatic slobber.

'Get off me, you damn mutt!' he shouted. 'He's crushing me to death!'

Miller hauled the gargantuan bulldog off of Jacobus, but not before it managed to urinate in unrestrained joy on Jacobus's leg.

'Get thee to the glue factory!' Jacobus hollered.

'Nothing like the love between a man and his dog,' Miller said.

'Yeah, nothing worse.'

Jacobus went into the kitchen to boil a pot of coffee for Miller and himself when Benson called.

'Late night, eh, Sigurd?' Jacobus asked.

'No thanks to you, Mr Jacobus. But I thought you'd want to know. After your meeting with Minerva Forsythe we tailed her to Berkshire Bliss Holiday Cottages, near Hillsdale. She's there under an assumed name.'

'Can you get someone into the next cottage to keep tabs on her? Her story doesn't add up.'

'If I had the personnel and the budget, I would. With Borlotti's body showing up in Italy inside Ubriaco's bass case, our friend Jimmy is currently my priority, and on top of that I have to work with the Italians. I also have to liaise with Saratoga police on that woman, Maggette. We've also been experimenting with Bunsen burners to see whether they can knock over paint cans.'

'And?'

'We've tried them at different levels, different sized cans, filled to different levels—'

'And?'

'And sometimes they can. Sometimes they can't.'

'Uncanny.'

'All I'm saying is the best we can do is keep an eye on Forsythe's comings and goings. We know the motel manager. He'll let us know if she does anything suspicious.'

'Make sure he does. She may be our canary in the coal mine.'

'Yes, but in the meantime, could you help me with my juggling act and pay another visit to Ubriaco?'

'You want me to end up in a bass case, too?'

'When you make jokes like "uncanny," Mr Jacobus, it's a tempting proposition.'

Miller was free to drive Jacobus to Jimmy Ubriaco's house in Egremont Falls, and Jacobus was happy to have the big man with him. As Benson had noted, Ubriaco's string bass case made him a prime suspect, and all the bonhomie in the world couldn't disguise it.

'Jake,' Miller said as they arrived at Ubriaco's address, 'he's got a For Sale sign out in front of his house.'

'He's moving fast, isn't he? See if he's inside.'

Unlike their previous visit, the driveway and sidewalks weren't shoveled. Miller rang the doorbell. There was no answer.

'Look in the window.'

'Spotless,' Miller said. 'And it's also almost empty.'

They drove to The Last Drop at the end of Main Street, where Ubriaco had told them he and Borlotti met daily, but he wasn't there either. Try the high school, the woman behind the counter said. It was back-to-school day after the Christmas break.

'Where's the school?' Jacobus asked.

'School Street.'

Jacobus and Miller inquired at the main office.

'You should find Mr Jim in the band room. You're just in time. He's gathering his things.'

'And where's the band room. Band Street?'

'No, it's right behind you.'

Miller shouldered the swinging doors, but halfway open they were blocked by Ubriaco, who, arms filled with cartons, was on his way out.

'Well, if it isn't the clowns who lost me my job!' Ubriaco said.

'What are you talking about?' Jacobus asked.

'Jesus! What did you think happens to an orchestra conductor when the orchestra has no instruments? And then our school board reads in the *Eagle* that a bass case belonging to Egremont Falls High School, in the possession of its orchestra and band director, James Ubriaco, had been recovered in Italy bearing the mutilated remains of local violinmaker and philanthropist, Amadeo Borlotti? I got hauled down to the office this morning and got the old heave-ho. They were nice enough to give me an hour to pack my bags.'

'You think their concern is unreasonable, Jimmy?' Jacobus asked.

'Your case, your friend. Friend's house burned down with everything but your case. Friend's body is packed in your case and is shipped off. I think an explanation is in order. Don't you?'

'To you? No. To them? No. They didn't even have the balls to say I was fired. Discontinued the music program until further notice. Indefinite administrative leave, they said. Sounds so much less painful that way, almost like they're doing you a favor. How do they say it in England? "Made redundant? Sorry old chap, no more instruments, no more orchestra, no more orchestra director. Redundant, you know."

'So my house is on the market and I'm selling everything. Off to start a new life. Go West, young man! Just like my folks did a hundred years ago when they left Italy. America, the land of opportunity! Well, I've never been to California but I can fantasize, right?'

'My heart bleeds for you,' Jacobus remarked loudly.

'Jake,' Miller intervened, 'you're attracting the attention of some of the students. Maybe we should go inside the band room.'

'Like hell I will!' Ubriaco said, amping up the volume. 'You want to keep hounding me? Hound away! Borlotti was my friend. I'd never hurt him, I didn't burn down his house, and I don't know how the hell that bass case ended up in Italy!'

'If not you, then who, Mr Jim?' Jacobus asked.

'How the hell do I know? Find out who shipped it! You ever try to ship a bass case? It's not like putting a postcard in the mail. You figure it out. Now, I'm outta here. My real estate agent said my house'll go in a trice and I might even get my asking price, so get outta my way, you two geniuses, before I run you over with a tuba.'

On the way back to his house, Jacobus and Miller stopped at Benson's office in the old schoolhouse and reported their meeting with Ubriaco.

'Another headache to add to the list,' Benson responded. 'Maybe I'm getting too old for this. Well, we'll do the best we can to keep an eye on him, too. But some good news for a change. The Carabinieri have been very cooperative. They've analyzed the bullet. Thirty-eight caliber from a Smith and Wesson Model Ten revolver. One shot to the center of the forehead. Classic gangland.'

'Gangland!' Jacobus said. *What would Borlotti, or Ubriaco, have to do with gangs?*

'But the mutilation,' he asked Benson, 'That can't be Mafia standard practice.'

'It does seem inconsistent, at least for now,' Benson replied. 'It was the bullet that killed Borlotti. Carving him up was window dressing. The Carabinieri also sent a tissue sample from Borlotti to the state forensic lab. DNA forensics is a new science and it's going to take time to analyze, but we're hoping for a match with the blood on the knife by Borlotti's doorway. If it does match that would not only confirm that the murder occurred at his house but would also make theory of an accidental fire even less plausible.'

'But that's not really hard evidence of arson, is it?' Jacobus argued. 'You're putting two and two together and just hoping it comes out to four.'

'You're basically right, though at this point it's hard to imagine that there would be an accidental fire on one hand and a cold-blooded murder on the other. The other thread we're working on is that whoever sent the bass case with Borlotti's corpse to Italy must have known who the Vassaris were. We're asking, very discreetly to be sure, who might have been privy to that information.'

'Ubriaco, for instance?' Jacobus asked.

'Very possibly. We'll check it out for sure. But as you say, we have little evidence of arson that's tangible. Which made me kind of curious about one thing. Last year there was a spate of fires in the Boston area. Dilapidated buildings that developers wanted to buy, tear down, and build upper end condos and shopping malls. There was one entire block in Somerville of two-family houses that went up in smoke. All of the investigations said the fires were of suspicious origin, but none of them were able to conclude arson.'

'What are the chances of them all being accidents?' Jacobus asked.

'Like turning up a royal flush on ten consecutive hands.'

'Maybe the very absence of evidence is in itself a fingerprint,' Jacobus suggested.

'An interesting thought, but how do you convict someone on nothing?'

'Ask Sacco and Venzetti.'

'You have a point. Anyway, all of the investigations were coming up with blanks, so the governor empowered law enforcement in several counties in the Boston area to form a joint task force to coordinate their police work. I think I'll find out who heads it and see if there might be something we can learn from them. If our case has any connection with theirs, we could potentially be on to something we can't handle all alone. I recognize that I'm almost out of my depth here already.'

'Don't be too hard on yourself, Sigurd,' Jacobus said. 'Life might be a bitch, but death's a lot worse.'

TWENTY

Tuesday, January 3

'Come with me to Boston,' Benson said when he called in the morning.'

'Why?' Jacobus asked.

'I've just arranged a meeting with a Lieutenant Russell Brooks, the commander of the Greater Boston Arson Taskforce, or G-BAT as it's called.'

'When?' Jacobus asked.

'Now.'

If Nathaniel or Yumi had been there, Jacobus would have said no, but with nothing better to do he allowed himself to have his arm twisted, primarily because Benson cajoled him with a promise of lunch at the Daily Catch. It was Jacobus's favorite seafood restaurant in Boston's North End, a unique neighborhood that combined Little Italy with Boston's seafront with colonial architecture and history.

'OK. Just don't expect me to drive, too,' Jacobus said.

While waiting for Benson to pick him up, Jacobus put a few logs in the woodstove for the day and set the thermostat to sixty degrees, so that even if the fire went out, the house wouldn't freeze in his absence. A simple task for someone with sight, Jacobus had needed to devise a creative method for adjusting a thermostat. He knew that the dial of his circular thermostat went down to a minimum of forty-five degrees, so he had Nathaniel insert pushpins into the wall for every five degrees above that. It became an easy task, starting at forty-five and feeling each pushpin, to turn the knob to the fourth one to reach sixty. With that done, he let Trotsky out for a final gallivant, so that when he returned from Boston in the evening there wouldn't be an unwelcome present waiting for him on the living-room floor.

The drive from the Berkshires, on the western border of Massachusetts, to Boston, on the shore, was a straight two-hour shot from Exit One on the Massachusetts Turnpike. Benson's company made the drive seem more like three.

'G-BAT was assembled to investigate all those fires I was telling you about,' Benson explained. 'Lieutenant Brooks has been on the Boston police force for over twenty years and is known as a straight shooter. Not that it makes a difference, but when they signed him on to head G-BAT it made him the highest-ranking African American law enforcement officer in the state. My feeling is if anyone can help us, he can. At least that's what I concluded after talking to him this morning. For some reason, he said he thinks we can help *him*.'

'By comparing notes on the absence of evidence?' Jacobus asked.

Benson laughed, pretending he wasn't offended.

'One other piece of non-evidence is the alarm system you were curious about, Mr Jacobus. Borlotti did indeed have one, both for security and fire. The company is StrataSystems up in Pittsfield.'

'Why didn't they respond?' Jacobus asked.

'Because they never got the alarm.'

'Someone turned it off?'

'You would hope so. That would at least confirm that someone was up to no good. But, you see, the way these things work is when something goes wrong in the house, the alarm automatically gets sent to the security office through the homeowner's phone line.'

Jacobus finished the thought.

'And since the phone lines were down because of the snowstorm, the message couldn't be transmitted.'

'Exactly.'

'Could someone have intentionally pulled down the lines that connected to Borlotti's house?' Jacobus asked.

'It's possible, but lines were down in several locations. I don't think we'll ever know.

'We did get one tidbit of good news that I shared with Brooks. The forensic lab got a positive match between the blood on the knife in Borlotti's house with the sample that the Carabinieri sent from his body. So now we can be reasonably sure Borlotti's murder occurred at his house on the night it was burned down. Even though it was the gun and not the knife that killed him, and even though we haven't found the gun, if we can determine who was holding the knife, we'll most likely know that person was the murderer. Assuming they were one and the same.'

This time it was Jacobus who laughed.

'What's funny?' Benson asked.

'It's the first time in my life that blood on a weapon was considered good news.'

As they approached downtown, they became mired in traffic, one of the constants of life in Boston. The Big Dig construction converting the central artery, which had split the North End from the rest of the city, into an underground freeway had been going on at a snail's pace for two decades and was costing the taxpayers billions. When finished it promised to improve the traffic flow, but for now it only made matters worse. It didn't bother Jacobus, who couldn't see it and didn't live there, but he sympathized with the commuters who had gotten stuck with both the traffic and the bill.

Benson had little else to report other than to update Dahlia Maggette's tarnished employment history, which included being fired from the Club Terrace and Back Stretch for soliciting. It reminded Jacobus that sometime soon he would have the unpleasant task of informing her that her beau and benefactor, Amadeo Borlotti, was dead, assuming she hadn't already read about it in the papers. He suspected she hadn't.

They arrived at the Daily Catch on Hanover Street after the lunch rush so there wouldn't be the customary wait for a table outside in the cold. The tiny seafood restaurant had been around for decades and had fended off all challengers, including the trendy new oyster bar, Awe Shucks, that had just opened down the block. Brooks, who had positioned two plainclothesmen outside the entrance, was already there, and gestured for them to join him.

They sat at the one table in between the front window and the open kitchen, where a single chef handled all the orders. Jacobus and Benson sat with their backs to the window. Brooks, with a vantage point to see anyone coming in, had taken the seat facing out.

'I'll keep my eye on the street traffic,' Brooks said to Benson. 'You can keep your eye on the calamari.'

Jacobus inhaled the aroma of simmering seafood, tomatoes, and garlic with pleasure.

'And I'll be the cockle-eyed optimist,' he said, and ordered his favorite dish, clams in red sauce over linguini, served in the pan in which it was cooked. It went perfectly with his glass of red wine, served in a plastic cup.

They small-talked about food and the weather for a few minutes. Then, with conversational appetizers out of the way, Brooks attacked the meeting's main course.

'Gentlemen, as I'm sure you're aware from reading the news, arson for hire in the Boston area has reached epidemic proportions. Hardly a week goes by when there isn't a suspicious fire. Until recently, casualties were minimal and we've had our share of successful prosecutions. But this year we've had four fatalities – five if we end up adding Borlotti – and there are still way too many that go unresolved.'

'Why?' Jacobus asked. 'How many arsonists can there be in one city?'

Brooks answered calmly.

'Partly because of bureaucratic gridlock, Mr Jacobus, which has improved greatly since the formation of G-BAT. And partly because some arsonists are extremely good at what they do. There is one in particular who my gut tells me is behind at least some, if not all, of the more recent suspicious fires. His name is Francis Falcone, but he goes by the names of Frankie the Flame and Saint Ignitius. He's a hoodlum, a narcissist, and a braggart, but he also happens to be the best in his profession.'

'What makes a good arsonist other than extra matches?' Jacobus asked.

'Much to our dismay, this Falcone's a chameleon. He's an innovator who transformed the trade. He doesn't bring his own flammables but utilizes materials he finds on site, assembling them in such an organic way that we usually can't even tell that arson had been committed. It's only when there's been a string of them that we figure the odds are that it was intentional.'

'OK. Arson is arson. But not all arsonists are murderers,' Jacobus said.

'True, but consider the skillset of a fine arsonist. Impeccable planning, expert craftsmanship, ice running through the veins. That lines up well with the profile of a professional hit man. We believe Falcone is not averse to occasionally being called upon to dispose of the occupant of a structure in addition to the structure itself. And why not? The payoff would be much greater for him without having to punch much more time on the clock.

'When Officer Benson called and told me about what happened out in your neck of the woods, it had all the earmarks of a Falcone job. If we can work together on this, we might be able to nail him.'

'What makes our case any different from the others you've been incapable of solving?' Jacobus asked.

'I see you live up to your reputation, Mr Jacobus,' Brooks said.

'What's that?'

'You're an asshole.'

Jacobus laughed.

'Just wait until you get to know me better,' he said.

'Here's what's different,' Brooks continued. 'You have actually found a body.'

'You said Borlotti's not the first fatality,' Jacobus pressed.

'That's right. But he's the first whose death was unquestionably homicide. All the others were categorized as accident victims, or questionable at best.

'Also, you've found a weapon, and the lab has connected those dots with the blood. Whoever used that knife killed Borlotti with it and, by extension, burned the house down. We need to figure out where Falcone was on Christmas Eve and what the connection was to Borlotti.'

'If any,' said Benson.

'If any,' Brooks repeated.

'Where does this Falcone live?' Jacobus asked.

'Would you believe a few blocks from here? That a hoodlum like him lives spitting distance from Paul Revere's house? He grew up in the North End in a one-bedroom apartment on Salem Street. Went to church at Saint Ignatius on North Street. Now he's got a lovely million-dollar condo with a great view of the harbor and his yacht sitting in the dock. And you know how he paid for it?'

'No.'

'Join the club. We've never been able to trace anything illegal in his bank accounts because it's all cash. He hasn't worked a day in his life that we know of, yet he's flush. Go figure.'

'Have you interrogated him?' Jacobus asked.

'He always has an airtight alibi. Never knows a thing.'

'Anyone at Saint Ignatius know him?'

'It's a little late for that. It's no longer a church. They shut down the congregation a year ago,' Brooks said, 'after a hundred-thirty-eight years. Couldn't afford maintenance and repair. Heating bills in the winter. AC bills in the summer. It's becoming an old song. No one goes to church anymore. It's a nice historic building.'

'They're going to tear it down?'

'Saved at the bell by an architect. He's going to convert it to an art gallery café.'

'Probably for the best,' Jacobus said.

'Why do you say that?'

'With the congregation turning out scum like Falcone, a gallery will probably serve mankind better.'

'I'm not sure Monsignor Gallivan would agree with that.'

'Probably not. Hard for him to save souls as a barista. Is it worth talking to this monsignor about Falcone?'

'They put him out to pasture when they closed the congregation. I heard he's not in great shape.'

'Then why not go and have a chat with Falcone directly?' Benson asked. 'Maybe if you tell him we've expanded our investigation and are gathering evidence from the Egremont Falls fire you can rattle him into making a false move. Telling him about the matching blood samples might get under his skin.'

'Sooner the better, I'd say,' Jacobus added.

'I understand how anxious both of you are to get results,' Brooks said. 'But I don't think going at Falcone will produce the results you want. Chances are he'd lie or clam up. Telling him where we are in the investigation will also give him information he does not yet have. And finally, I can't overstate how dangerous this guy is.'

'You have a better suggestion?' Jacobus asked.

'Yes. Keep our distance and get some information at the same time. And if you accompany me down the street to the Café Paradiso for espresso and the best cannoli in the North End, I'll introduce you to someone special.'

'Say no more,' Jacobus responded.

TWENTY-ONE

'I hope this isn't far,' Jacobus said, beginning to reconsider the relative value of a cannoli. He hadn't anticipated having to walk through frozen slush in downtown Boston, and every time he stepped off a curb into the street he felt Italian ices seep through the soles of his old shoes.

'We're almost there,' Brooks assured him. 'And I think you'll find the effort worthwhile, and not just for the dessert. We definitely need information, and I think we'll be able to get some from Sammy Rocchinelli, one of our more dependable informants.'

'You invited him to be part of our coffee klatch?' Jacobus asked.

Brooks laughed.

'That would be a little obvious,' he said. 'No, Sammy's hangout is the Paradiso. He's almost always there this time of day. I'd be surprised if he wasn't. I think you'll find him a colorful character.'

'What does he do for a living?' Benson asked.

'Why, he's an arsonist!' Brooks said, sounding surprised by the question.

'So why don't you put him behind bars?' Jacobus asked. 'Voila! Epidemic cured.'

'If only that were the case,' Brooks answered. 'Believe me, Sammy did more than a few years in Walpole. But we got him out early for good behavior once he agreed to cooperate with us.'

'How did you get him to do that?' Benson asked.

'The usual,' Brooks replied. 'Money. Sammy is predisposed to wager on sporting events.'

'Horse racing?' Jacobus asked. Maybe there was a connection.

'Any sport. From football to foosball and everything in between. Sammy never met a hot tip he didn't like. To our good fortune, he almost always loses. He needs us to help maintain his cash flow.

Sometimes he's loose and easy with the facts, but he's got a memory for detail that fortunately hasn't been beaten out of him yet.'

'How is he still alive?' Benson asked. 'For a crook, there's nothing worse than having a reputation as a rat. Look what's going on right here in Boston. The Herald's saying Whitey Bulger's killing anyone who even smells like an informant.'

'We never asked Sammy to turn state's witness, so no one knows he's providing us with information,' Brooks said. 'Plus, we make him look good.'

Benson beat Jacobus, asking, 'How do you do that?' as Jacobus put his foot into yet another moat of slush.

'We keep him gainfully employed to burn things down once in a while. We tell him when and where. Mostly small jobs – condemned apartments, a shuttered up store here and there. Make sure no one's in them, of course. We make sure the fire department is on the scene pronto to keep things contained. It's enough work for Sammy to keep his street cred without questions being asked. And, to be honest, it's been good for urban renewal. Some of those property owners would never fix their places up unless they got the insurance money. And I should mention, there aren't many people who would mess with Sammy Rocchinelli whether they knew he was a rat or not. There's good reason they call him Sammy Rock. Here we are, Mr Jacobus. Just let me do the talking,' Brooks said to him and Benson.

Brooks took Jacobus's arm and entered the café. The weather had evidently shooed away the tourists, as the conversations Jacobus heard were mostly in Italian. Brooks escorted Jacobus past the tables and past a television set broadcasting a soccer game on low volume, to the bar at the back of the café where a Mario Lanza medley held sway. Jacobus felt for a stool and sat on it, placing his hands on the counter for stability. Benson sat to his right, Brooks to his left.

'Hey, Sammy,' Brooks said. The volume of noise in the café was soft enough for quiet conversation and loud enough for it not to carry more than a couple feet. Ideal for passing information.

'Hey, you bring your blind grandfather today?' Rocchinelli said. The voice came from Brooks's left, even farther to the back of the café. Maybe the last seat at the bar. Though the voice was hushed, the brutality was undisguised. 'Better not tell him you're a black boy.' Rocchinelli apparently thought that was a great joke and started wheezing with laughter.

'Now you've done it,' Brooks replied with a chuckle. 'I've been trying to keep it a secret from him.' He then introduced Jacobus and Benson.

'Espresso for everyone? Cannolis?' Brooks asked. Jacobus and Benson nodded their assent.

'Grappa,' Rocchinelli said.

'Starting early today, Sammy?' Brooks asked.

'Today, tomorrow, yesterday. Plus, you're buying.'

The barista, a large woman in her sixties who seemed to be serving all the customers in the café simultaneously, took their order and went off.

'You seen Frankie lately?' Brooks asked Rocchinelli.

'What, aren't you gonna ask me about the weather first?'

'Look, Sammy,' Brooks said, suddenly with gloves off. 'I don't have all day. You've seen him or not?'

The change of tone must have surprised Rocchinelli. He answered quickly.

'Nah. He's down at some Caribbean resort with the wife and kids. Celebratin' the holidays.'

'How do you know that?'

'Because I saw him before he left, Einstein.'

'When was that?'

'Christmas. Christmas day. We was watchin' football at Johnnie's on Salem Street. Fuckin' Lions lost again. You know how much I lost on them?'

'Don't give up on them, Sammy. That Barry Sanders kid they got can run. They'll turn it around. Just you watch. Did Frankie tell you about anything other than his vacation plans?'

'Not much.'

'Sammy, you want to earn back what you lost on the Lions, you'll have to unburden yourself more than that. "Not much" just ain't gonna cut it.'

'OK. So he says he can't wait to get to the sun because the night before he was so fuckin' cold.'

'So Frankie was cold on Christmas Eve. Him and ten million other people. Go on.'

'OK, he was pissed because he was stuck in some delivery truck somewhere out in the sticks with only his leather jacket and didn't have no gloves. He said every time he was cursin' that he shoulda been home in his condo, all it did was fog up the fuckin' windshield.'

'You've ever been in his condo?' Brooks asked.

'Sure I been there. More than once, too. Six bedrooms. Overlookin' the harbor. Can you imagine how much that costs?'

'Sounds like a nice place.'

'He keeps it nice and warm there. Never lower than seventy-five. No wonder he felt so fuckin' cold. The only ice in his condo is in his martini.' Rocchinelli laughed through his nose at his joke. Brooks joined in.

'There's one room you'd really, really like, Lieutenant,' Rocchinelli continued, with false mirth. 'Frankie's trophy room.'

'Tell me about it,' Brooks said.

'He got his favorite newspaper stories in frames. Shows 'em off. You know: "Faulty Wiring Sparks Warehouse Fire." "Smoking in Bed Dooms Victim, Building." He brags that none of them newspapers ever mentions his name because the cops got nuthin' on him. A couple stories said 'suspicious, under investigation,' but they got nowhere. As you well know.'

'Proud of his accomplishments, is he?'

'Yeah. He sure has got you guys chasing your asses. The only thing that bugs him is he's so good at what he does he'll never get no credit for it. He's pissed no one's ever gonna know his legacy.'

'That's what he said?' Brooks asked.

'That's what he said.'

'Life is tough.'

'Fuck you, Brooks,' Rocchinelli said, but there was no heat behind the comment.

'So he'd like to be able to leave some kind of trademark? Some indication of his handiwork?'

'Trademark. Yeah. That's exactly the word he used. But not enough to get caught.'

'Of course not. Just something to burnish his reputation. His calling card, so to speak.'

'Yeah, like that bounty hunter in that TV western. I liked that guy. With that mustache and that black outfit he wore. What was his name?'

'Palladin? "Have Gun, Will Travel"?'

'That's it! You should be on Jeopardy, Brooks. You'd make more than being a fuckin' cop.'

Rocchinelli's laugh started in his stomach and bubbled up to his throat before he squelched it. 'I should've been a comedian,' he said.

'Yeah, you're another Rodney Dangerfield,' Brooks said. 'But you want some respect, you tell me more than the bullshit you've given me so far. The more detail, the more you'll have to lose on the Bowl Games.'

'OK. It's your dime, pal. Sure is crummy weather we're havin'. Think we'll be gettin' dumped on again?'

Jacobus noted that the change in subject matter coincided with the barista arriving at the counter with their order. *Cautious son-of-a-bitch, anyway,* Jacobus thought. Feeling for the cannoli, he accidently inserted his finger into the ricotta cheese, licked it off, and mentally agreed with Brooks's assessment of its quality.

As soon as the barista left, Rocchinelli returned to the narrative.

'So Frankie was stuck in this truck. On Christmas Eve. He says *Feliz Navidad* was on the radio. You know it?'

Rocchinelli did a bad impression of Jose Feliciano. '*We wanna wish you a Merry Christmas. We wanna wish you a Merry Christmas. We wanna wish you a Merry Christmas, From the bottom of our heart.* Frankie said he loves that song, but that night everything was pissing him off. It was dark as hell and the snow was coming down. Hard. So he turns on the wipers to clear it off before the truck turns into a fuckin' igloo. He has to rub the inside of the windshield with his sleeve just to see out.'

Jacobus was about to ask the essential question: Where was Falcone parked? But just as he was clearing his throat, Brooks put a restraining hand on his leg. Jacobus took another bite of cannoli.

'Frankie didn't understand why his boss contracted him to deal with a punk yokel in the first place,' Rocchinelli continued. 'He was so pissed he punched the steering wheel.'

Rocchinelli, imitating Falcone, delivered a series of blows to the bar's counter with his fists that made Jacobus's espresso cup rattle. Rocchinelli laughed and took a sip of grappa.

'But then he decided he wouldn't let it get to him. One way or the other, his job would go off without a hitch. It was a piece of cake. Chump change. He said he wouldn't have taken it at all unless he really wanted that extra cash. Wouldn't be sitting there in the freaking cold. But he'd promised Nadine and the kids to celebrate the holidays in style as soon as he finished taking care of business. He said with his paycheck he'd give them a Christmas present they'd remember for a long time. Lying on the hot sand with Nadine turning red as a lobster next to him – hey, don't tell Frankie I said this, but

I bet she still looks great in a bikini – and the kids doing chicken fights in the clear blue sea, warm as bathwater. He's one lucky prick. He said maybe he and Nadine would make another baby.'

'Could you get back to the night in question, please?' Benson quietly asked from Jacobus's right.

'Who the fuck—?' Rocchinelli said, his voice exploding.

'Calm down, Sammy,' Brooks said. Jacobus could imagine him patting Rocchinelli's arm the way he had patted his leg. 'You take your time. No more interruptions.' Brooks's message to Benson was clear.

'Another grappa,' Rocchinelli demanded, and Brooks ordered it. 'You were saying.'

'I don't remember what I was saying.'

'You were saying how Frankie and Nadine might make another baby. Once he took care of business.'

'All right. So Frankie congratulated himself for comin' up with using a delivery truck. No one would think twice about a delivery truck during Christmas. He said it hardly mattered. Except for the runty house there weren't any buildings around, and the snow covered everything like white sand dunes. Like it looked like a beach, but it sure as hell wasn't the Caribbean. Like it was like a beach on fucking Mars. No people, no noise, no nothing. No city lights to cheer him up. Not even any fuckin' Christmas lights.

'He said he tried to keep positive. That all of that nothing out there in the sticks would make taking care of business with this guy that much easier. And what was a little cold? Soon enough he and Nadine would be laughing at how he froze his ass off on Christmas Eve, right?'

'That *is* pretty funny,' Brooks said, whose deep belly laugh seemed genuine even to keen-eared Jacobus. 'And Frankie's such a skinny guy. I'm just picturing him sitting in that truck with his teeth chattering like a baby rattle. "What the fuck am I doing here?"' Brooks wailed, and laughed so hard even Jacobus started snickering.

'Oh, my! Oh, my!' Brooks said, and blew his nose.

'Frankie said it was so fucking cold his balls were turning blue!' Rocchinelli could hardly choke the words out, he was laughing so hard. Jacobus wasn't sure any longer what Rocchinelli was making up or had actually remembered. 'He said it took a week on the beach to thaw them out!' The floor actually shook. Jacobus could picture Sammy Rock wiping tears off his rock hard cheek.

'So he did finish his assignment, then,' Brooks said, traces of laughter still audible.

'What's that old G.E. jingle?' Rocchinelli asked. 'You know, for their clock radios? "When the sun goes down, the dial lights up." Well, the dial lit up, baby! Frankie said he never had such a natural torch.'

'What did he mean by that?'

'It means the place already had stuff in it. Burn, baby, burn! Frankie said even Mother Nature helped him. He'd planned to disconnect the power before going in, since he figured there was some kind of security alarm. But the gods were with him and the storm knocked out the power and the phone lines. He said it was meant to be!'

Jacobus thought quickly but kept his mouth shut. What was the likelihood that more than one house burned down on Christmas Eve where the power was down?

'I suppose so,' Brooks said. 'I suppose so. Funny, though. We didn't get any reports about arson on Christmas Eve. You sure Frankie wasn't pulling a fast one on you?'

'What do you mean?' Rocchinelli answered.

'Either you got the date wrong or he was just trying to make himself look big. Making up stories. You sure it was Christmas Eve and not Thanksgiving or Labor Day?'

'Fuck you!' Rocchinelli said. 'Look who's trying to pull a fast one! You're trying to jew me out of paying me, you black prick!'

Jacobus heard a stool scratch angrily.

'Easy, Sammy,' Brooks said. 'Down, boy. No one's trying to cheat anyone. Now sit down so we can sort this out, OK? It's just that without more information, we can't really use what we've got here. What we need is a location.'

'All he said was it was out in the boondocks.'

'You sure?'

'Yes, I'm fuckin' sure.'

'Did Frankie mention anything about anyone being killed? Any names at all?'

'No. He's too smart for that.'

Jacobus finally opened his mouth for something other than cannoli and espresso.

'Hey, junior,' he said. 'You mentioned that your pal, Frankie, worked for someone. Who might that have been?'

Rochinelli took time to respond.

'Stu,' Rocchinelli said seriously. 'He worked for Stu.'

'Stu who?' Jacobus asked.

'Stu Gotz,' Rocchinelli said and burst out laughing. Jacobus understood enough street Italian to know that stugots was slang for prick.

'Is that all you have for us, Sammy?' Brooks asked. 'Can you tell us where Frankie went for his fun in the sun?'

'Hello! Read my lips! I. Don't. Know.'

'Sammy, I really could use something else. What can you give me?'

'You gonna pay me or not?' Rochinelli whispered.

'Have I ever not come through?'

'OK. There's gonna be a second part to Frankie's assignment. After he gets back. Big payday. Double the first one.'

'For what?' Brooks asked.

'Don't know. Except he said it would be a win-win.'

'All right,' Brooks said. 'For now. Wait! Sammy, if I need you to, what would it be worth to you to take another look at Frankie's Hall of Fame?'

The question apparently took Rocchinelli by surprise. He remained silent. Brooks let him take his time.

'Ten Super Fucking Bowl tickets,' he said at length.

'That's not just a drop in the bucket,' Brooks said. 'Why not just take the cash?'

'Because I can scalp those tickets for twenty times what they're worth. I don't guess you cops got *that* much in the piggy bank. Am I right?'

'As always, Sammy, as always.'

Brooks paid the bill to the barista. Jacobus and Benson followed him out the Café Paradiso. Sammy 'Rock' Rocchinelli stayed behind.

As soon as they were outside, Benson apologized to Brooks for having interrupted his questioning of Rocchinelli, which Brooks accepted with a wave of his hand.

Benson asked, 'How credible do you think Rocchinelli's testimony would be in court?'

'If it didn't get thrown out by the judge,' Brooks responded, 'Falcone's defense attorneys would tear him to shreds in a minute. Hearsay, unreliable witness. They'd have a field day.'

'Then what good does he do you?' Jacobus asked.

'I basically believe him, though at times it's clear he's playing to the audience. We just have to find some corroborative evidence in order to make his testimony credible. Don't worry. We'll get there.'

Brooks then surprised Jacobus.

'I might not have Super Bowl tickets, but I've got a couple for the Boston Symphony tonight. Would you and Officer Benson like to join me?'

'What are they playing?' Jacobus asked.

'Stravinsky "Firebird".'

'How about it, Sigurd?' Jacobus asked. 'You a music lover?'

'Sorry. "Sweeny Todd" is about as longhair as I get. And I need to be back home tonight.'

'Rain check, then?' Brooks offered.

'Rain check,' Jacobus said.

'Here's my direct line.' Jacobus felt a business card pressed into his hand.

'Call me anytime,' Brooks said.

'We getting anywhere?' Jacobus asked. 'Are you sure you shouldn't just go after Falcone?'

'Not yet,' Brooks replied. 'We push too hard, he either disappears, or . . .'

'Or what?'

'Or worse. I'm not even sure we haven't already gone over some invisible line.'

'When do you pay off Rocchinelli?' Benson asked.

'Done and done,' Brooks said. 'I didn't see you give him any money,' Benson said.

'You're damn right. If anyone saw that, Rocchinelli would be dead before tomorrow.'

'Then how?'

'I gave it to the barista. She'll give him the money and take her cut.'

'How do you know she won't talk?' Benson asked.

'She's his sister.'

TWENTY-TWO

Benson turned off the ignition in front of Jacobus's house and thanked him for taking the day to go to Boston. For Jacobus it was a relief to be back, away from a city congested with grime and crime. As soon as he opened the car door, the fresh scent of burning pine commingled with the enticing, savory aroma of Asian cooking entered his lungs. With Yumi in Italy it must be Nathaniel in the kitchen. The house would be warm and his stomach would soon be full.

Jacobus thought about inviting Benson in, but didn't. He thanked him for lunch and closed the car door. Benson drove off, skidding slightly as he tried to maneuver up the icy driveway. But like many people in the Berkshires he knew how to deal with winter weather. He eased up on the gas until the tires gripped and then revved the engine just the right amount and was soon back on Route 41.

'Where have you been?' Nathaniel asked as Jacobus entered the house. 'We've been waiting for you.'

'We?'

'*Buona sera*, Jake,' Yumi said.

'Back so soon?'

'Marcello wanted me to meet his mother. I had to break the news to him that buying his violin was not a marriage contract.'

'Were you heartbroken?'

'Only at seeing a grown man cry.'

Jacobus sat down at his kitchen table. He knew its dimensions so well that he no longer even needed to extend his arms to the corners to know when he was sitting in the middle.

'Who made the sukiyaki?' he asked.

'There's a nice-looking new Japanese place on Main Street in Great Barrington,' Yumi said. 'It's called Get Bento.'

'It was either that or Vietnamese,' Nathaniel added. 'And we've already been to Friend And Pho.'

As usual, Nathaniel had bought enough for a small army. They didn't talk much business – in fact, they didn't talk much at all – until after they had polished off the last rice noodle of their dinner, which, when they started, they said they'd never be able to finish.

Afterwards, Jacobus told them about what he had learned about the possible connection between the suspected Boston arsonist, Francis Falcone, and the Borlotti case.

'Well, from what I found out,' Nathaniel said, 'it's hard to imagine why a big shot like this Falcone would want to take such a risk with Borlotti.'

'What have you got?' Jacobus asked.

Nathaniel had personally gone to every customer on the Rolodex who was willing to see him. With everyone having heard the news that Borlotti had been killed, no one – whether out of self-interest, a desire to help, a perverse thrill of being in a murder investigation, or fear of potential dust-ups with the police – declined his request for a meeting.

Compared to their initial reluctance, the customers were now only too happy to divulge their relationship with Borlotti. Some even confessed that their instruments had been at Borlotti's for repair on the night his house was burned down. The insurance labyrinth had been a nightmare ever since, and they didn't know when, or if, they would ever be reimbursed for the loss of their instruments. Jacobus again made a mental note that, other than Ubriaco's school instruments, no trace of any others had been found in the rubble.

Nathaniel took a three-pronged approach with those customers who did have instruments in their possession. First, he studied any documentation they had pertaining to authenticity, insurance appraisals, and repairs. Then he took a careful look at the instruments themselves. Though he wasn't an expert like Boris Dedubian, he had developed discerning eyes and ears and was more often than not able to detect an imitation. Third, he asked the owners to play the violins for him. Some of them were rank amateurs, others were good students, and a few even rose to the level of modest professionals. With such a disparity it was difficult to draw any strong conclusions about sound quality.

'But I have to admit, they all sounded good, Jake,' Nathaniel said while Yumi cleared the table of cardboard containers and packets of unused soy sauce. 'And looked good.'

'Signs of wear and tear?' Jacobus asked. 'Two-hundred-year-old violins have to have scratches or cracks somewhere.'

'They did, and in the places you'd expect. A couple had soundpost cracks that had been repaired.'

'How about the wood? Was it the same wood the Vassaris sent him from Italy?'

'It could have been, but there's no way for me to really know. The finished product just looks too different from the raw planks we saw. But maybe Boris could help us with that.'

'How were the labels inside the fiddles?'

'That's one place it's easy to tell a fake, but they looked right and had dust on them so I suspect they're the originals,' he said. 'They looked authentic. As did the certificates.' Nathaniel went down the list:

'Wurlitzer—'

'Rembert?' Jacobus asked.

'No, Rudolf. Francais—'

'Jacques?'

'No, Emile. Vatelot—'

'Etienne?'

'No, Marcel. Dedubian.'

'Boris?'

'No, Aram.'

'What about repairs, insurance?'

'That's even more Dedubious,' Yumi joked.

'That's even worse than *my* puns,' Jacobus said.

'I learned from the worst,' Yumi said and punched Jacobus in the arm.

Nathaniel continued.

'There's some evidence that Borlotti inflated the estimated repair costs when he sent them in to the insurance companies. Two of his customers as much as admitted to that when they told us Borlotti had received overpayments and offered to split it with them. They were delighted because not only had their instruments been repaired well, they also made a little profit.'

'Is that a reason to kill someone?' Jacobus asked.

'No, by no means,' Nathaniel answered. 'But there's another thing that got me thinking. Some of the minor repairs, no big deal. Everyone expects those. But there were a couple bigger ones, like those soundpost cracks, that also depreciate the value of the instrument. When that happens, the insurance company not only reimburses you for the cost of the repair, you get compensated for the instrument's diminished value.'

'Everyone knows that,' Jacobus said. His patience for the minutiae of insurance policies was at the same level as with students who didn't practice their scales. None.

'Yes, but with these instruments I'm talking about, the insurance companies agreed to a much greater loss of value than normal. Somehow, Borlotti was able to convince them he knew something about the market that no one else does. Or he was skimming.'

'How much?'

'Well, we can hardly guess because we only saw a couple instruments. The repairs on them cost from five to fifteen hundred, but the loss in value amounted to thousands.'

'Again, enough to kill someone for?'

'Only if you were a really mean bugger.'

'There'd have to be an additional reason to kill someone,' Yumi mused. 'It wouldn't make sense. Just the risk alone, even if it were tons of money. And it's not.'

'You notice something interesting about those certificates?' Jacobus asked.

'By all means!' Nathaniel said. 'They were written by the most reputable dealers of the twentieth century. Ironclad. You wouldn't get much argument about them, even today.'

'How about you, Yumi? Anything strike you?'

'Only what Nathaniel . . . Oh! I know what you're thinking! They're all experts who were the fathers of living experts.'

'Or to put it more bluntly, the writers of those certificates are all dead as a doornail.'

'But their reputations were at least as strong as their sons,' Nathaniel argued, 'and their certificates are still considered valid. More than valid. Authoritative. They help establish the provenance of the instrument.'

'But there's no one in the first person to corroborate the authenticity of the documents themselves. Even if someone were to question what looks like a perfectly valid certificate, they'd have to go to a helluva lot of trouble to prove or disprove it.'

'And who would want to disprove it if it's for their own instrument?' Yumi asked. 'It would only make the value of their instrument go *down*!'

Jacobus had an idea.

'Who owns the violin with the Dedubian certificate?' Jacobus asked.

'Someone in Millerton, New York, I think,' Nathaniel said.

'An hour from here, give or take,' Jacobus said. 'And on the way to the city. Nathaniel, do you think you could persuade the owner to lend us his violin and certificate for a day while we take a little trip to see Dedubian?'

'Boris?'

'Yes, the grandson.'

TWENTY-THREE

Wednesday, January 4

Jacobus was too antsy to wait for dawn. He woke Nathaniel and Yumi and hounded them out of bed, insisting they start for the city right away. He was sure that the pattern of old certificates was an important indicator. Of what, he wasn't sure, but he wanted to find out.

As they left the house, the phone rang. It was Benson.

'We're out the door,' Jacobus said. 'Research. Determining the relationship between a piece of paper and a bullet in the head.'

'Intriguing,' Benson said. 'So I won't keep you. But before you hang up I just wanted you to know that Frankie Falcone returned to Boston two days ago. Lieutenant Brooks asked Sammy Rocchinelli to talk to him wearing a wire if—'

'Let me guess. If the price was right.'

'Exactly. And he did it. Would you like me to see if he got a tape of the conversation?'

'No time now. Later.' Jacobus hung up. He reignited the embers in the woodstove and threw enough logs into it to keep it going for the day.

Yumi drove. They stopped in Middleton, New York, just off Route 23. Nathaniel had cajoled Abe Spellman, a retired pharmacist and the owner of the violin, to lend it to them for the day. Without saying anything definite, Nathaniel had suggested that Boris Dedubian might be in the process of writing a book on Milanese violinmakers and might want to use photographs of Spellman's Testore for it. If it all worked out, he hinted, the violin would be worth that much more. Spellman reluctantly handed it over to Nathaniel. 'Take good care of my baby,' he said as he parted with it.

They arrived at Boris Dedubian's elegant midtown Manhattan violin shop and showroom as its doors opened at ten o'clock. Dedubian examined the violin and was baffled. Everything about the violin, bearing the label Carlo Giuseppe Testore, Milan, 1724 looked right. Everything about it appeared authentic. The dimensions, the description of the grain and varnish were exactly consistent with information on the certificate, written and dated on June 28, 1924 by his grandfather, Aram, and passed along with the violin to newer owners ever since. The handwritten certificate, No. 4005, had the proper letterhead with the address of Aram Dedubian's New York shop on West 42nd Street – a branch of his business that had originated in Paris – in a building that had long ago been torn down:

> *We certify that the* violin *in the possession of* Mr Lucien Frawley, *of* New Haven, Connecticut, *was made by* Carlo Giuseppe Testore, in Milan, in 1724, *whose original label it bears.*
> *Description: The back is formed by two pieces of very hand-some maple joined at the center, having a broadish figure, which extends upward toward the edges. The sides are of the same material and match the back. The front is of spruce of the choicest selection known to this maker, of fine, even grain. The varnish is of a rich, brownish red and is unusually plentiful. The scroll is in the Maker's best style. It is a thoroughly representative example of the year in which it was made.*

The certificate bore the distinctive signature, *Aram Dedubian*. It was on the basis of the certificate and the fine condition of the instrument that Borlotti had written an insurance appraisal for one hundred and fifteen thousand dollars.

Boris Dedubian remeasured the instrument. It was exactly the same as what his grandfather noted on the certificate:

> *Length:* 14 inches; *Width (upper bout):* 6 9/16'; *Width (lower bout):* 8 3/16'; *Width (middle bout):* 4 3/8.'

'Everything about this instrument is right,' Dedubian said. 'But something about it is not right. Do you think Mr Testore would mind if we performed some minor surgery?' Dedubian asked.

Jacobus knew what Dedubian was about to propose.

'As long as we don't tell the owner,' Jacobus said. 'We assured him we'd take care of it like it was his own baby.'

'Well, don't sometimes babies have their tonsils out?' Dedubian asked, removing the strings, bridge, and chinrest from the violin. Then he proceeded to slide a tool that looked like a palette knife in between the top of the violin and the ribs, digging into the glue with a gut-wrenching crunch. After a few minutes, he gave the knife a twist and the top of the violin came off with a pop.

'He'll be none the wiser after I've glued it back on. It doesn't hurt the violin a bit.'

Dedubian inspected the inside of the violin. Everything looked right there, too. Almost.

'Look at this,' he said to Nathaniel and Yumi. Jacobus could only listen.

'The repairs here on the inside of the top. They're well done, but it's not my grandfather's work. They didn't make wooden cleats like that back then.'

'Well, couldn't that have been a later repairman's work? Or Borlotti's?' Yumi asked.

'I would say yes. But look, there's as much dust on the cleats as on the plate. If the repair were more recent there would be less dust, no?'

'Not necessarily,' Jacobus said. 'It could all have accumulated since the repair was done.'

'I suppose that's possible, but it looks like it has been there for as long as the dust on the label. Long Before Borlotti. It doesn't add up that he did the repair but the dust was on there before.'

'I'm not sure that's very convincing,' Jacobus said.

'No. I confess, to me, either,' Dedubian said.

Jacobus heard Dedubian tapping his fingers. On the top of the violin, he wondered?

'I should have the original certificate in the vault,' Dedubian continued. 'Let's see if they match.'

Dedubian had his receptionist, Mrs. Prince, bring some tea for everyone and retreated to his inner sanctum. He returned fifteen minutes later. His footsteps were quick and more decisive.

'Dear friends,' he said. 'I can tell you with confidence that both the violin and the certificate are genuine. Genuine forgeries!'

'Lay it out for us,' Jacobus said.

'Jake, I am putting the two documents side by side. On the left is the certificate you brought me from the violin's owner. On the right is the one from my vault. For the most part they are quite the same. Since these were the days before copy machines of course there will be some minor inconsistencies, but the hand-writing is the same, the paper, the ink. It is virtually identical for all intents and purposes. I am asking your friends to look closely at the filing number of the two certificates, which is found in the upper left-hand corner.'

Nathaniel and Yumi together said, 'Four-zero-zero-five.'

'That is exactly right,' said Dedubian. 'And that's how I know the one you brought me is a forgery.'

'I must be slow. I don't get it,' Jacobus.

'Mr Williams,' Dedubian said. 'Fraud in this field is your expertise. Is it not?'

'Yes!' Nathaniel said after a lengthy pause. 'You're right! The ones your grandfather kept in the vault were the originals. The ones he gave to his customers would have had the word "Duplicate" or "Copy" after the number, or at least some indication that they were copies. Whoever forged this must have found a picture of the certificate at a library or on the Internet and made a hand copy.'

'How could he have known about the paper and ink from the Internet?' Yumi asked.

'Easy,' Jacobus said. 'He could have gotten his hands on a hard copy of any other authentic Aram Dedubian certificate to give him that information. Once he had that much he could write as many of Grandpapa's certificates as he wanted.'

'That's exactly right,' Dedubian said.

'Wait a moment,' Nathaniel said. 'It may be that the duplicate certificate is false, but the violin still is exactly what both of the certificates say it is. So you might not approve of the forger's tactics, but the violin is still a Testore worth a hundred-fifteen grand.'

'I'm afraid that's another deception,' Dedubian said. 'And here's the proof. Jake, I have a photo here of the violin for which my grandfather wrote the certificate. He took the photo himself and put his stamp on it. He did that with all the violins of value for which he wrote a certificate. The photo is black and white, but it is clear. Believe it or not, they had surprisingly good cameras in those days. Ms. Shinagawa and Mr Williams. Would you kindly look at the violin on the table and the violin in the photo?'

'They look similar,' Yumi said.

'I agree,' Nathaniel said. 'But the photo is old.'

'Then take this magnifying glass and look again at the photo.'

'There's some of the usual wear on the upper right bout in the photo,' Nathaniel said, 'where the varnish is lighter.'

'And on this violin?' Dedubian asked.

'On the upper left bout.'

'Precisely. Now, you can have wear on either the upper right or the upper left, or even on both bouts. But, lady and gentlemen, the wear cannot move from one side to the other.'

'What you're suggesting then,' Jacobus said, 'is that someone first forged an otherwise genuine document, and then made a violin to fit its description. The current owner of the real Testore, who may be in China for all we know, has the real duplicate certificate, and would be none the wiser.'

'That's right. When we write a certificate we try to describe an instrument as accurately as we can using words. But words can be interpreted. It's like trying to use words to describe a melody. One would have to be an exceptionally accomplished author to do that. What, really, is "handsome maple," "broadish figure," or "choicest spruce"? That description could be applied to hundreds of violins.

'Mind you, though. This would not work with a Stradivari or Guarneri.'

'Why not?' Yumi asked.

'Because we know of the existence of every one of their instruments. We know them like we know our own children. The documentation is much more extensive and the provenance goes back for generations, even centuries. They are almost like birth certificates. But Testore? A fine maker, yes, but no one would ever have reason to question the authenticity of this violin you brought me today when accompanied by this certificate.'

'Then, is this violin worthless?' Yumi asked.

'By no means,' said Dedubian. 'It's a lovely instrument. I would say it's worth about fifteen thousand dollars.'

'So if Borlotti made a dozen of these fakes with the fake certificates to go with them,' Jacobus considered, 'and he made a hundred grand on just the Testore, then Mr Borlotti made quite a nice nest egg for himself.'

'Perhaps,' Dedubian said. 'It doesn't necessarily mean he sold the violins for that much. Only that he wrote the insurance appraisals for that value. But, as you suggest, this Testore could well be only the tip of the iceberg,' Dedubian said.

Could dollars like these be a motive for murder? Jacobus asked himself. *And what could violin fraud have to do with arson? Perhaps nothing. Maybe that Boston thug, Falcone, had nothing to do with it. It still didn't fit.*

While Dedubian reglued the violin and put the strings back on, Jacobus recalled his dustup with Jimmy Ubriaco.

'There's one other thing you can help me with, Bo. When you ship instruments overseas, how do you do that?'

'Very carefully, Jake, very carefully.'

'You're a real comedian. It's like that joke about Carnegie Hall.'

'You mean, "How do you get to Carnegie Hall?" "Practice! Practice!"?'

'No. I was thinking about the one where there's a tourist who's in New York for the first time. He's frustrated after a day of getting lost and goes up to a cabbie and asks, "Can you tell me how to get to Carnegie Hall or should I go fuck myself?"'

'Ha! I'll have to tell that to my wife, Jake!'

'Why? Is she a cabbie?'

'I guess you really don't need information about shipping.'

'Truce! Truce!'

'If you insist. First, you see, the instrument is packed very carefully, in its own case, using Styrofoam peanuts or bubble wrap, and then in a larger box – usually plywood – that is also stuffed with shock-absorbent material. The box is labeled accurately, with many "Fragile" signs that are usually ignored, and we fill out a commercial invoice describing the contents and its value. Of course, we make sure the instrument is insured both with the owner and the shipper.'

Dedubian put the fake Testore back in its case.

'What are we going to say to Mr Spellman?' Yumi asked. 'It will break his heart when he learns his violin isn't a real Testore and that it's worth a tenth of what he thought.'

'I'm a very lucky man,' Dedubian said.

'Why do you say that, Bo?' Jacobus asked.

'Because I'm not the one who has to make that decision.'

TWENTY-FOUR

Before they left New York in mid-afternoon, Yumi called Marcello Bertoldo in Cremona and first apologized for calling so late at night.

'But you didn't!' Bertoldo said. 'Mama and I are just finishing our supper. Have you changed your mind? Are you coming back to me?' he pleaded.

Yumi managed to avoid a direct no in order to ask him for a favor, to call the police and ask them what shipping information was on the bass crate that contained Borlotti's ersatz coffin.

'But there is no need to go to the police, *princessa*! The Vassari are back home and they still have the crate and the case. I will go there tomorrow myself and report back to you.'

'But I thought they turned themselves into the authorities for their smuggling.'

'Yes, yes. But you know, here in Italy things take time . . .'

Except courtship, Yumi thought.

'Their case probably will not come before the magistrate for years.'

Yumi thanked Bertoldo and wished him and Mama goodnight.

When they returned the violin to Abe Spellman in Middleton, Nathaniel took a most diplomatic approach to breaking the news that his beloved Testore was an anonymous maker's bastard son.

'Mr Dedubian wanted us to convey his appreciation for letting him study your fine instrument,' Nathaniel said. They left quickly afterward, before Spellman had a chance to ask when the book on Milanese makers would be in print.

As they passed through Main Street in Great Barrington, Jacobus asked Yumi to make a quick stop at Fly By Night, the local packing and shipping store and outlet for UPS, FedEx, and Western Union. He had thought of some questions that he should have asked Dedubian, but Simon, the manager of Fly By Night, knew everything there was to know about shipping in general.

'Simon,' Jacobus said, 'I understand how instruments are packed for shipping, but now I'm thinking more about what happens after that. Once you take it to the shipper. Who exactly *is* the shipper, by the way?'

'That depends,' Simon said. 'If it's a small instrument it could be any airline cargo, though sometimes it's safer and cheaper just to buy a plane ticket for someone to take it on the plane and deliver it in person.'

'What about larger instruments, like a cello or bass?'

'That also depends. If the total inches – length times width times depth – is over one-hundred-thirty inches it has to be shipped as freight,

as opposed to regular air. We usually use FedEx Air or UPS Air –
they're the most reliable – and they'll deliver it directly to an address.
If you send it DHL they'll deliver it to an airport, which makes it a
little cheaper, but it would be your responsibility to pick it up.'

'How much would it cost?'

'For what, specifically?'

'Let's say to ship a bass in its crate overseas. In two or three
days.'

Simon whistled.

'Whew! A rough guess would be fifteen-hundred to two-thousand
dollars.'

'Would there be a customs charge?'

'That really depends on the country.'

'Italy?'

'It could be exorbitant. Unless you knew the right people.'

Simon gave a little chuckle.

Jacobus thanked him. Since it was nearing the close of the business day, before going home Jacobus asked Yumi to make a call.
He suggested they go to Cuppa Cabana, a new coffee shop just
down the block near the Mahaiwe Theater, which would be a warmer
place to call from than out on the street.

Because Ansaldo Vassari had needed to drive to the airport to pick
up the crate, Jacobus discounted the likelihood it had been shipped by
FedEx or UPS Air. He asked Yumi to call the DHL customer service
representative and ask whether they had shipped a box – she gave him
the approximate dimensions – from somewhere on the east coast, probably Boston or New York, to Rome on December 25th or 26th or
thereabout. She offered to give the DHL representative her cell phone
number and said he could call back when they had the information.

'Can you wait two minutes?' the rep asked. 'I can get it up on
the computer in a jiff.'

Yumi waited. Hopeful.

'Ma'am, the computer's slow as molasses today. Can you hold
another minute?'

She waited some more, hoping that the longer the wait, the better
the news would be.

'I'm sorry, ma'am,' the rep finally said. 'We have no record of
anything approximating that size going from New York-New England
to Rome on those dates. I even checked the twenty-fourth and
twenty-seventh. Is there anything else I can help you with today?'

Yumi thanked him and hung up. At least the coffee was good.

They made one more detour before returning to Jacobus's house, stopping in Egremont Falls to fill Sigurd Benson in with the day's progress, incremental as it might be, but he was neither at home nor at the schoolhouse.

'Maybe he's out fighting a fire,' Jacobus said.

'That's not funny,' Yumi replied.

Coming up the hill on Route 41 in Yumi's Camaro, about a half-mile from Jacobus's house, they were in the midst of discussing the inimitable quintuple counterpoint at the end of Mozart's last symphony, the Symphony No. 41 in C, nicknamed the 'Jupiter.' They tried singing it, even though there were only three of them. So they were distracted – Nathaniel was mentioning something about it being Mozart's legacy to the music world – when Jacobus, whose sensory apparatus was always on alert, smelled the smoke first.

As they approached the top of the hill from which Jacobus's precarious driveway descended into the woods, the smell of smoke came through the air vent, growing acrid and stinging their eyes, bringing an uncomfortable cadence to their homage to Mozart.

'I think it's coming from your property, Jake,' Nathaniel said. His voice was tense.

'The Burkes must be having a bonfire,' Jacobus said of his closest neighbors, whose house was located in the woods just before his own. His thoughts turned to Borlotti's house as he continued to inhale the smoke.

'A little late to be celebrating New Year's, don't you think?' Nathaniel said. The levity in his voice was strained.

'How often have they had bonfires?' Yumi asked.

'Never,' Jacobus said.

'Maybe they're Druids or something,' Yumi said, trying desperately to maintain the humor. 'There's a lot of smoke.'

'Roasting a bullock,' Jacobus said replied, but the joke fell flat. He began to fear the worst.

As they passed the Burke's place, Yumi looked into the woods and saw Mr and Mrs Burke around a massive pile of burning leaves and brush. The cloud of smoke rose as high as the top of the hill and then the breeze blew it across Route 41. The Burkes waved in greeting. By the time Yumi's car reached the bottom of Jacobus's driveway, they had passed through any remaining smoke.

They sat in the car, shaken.

'Well, I guess it wasn't a bullock,' Nathaniel finally said, and they all laughed more than the comment warranted. 'But the thought of one gave me an appetite.'

'What *doesn't*?' Jacobus said.

'What do you have in the house?'

'A selection of fine canned goods. Veg-All. Dinty Moore beef stew. Campbell bean with bacon soup. And a jar of sauerkraut.'

'How about we get a pizza?' Yumi suggested.

'If we must,' Jacobus replied.

TWENTY-FIVE

Thursday, January 5

There was a freshness in the air when Jacobus awoke. He couldn't tell whether the sun had risen or not but judging from the quality of the quiet he guessed it hadn't. Dressed in his flannel pajamas and new gloves, he went out to the woodshed, piled a load of logs into a big plastic bucket to which a rope was attached, and dragged it over the snow-packed driveway back to his house. Once inside, he fanned the embers of the woodstove and loaded it for the day. As he filled the stove he noticed some of the logs were icy with blown snow, but rather than let it melt and make puddles on the pine floor, he just threw them in the stove. He was in the process of making a pot of coffee when the phone rang.

'Brooks here.'

'What's up?'

'Frankie Falcone got back on Monday. We arranged for Sammy to "coincidentally" bump into him as he was leaving his condo. Sammy invited him to join him for a beer and they had an interesting conversation. I want you to hear it. I've already spoken to Benson. I don't want you to have to drive all the way to Boston, so how about we meet halfway? There's an inn in Sturbridge. Right off the Pike. The Publick House. I think you'll like their lunch menu.'

Jacobus got dressed. He didn't bother with breakfast. He decided not to wake Yumi or Nathaniel, but he couldn't leave much of a note for them, either. He had given up trying to maintain his handwriting over the years after Nathaniel generously described his efforts as cuneiform-like. So Jacobus grabbed what he hoped was a blank piece of paper and a pen that still had ink, scrawled 'BACK LATER,' and hoped he hadn't written half of the message on the table.

Jacobus waited outside for Benson so that he wouldn't honk the horn and wake his friends. When the car pulled up he felt for the door handle and eased himself in.

'Where were you yesterday evening?' he asked.

'What do you mean?' Benson asked.

'We looked for you on our way back from the city.'

'Oh. We were putting out a fire.'

'Arson?' Jacobus asked, still skittish from the false alarm the day before.

'Parson,' Benson replied.

'Larson?'

'Who's Larson?'

'No one. Just a joke. What happened?'

'The parson at the Congregational Church fell asleep on a pew and a candle he was holding started a fire on the cushion. We had it out in a minute.'

'Just out of curiosity, what was the parson's name?'

'Carson,' Benson said seriously.

Jacobus smiled. No one would ever accuse Benson of a sense of humor.

After a lunch of the Publick House's open-faced, freshly roasted hot turkey sandwich with all the fixings, Jacobus, with Brooks and Benson, retired to a conference room in the restored eighteenth-century inn. They sat at a good imitation of a Chippendale table in imitation Chippendale chairs that made Jacobus's back ache. *At least imitation violins sound good*, Jacobus thought.

'We prepped Sammy before he went in,' Brooks said, setting up the recorder. 'Told him what to say and not say. I'll skip the preliminaries on the tape, unless you want to hear the details of Falcone's Cabo frolic, sipping piña coladas on the beach next to his hot wife in her white string bikini, giving his kids a hundred-fifty bucks each to get lost while they screw on the—'

'As you said,' Jacobus interrupted, 'skip the preliminaries.'

Jacobus heard Brooks push some buttons, fast-forwarding the conversation.

'. . . those fucking Patriots.' It was Sammy's voice. There were typical bar noises in the background. A low hum of conversation, beer being poured, a sporting event on television, an occasional cheer or moan. 'I dropped a bundle on those bums.'

'You can't win them all,' someone replied.

'Falcone,' Brooks whispered to Jacobus and Benson.

'Yeah, our boy Grogan bit the big one,' Rocchinelli said. 'Three interceptions.'

'I hadn't heard.' Falcone didn't sound interested in football.

'There was a big story in the Globe,' Rocchinelli said.

Silence of several seconds.

'Since when do you read the Globe?' Falcone asked.

'What do you mean?'

'Most people who read the Globe graduated junior high.' More silence.

'Globe, Herald, whatever,' Rocchinelli said. 'How about another beer?'

Brooks stopped the tape.

'What was that all about?' Benson asked. 'What did we need to hear that for?'

'Because Rocchinelli already screwed up,' Jacobus surmised. 'Who knows if he'd ever read the Globe on his own? But he sounds nervous. It put Falcone on guard.'

'That was my observation as well,' Brooks said. He fast forwarded, stopping and starting until he found where the conversation resumed.

'Speaking of news' – it was Rocchinelli again – 'did you read about that guy they found in Italy?'

'There are a lot of guys in Italy.'

'The one that got whacked. Said he made violins out in the Berkshires. Bullet between the eyes. Carved up nice, too. To look like a violin.'

Rocchinelli tried to laugh, but it evaporated before it even got started.

Yet another extended silence. Jacobus was getting uncomfortable listening to this.

'Why should I be interested in that?'

'Well, the guy's house was burned down on Christmas Eve, and you said—'

'What did I say?' Falcone said, clearly irritated.

'What's your fuckin' problem?' Sammy wasn't a happy camper, either.

'*What the fuck did I say?*' Falcone repeated.

'Only that you had a job in the boondocks and you were fuckin' cold. That's all. Hey, you don't wanna talk about it, we won't talk about it.'

'Talk about what?'

'You know. It.'

'I can talk about it,' Falcone said. 'Better than talking about fuckin' football all day. So a guy gets shot and then gets carved? Who needs to kill someone twice?'

'They said it might've been the violinmaker's own knife.'

Falcone laughed without humor.

'Carved to look like a violin?' he asked, as if savoring the image. 'That's fuckin' artistic. Wouldn't you say?'

'Shit, yeah.'

'Picture this,' Falcone said. 'Picture a little prick trying to defend himself with a wood-carving knife against a guy with a gun. Let's see: little knife, big gun. Hmm. Gun wins every time. Right?'

Both laugh now, Rocchinelli harder than Falcone.

'OK, Sammy,' Falcone continued. 'Let's say you whack someone with a bullet in the head. You gonna leave him lyin' there or you gonna get rid of him?'

'If I whack someone I gotta get rid of him.'

'Even if you burn the place down?'

'Shit, yeah. You don't wanna leave a trace.' Jacobus could hear the growing confidence in Rocchinelli's voice. He clearly thinks he's overcome his stumble out of the gate and has finally found common cause with Falcone. No doubt he is already counting the dollar signs from Brooks as a reward for his success.

'So, maybe you ship him overseas, right?' Falcone asked. 'What better way?'

'Makes sense!'

'Let's say you send the rube to an address that you'd found lying around the place before you torched it, right?'

'Right.'

'You wouldn't expect someone here to find that body, ever. To ever connect the dots. And it would send a message to whom it may concern not to fuck with the boss. Right?'

'Never. It's fuckin' genius.'

'But then if someone did, somehow, find it, it wouldn't be your fault, would it?'

'Not in a million years.'

'Yeah, you've covered your tracks. So would it be right for your boss to get on your case? Call you while you were celebrating the fucking holidays with your family and tell you you fucked up?'

'Wouldn't be fair.'

'I don't think so either. Sammy, did you celebrate the holidays?'

'Sure.'

'Did you celebrate the holidays with your family?'

'My sister and her kids. Yeah. She made lasagna.'

'So, Sammy, why you do it?'

'Do what?'

'Kill the prick and ship him to Italy.'

'What are you talkin' about?' Rocchinelli asked, clearly confused.

'You just told me you whacked him. Didn't I hear you just say that? And that you got rid of the body because you didn't wanna leave a trace? And your boss called you while you were celebrating the holidays with your family to tell you you fucked up?'

'You know that's not what I meant,' Sammy said, sounding desperate.

'I know what the fuck you meant, sports fan. Enjoy the game.'

Brooks stopped the tape.

'End of conversation,' he said.

'I'm no cop,' Jacobus said. 'What can we prove from this?'

'At this point, nothing,' Brooks said.

'I have to agree,' Benson said.

'So, what's your next move, Sherlock?' Jacobus asked.

'Keep up the police work. Follow all the other leads. One step at a time.'

'Well, good luck to you gentlemen,' Jacobus said. 'I've done my community service. From this moment on, I'm retired. Home, James!'

'I smell smoke,' Benson said as they climbed up the hill on Route 41.

'Yeah, I smell it, too,' Jacobus said. 'Don't worry. It's the Burkes burning their brush.'

'I don't think so,' Benson replied. 'There are lights flashing from your property.' He braked his car and slowly turned down Jacobus's steep driveway.

Jacobus did not need to be told anything more. This smoke was different from the Burke's. But it was the same gut-churning smell as the ruins of Borlotti's house. And now the noises the woods around his house had blocked out were clearly audible. Above the churning of engines, men barked incomprehensible orders to one another, but the tone of defeat was as redolent as the smoke. Jacobus pressed his thumb and forefinger into his sightless eyes and tried not to think.

Benson wrenched his car into low gear so as not to skid on the sheet of ice created by water from the fire hoses, and slowly descended the driveway, coming to a stop a safe distance from the smoldering wreckage. He flung his door open and rushed out. Jacobus remained immobilized, half-hearing Miller yelling orders to the fire crew.

'Jake, I have bad news.' Miller placed his hand cautiously on Jacobus's shoulder. 'Real bad. I hate to tell you this. It was a chimney fire. It's a total loss.'

'But I put hardwood in the stove this morning,' Jacobus said. 'Not pine.' Desperately wanting, by the simple force of reasoning, to undo what couldn't, what shouldn't, have happened.

'Doesn't matter, once the creosote's built up in the chimney. There was years' worth. It got so hot the chimney just exploded.'

Jacobus tried to stay calm.

'Anything left?'

'I'm sorry. Your books, your music, the whole house. I'm sorry. It was all tinder.'

'All gone.' Jacobus mouthed the words, but hardly a sound escaped. 'The violin?'

'I'm afraid so.'

Jacobus was suddenly light-headed. He almost lost his balance, though he was still sitting in the car.

'Where's Yumi? Where's Nathaniel?' he cried out and tried not to picture them if they were still in the house.

'No trace. They must have been out. That's the good news.'

'Grane!' Jacobus cried. 'Where's Grane?'

'What?' Benson asked, jogging to the car. 'Who's that? Who's Grane?'

'My horse!' Jacobus said, perplexed that Benson didn't understand. Then he recovered himself. 'I mean the dog. Where's Trotsky? Where's my damn dog? I left him in the house!'

Jacobus pushed himself out of the car and stumbled through snow and rubble.

'Trotsky!' he yelled, his voice hoarse. 'Trotsky! Well the hell are you, you damn mongrel?'

Miller surrounded Jacobus, still shouting for his dog, with a bear hug to prevent him from slipping on the slickened ground, or tumbling into the simmering remains of his house, its stone walls, still sizzling hot, not yet finished collapsing upon themselves.

'I haven't seen the dog,' Miller said, his voice tense.

Above the muted exertion of the fire crew, the hiss of steam as hoses discovered new hot pockets, and the groan of a building in its death throes, Jacobus heard Miller shouting for the dog, growing distant. 'Here, Trotsky! Trotsky, come!'

But there was no response. His house, gone. His violin, gone. His dog, gone. It was the first time that Jacobus ever felt truly blind.

'I'm sorry, Mr Jacobus,' Benson said.

Jacobus had no idea how long he stood there, numbly, as a world he was no longer part of swirled around him.

'C'mon, Jake,' Nathaniel said.

'Where've you been?' Jacobus asked. Why hadn't Nathaniel prevented it from happening? What kind of a friend was that?

'Yumi and I have been here for the past half hour,' he said. 'Talking to you.' *Could that be?* Jacobus asked himself. Through his fog he heard Nathaniel continue. 'Roy called us to tell us what happened. C'mon, it's getting cold. We best be going.'

Jacobus let himself be led by the arm somewhere. He supposed it was to the car, though it didn't really matter. Sounds made no sense to him anymore. They came from the place that used to be his house, but they were foreign. Things bubbling. Things cracking. Things moaning. Things from hell.

Jacobus wiped his nose, which was running. He heard snow slough off a tree and thud to the ground in the woods, probably the effect of heat generated by the fire. Then off another tree, and another, sounding like distant mortar fire. Then he heard some rustling in the brush at the edge of the forest. Then, was it grunting? That familiar, offensive grunting?

Something crashing out of the woods barreled into Jacobus's knees and knocked him over. Trotsky pinned Jacobus on his back, his whimpers so loud that no one could hear Jacobus's. Jacobus flailed with his arms, an unwilling snow angel.

'Get the hell off me, you damn dog!' Jacobus cried, pushing against its massive head. There was something hanging from the dog's mouth flapping on Jacobus's face.

'Get that off my face!' he shouted.

Jacobus pulled at it. Trotsky's pulled back. A new game!

Trotsky gave up his trophy to Nathaniel, who passed it to Benson.

Jacobus tried to stand up on his own but couldn't. Yumi helped him to his feet. He pushed her away.

'It's a piece of cloth,' Nathaniel said. 'Torn. Looks like it's from someone's pants.'

'More than that,' Benson said. 'There's blood on it. A lot. It's not even totally dried yet. Your dog got a little singed, Mr Jacobus, but he took a big chunk out of someone's leg. I'd say he got the better of our arsonist.'

Arsonist? What arsonist? The fire wasn't his own fault? It was too confusing. But that was no longer even on his mind. The only thought that occupied his mind was that for the first time in his life he hadn't been able to stand up on his own.

Benson called Lieutenant Brooks on his cell phone, certain that whomever Trotsky had bitten would require medical attention. It was an opening.

'Brooks wants to talk to you,' Benson said to Jacobus, who was back in Yumi's car.

'Mr Jacobus, Officer Benson has informed me what has happened. I'm convinced this is Francis Falcone's doing. He must have seen your name in the papers and, frankly, I'm sure Rocchinelli didn't help. May I say I am sincerely sorry he got to you before we got to him. I have no doubt that not only your home, but your violin meant a great deal. I pledge to do everything I can to make it up to you.'

'How the hell would you even pretend to know how much things mean to me?'

'Mr Jacobus, I'm originally from South Carolina. When I was a child, the church my family attended was burned to the ground by people with no more conscience than Francis Falcone. And you can be assured the folks who perished in that fire were no less dear to me than your violin was to you. You could say that my mission in life was determined on that day.

'This is a tragedy, Mr Jacobus, but out of that tragedy we may have just obtained our first solid evidence of Falcone's involvement, the result of your dog's tenacity, which no doubt is a reflection of his owner. I am immediately placing all my resources at G-BAT on full alert. We're going to spread Francis Falcone's photo at every hospital and every clinic and every gas station and at every rest stop between you and Boston. I'm also ordering extra patrols in the North End and a stakeout on his home. You flushed him out of his hole, Mr Jacobus, and now we've got him on the run. I vow to you that I'll get him. I vow I'll catch him and put him behind bars.'

'And you're going to do that how?' Jacobus asked.

'One match at a time, if that's what it takes.'

Roy Miller insisted that Jacobus, Nathaniel, and Yumi come to his house and stay as long as they wanted. When they arrived, Miller's wife, Martha, had already put steaks on the grill and reiterated her husband's invitation. Jacobus and Trotsky would stay there until he was back on his feet, and she wouldn't accept any argument.

At first, conversation was light, even gossipy. It floated around Jacobus, who ate little and responded even less. No one wanted to face the enormity of his loss. At least not yet. But with dinner finished, the talk and the adrenaline disappeared along with the dishes, and Jacobus's mind wandered from the unbearable present to the unimaginable future. Martha helped him to his room and made him as comfortable as possible, giving him an extra pair of Miller's pajamas, which billowed on his sunken frame. Jacobus, disoriented and not caring, soon fell into a surprisingly deep sleep, Trotsky at his bedside.

TWENTY-SIX

Friday, January 6

Jacobus awoke in a panic, clutching at his suffocating blankets. *Where am I?*

The sounds and smells were faint and unfamiliar. He flailed in all directions and touched nothing. His breathing became stertorous as he gasped for air.

Is this a hospital? A prison? An insane asylum? What time is it? Why am I here?

Recollection returned piecemeal, isolated fractals of events. The more he remembered the worse it got.

As he lay panting, Jacobus heard the clink of Trotsky's ID tag at the foot of his bed. That comforted him for a moment, but then full consciousness suddenly flooded back and he was consumed by uncontrollable rage. Rage at Falcone for violating his life. His sanctuary. Rage at himself for being the cocky instigator of his own disaster when he pressed Brooks to intimidate Falcone. His urge to destroy anything within reach was tempered only because he was in Miller's house and not his own.

Visitors had laughed at his house. 'Your traditional Berkshire hovel.' 'It needs a little TLC, but TLC doesn't need *it*.' And on and on. He let them laugh. Joined in on it. He hadn't given a damn. What they hadn't understood was that over the years, piece by outmoded piece, he had assembled his surroundings so that he knew exactly where everything was. It didn't matter what it looked like, God damn it! He was a goddamn blind man! He had lights in his house only so his goddamn friends wouldn't fall down. He had a gardener tear down the ivy climbing over his windows only so his goddamn visitors could see out them! He could navigate from his living room, with his LPs scattered everywhere, where he knew that Mischa Elman's recording of the Mendelssohn violin concerto was the fourth one down in the pile underneath the second window from the left; to the kitchen where he could make coffee by himself from the pot in the cupboard above the sink next to the can of Folgers instant; up the eleven-and-a-half steps, yes eleven-and-a-half, that people with goddamn sight tripped on and he didn't even need his cane, up to his bedroom where he had been comfortable in the bed that everyone said was too soft and would hurt his back, which it did but which he would never admit to anyone and would never sleep in again.

But now it was gone. His sanctuary was gone. His detractors would laugh no more. The comfort of the second movement of Vivaldi's 'Winter,' *'resting contentedly by the hearth,'* was over. The gracious violin cantilena, over. He was now living the third, the final movement. Troubled. Dangerous. Unsafe. Jacobus was now on the outside, exposed to the elements.

'We tread the icy path with greatest care for fear of slipping and sliding. With a reckless turn we fall crashing to the ground and, rising, hasten across the ice lest it should crack.'

For Jacobus, the ice had cracked.

Proving people wrong about him had given meaning to his life. Proving that a blind man could live among those with sight. Proving that a blind musician had more to offer than those with superior eyes but inferior ears. In the country of the blind, he had been king. The unending effort had hardened him. He reflexively confronted every challenge with an obsessive, relentless determination to prevail. It wasn't even a thought. It was his being. Now, he had been cast adrift.

But that was not the worst. No. The worst was that he had lost his violin. It would have been much easier to lose a leg. Both legs. His true voice was not the ugly, nicotine-scarred croak that came out of his mouth. His voice had been his violin. With his violin he had been able to connect to his true self, to reach far deeper than thought or consciousness could take him; and what emerged were emotions more complex and profound than the ones that he could express with mere words. If the words – even when partially disguised by dry humor – that spewed from his mouth reflected bitterness toward an amoral world; if they occasionally hinted at, but never admitted to, love for Nathaniel and Yumi; if from time to time they disseminated well-considered truths or half-truths or non-truths, the sounds he had made on his violin had cut through his façade, his protective armor. His violin was the *only* thing that could. There is no deceit in a C-major chord. In Bach, there is no cynicism. With the loss of his violin he had lost the connection not just to the world, but also to his own soul.

I'm going to kill him. Jacobus spent the rest of the day in his room. His only human contact was when Yumi had to drag Trotsky from Jacobus's bedside for a walk, and when Martha brought him food, which he didn't eat. He turned his back on both of them.

TWENTY-SEVEN

Saturday, January 7

Someone knocked on his door. Jacobus didn't respond, but someone opened the door, anyway. Along with that someone, through the opened door, wafted the smell of wood smoke from Miller's stove downstairs. It made Jacobus want to throw up, and if he could have remembered where the bathroom was, he would have.

'Jake, sorry to disturb you. But we got some news we thought you might want to hear,' Nathaniel said.

'What day is it?'

'Saturday. Saturday morning.'

Jacobus uttered no response.

'Brooks got a positive ID on Falcone,' Nathaniel continued. 'Someone went to the emergency room at Harrington Memorial Hospital in Sturbridge the night of the fire with a leg wound. He refused to give his name. They stitched up his left leg and gave him a rabies shot. They wanted him to stay overnight because he was bitten pretty badly, but he paid cash and left immediately. Brooks's guys showed Falcone's photo to the on-duty physician, who said it was him.'

'Get me some water.'

Nathaniel returned with a glass of water. Jacobus sat up and drank a quarter of it.

'There's some other news.'

Jacobus held out the glass. Nathaniel took it.

'That informant. Sammy Rocchinelli?'

Jacobus shrugged.

'He's dead. A single bullet to the head.'

'Falcone?'

'Probably. They think Falcone suspected Rocchinelli was on G-BAT's payroll. But they don't know for sure.'

'Where's Falcone now?' Jacobus asked.

'They don't know. He hasn't returned to his house, but even before he left the hospital, his wife bundled up the kids and left their condo for Logan Airport. They got on a plane to LA. Brooks put one of his men on the plane with them.'

'Falcone headed toward Boston?'

'At least to Sturbridge. But from there, they lost the scent. He could've gotten on to I-84 and headed to New York. It's their working theory that he's going to meet his family in California.'

'Eh. Leave me alone.'

Jacobus lay in his bed, fluctuating in and out of consciousness. How would he get from his present position as a helpless invalid, Point A, to Falcone dead, Point B? His mind wandered, devising one scenario after another, embellishing then irritably discarding each, like a losing hand in poker. Working with law enforcement would be impossible because that meant his plan would have to be legal. No. He would design a secret plot. At times his wild ideas had such a bizarre logic he thought they must have come to him in dreams, as when he hallucinated that he had trapped Falcone in a dark room, slit his throat with Borlotti's woodcarving knife and stuck a lit candle in the gaping wound.

TWENTY-EIGHT

Sunday, January 8

After a sleepless night Jacobus lay in his bed, his back propped against a pillow. Barely able to lift his head, he was emotionally and physically spent. Yet his mind had a mind of its own and spun at an uncontrollable pace.

There was a knock on the door.

'Yeah?'

'It's me,' Yumi said. 'I've brought you a new wardrobe. It's about time you got some new clothes. I'll put them next to your bed. You can try them on when you feel like it. I think you'll like them. Some nice flannel shirts and corduroy pants.'

'New wardrobe.'

'And Nathaniel has set up an office in Roy's basement. He's been doing a lot of research on the violins Borlotti bought and sold. And he's started the claims process for you with the insurance company. Your house should be totally covered.'

'Totally covered. You mean all fifty bucks?'

Jacobus coughed and his head sank deeper into the pillow. He felt Yumi take his hand in hers.

'Don't worry, Jake,' she said. 'Everything will be all right. You'll always have Nathaniel and me.'

Jacobus didn't respond. His future seemed as blank as his eyesight. Nothing.

'Do you think we should get you some grief counseling?' Yumi asked.

He would have laughed had he been able.

'Too late for counseling,' he said.

Yumi squeezed his hand more tightly.

'Get me Father Gallivan,' he said so quietly that Yumi had to ask him to repeat it.

'Father Gallivan. Get me Father Gallivan.'

'No, Jake, no!' she cried. 'It's not your time yet. You'll get better. I promise!'

Jacobus laughed but it came out as a sputtering cough.

'Gallivan was Falcone's priest. I need to talk to him so I can nail that motherfucker.'

Yumi's laugh mixed with her sobs.

'I can't tell you how wonderful it is to hear you talk normally again,' she cried. 'I'll call Lieutenant Brooks and find out what he can do.'

'You do that.'

'I'll let you rest now,' Yumi said, and got up from Jacobus's bedside.

Before she left the room she said, 'And I just wanted to let you know, I took Trotsky to the vet. He's fine.'

'Great, but how's Trotsky?'

Jacobus felt Yumi's arms around him.

'I'm so glad to hear your bad jokes again,' she said, and he could feel her tears on his cheek.

'What do you mean bad?' he said.

'We're so worried about you.'

'Nothing to fret over. I'll emerge from the ordeal miraculously scathed. Any day now and I'll be as crepit as I used to be.'

Once Yumi left, Jacobus went to the bathroom, the path to which he had become well-acquainted, and threw up.

Jacobus couldn't be dissuaded. He threatened to walk to Springfield if someone didn't drive him there, so they had no choice but to bundle him up and help him into Yumi's car, since that was the most comfortable one.

Lieutenant Brooks had traced Father Gallivan to the St Thomas of Loyola Convalescent Home, where he had been a resident for over a year. Brooks gave Jacobus a heads-up that Gallivan was reportedly showing symptoms of dementia. They said his behavior started to become erratic during the final years he shepherded his flock at St. Ignatius, which might have been one reason the lambs wandered off. Gallivan might well have no recollection of Falcone at all. Brooks again questioned the wisdom of Jacobus going out into the bitter cold for what seemed a fool's errand.

'The bad news is, it won't be my first,' Jacobus said, 'and the good news is it'll likely be my last.'

Brooks finished their conversation by informing Jacobus that Falcone's wife, Nadine, had arrived in Los Angeles. G-BAT agents had searched Falcone's now-vacant North End condominium. Though they discovered nothing that could tie him to the recent crimes, it was Brooks's prediction that the wife would lead them to Falcone.

'Was there any food in the condo?' Jacobus asked.

'We haven't checked yet. Why?'

'Might tell you whether she plans on it being a long trip. You and I, we're men. We might not give a second thought to letting the milk turn green in the fridge, but you know what women are like.'

'Good point. We'll check.'

Sweet Sister Agnes ushered Jacobus into a common room that smelled of Mr Clean. It was warm and quiet and the chair was comfortable, and Jacobus thought, *this wouldn't be such a bad place to die*. In the background, the PA softly played a medley of Bing Crosby favorites and Jacobus changed his mind. Sister Agnes cautioned Jacobus that although Monsignor Gallivan was in good physical health, from time to time he spontaneously combusted into language not representative of his holy calling.

'Don't worry,' Jacobus said. 'We'll get along just fine.'

A door opened. Long strides approached him.

'Ah! And it's Mister Daniel Jacobus, is it?' came the Irish-inflected voice. 'Don't get up! Don't get up! No formalities here!'

Jacobus, who had neither any intention of getting up nor energy to waste words, came straight to the point.

'Tell me about Falcone.'

'Ah, yes. Young Francis. They told me you were curious about our young Francis.'

Yes. I want to kill young Francis, Jacobus thought, but said nothing.

'Francis was only far and away the finest boy soprano in the history of the Saint Ignatius parochial school choir, wasn't he?' Monsignor Gallivan clucked, with as much paternal pride as was publicly permissible for a priest. 'Only the angels themselves could sing *Panis Angelicus* sweeter than our young Francis.'

'The Cesar Franck version?' Jacobus asked, referring to the noted nineteenth-century Belgian organist and composer, whose tear-jerking *Panis Angelicus* was one of his most beloved compositions.

'Surely! Would there be any other?'

Gallivan began to recite with fervor: '*The angelic bread becomes the bread of men. The heavenly bread ends all prefigurations: What wonder! A poor and humble servant consumes the Lord. We beg of You, Triune God that you visit us, as we worship You. By your ways, lead us who seek the light in which You dwell. Amen.*'

'Whatever,' said Jacobus. 'You're giving me this image of a cherubic, squeaky clean altar boy. What happened to dear Francis?'

'He was a beautiful boy, was Francis. But his voice and his comeliness attracted the attentions of others. Francis became addicted to fame and adulation and he led others into temptation. It would forever stamp his character, poor boy. Nadine Esposito, girl of his wet dreams with the peaches and cream complexion, followed him everywhere. Even let Francis feel her up for free.'

'How do you know that?'

'Because she made me pay!' Gallivan blurted out, as if it were an oft-repeated punchline. 'Sorry, that was only a joke. Truly. It was at her confession she told me, I must confess.'

Gallivan fell silent. For some reason, Jacobus had the sensation that Gallivan had fallen asleep. He cleared his throat.

'Next chapter, padre?'

'Yes, of course. Pardon me for ruminating. At thirteen, young Francis's voice broke according to the dictates of God and nature, and his voice was transformed overnight from the dulcet tones of a prince to the raucous croak of a frog. His musical aspirations plummeted from heaven to the realm below. But young Francis was undeterred and made the smoothest of transitions into his second passion.'

'Lighting things on fire.'

'Just so, Mr Jacobus.' Gallivan sighed. 'It wasn't long before Francis began accepting money to convert buildings into piles of ash. He was soon recognized to be as talented in his new field as his old, though my heart broke to think of the fuzzy-cheeked lad he had been not so many years earlier. He stopped going by the Christian name he was baptized with.'

'His preferences being Frankie the Flame and Saint Ignitius,' Jacobus prompted Gallivan.

'Yes, the latter in fond memory of his choirboy days. I was not pleased by the association, to be sure. By twenty-one Francis had saved enough cash burning down the pizza joints, the paint stores, and the pool halls to marry dear Nadine, the lass with the ass, who bore him four cherubic children in his image. It was that she-devil who took him from me.'

'From you?'

'As representative of the congregation, I mean. And a devoted couple they are to this day. They deserve each other.'

'Did Falcone continue to attend church after finding his true calling?'

'Only until the day of their wedding. Francis, alas, chose to follow the flaming path of the devil. Rest assured, Mr Jacobus, though he may have parted ways with the great Almighty, the Almighty will never abandon Francis, or anyone else.'

That gives me a great deal of comfort, Jacobus thought.

'It pains me still,' Gallivan said, 'from my heart to my aching . . . well, from my heart, to think that such an angelic voice would sing the song of a sinner. If only he could have kept his God-given gift, who knows what might have been? Who knows?'

'If every boy whose voice changed left the church,' Jacobus noted, 'there wouldn't be too many men in the congregation, would there? But, then again, maybe you preferred the boys.'

'What are you suggesting?'

'Maybe that you're partly responsible for the demon Francis Falcone turned into. When's the last time you went to confession?'

'Do you accuse me of transgression, sir?' Gallivan asked.

'Should I?'

Jacobus heard Monsignor Gallivan rise so abruptly from his folding chair that it skittered across the room. The old priest then strode out of the common room even more hurriedly than when he had entered.

Just as quickly, new, lighter footsteps approached, which Jacobus recalled as Sister Agnes's.

'I'm sure the monsignor didn't mean everything he said,' she said, clearly anxious.

'How do you know what he said?'

She mumbled something he couldn't decipher.

'Don't worry about what I think,' he said. 'The good monsignor has a higher power to answer to.' *Too bad there really isn't one*, he thought. 'You can escort me out now.'

When he arrived back at the Millers, Nathaniel told him Lieutenant Brooks had called.

'He said, "for what it's worth, tell Mr Jacobus there was no food in the refrigerator." Do you know what he means?' Nathaniel asked.

'Means the Falcones might be away for a long time,' Jacobus said. It also meant something else, but the half-truth was as far as he was willing to go.

Jacobus typically let others make phone calls for him, but there was one he didn't want anyone else to know about. After Yumi drove him back to the Millers, he asked Yumi to take Trotsky for his evening walk. In the makeshift office Nathaniel had assembled, he made sure everyone else was out of earshot, and closed the door before dialing 411 for directory assistance.

'Harbor master, Boston,' he barked into the recorded message that requested the name and city of the party in question. *Whatever happened to human telephone operators?*

'There is no current listing for anyone by that name in your city,' was the response. After his fourth attempt to bridge the gap between man and machine, Jacobus was about to hang up when a human voice finally interceded.

'Name and address,' it said.

'I want the number of the Boston harbor master.'

'Is that a first or a last name?'

'It's neither. It's the title of a position. I believe it's in the Boston police department.'

'Do you want the number of the Boston police department?'

'No, I want the number of the harbor master. Maybe you can search the Boston police department directory and tell me what it says?'

'Please don't tell me how to do my job, sir.'

'Actually, yes I will. Search the Boston police department directory and tell me what it says.'

Jacobus dialed the number the operator gave him and hoped he hadn't been given one to the city morgue. As he told Nathaniel, no food in the condominium might have meant the Falcone family was taking a long vacation. But it could have meant something else entirely.

'Can I help you?' a woman asked.

'Harbor master, please.'

After dinner, Miller turned on the television. Though Lieutenant Brooks had tried to keep it off the airwaves, reporters had gotten wind of the Falcone manhunt and were drooling to be the first to break the story. Andrea Montcrief on Channel 4 News 4U was the one who took the leap. She only had bits and pieces of the story, but she filled the gaping hole with innuendo. She didn't even mention Jacobus's name. But if Falcone had not known he was being pursued before – unlikely as that was – he knew it now. The report played up the fact that Falcone, a dangerous fugitive, was on the loose and the authorities hadn't the slightest idea of his whereabouts.

'Do you think we're in danger?' Yumi asked when the report ended.

'If I were Falcone, this is the last place I'd be,' Miller said. Though it was logical, no one seconded the thought. Miller made a dispirited attempt to channel surf. Finding nothing but football and the weather report, they all went to sleep early.

TWENTY-NINE

Monday, January 9

Nathaniel and Yumi dragged Jacobus to K&J's for breakfast, hoping that an outing to his favorite dive would raise his spirits and stabilize his drastic mood swings. He ordered unbuttered whole wheat toast and tea, a clear indication to them that though Jacobus might be recovering he still had a long way to go.

'Marcello called me,' Yumi said. 'We've got some news about the shipping company, but it's not very good. And he said the crate had no labels on it, except for the Vassaris' address.'

'That's odd,' Jacobus said. He wasn't all that interested. He wasn't too interested in the whole wheat toast, either.

'No labels on a shipping crate is as kosher as ham on Hanukah,' Yumi said, doing her best Jacobus imitation to cheer him up. 'Marcello even called Fiumicino and tried to find out what company shipped it. No luck.'

'Wonderful.'

'What do we do now? We stumped?' Nathaniel asked.

Jacobus thought for a minute.

'If you must, have your Casanova contact the Carabinieri. They might be able to coax Ansaldo Vassari to identify the airport agent he bribed to get the bass case. Maybe part of a plea deal for a lighter sentence, like a week without espresso. If they can track the agent down, maybe they can strong arm him into telling them what label-challenged company delivered Uncle Amadeo to the old country.'

'Mr Jacobus.' Jacobus recognized Benson's voice. 'Might I join you?'

'It's a free country.'

'Roy told me I'd find you here. I've got some news about Minerva Forsythe.'

'Let me guess. "But it's not very good." '

'Yes. How did you know?'

'I play the odds.'

'Well, it seems she's disappeared. She parked her rental car at the Metro North station in Wassaic and got on the train to New York. My deputy who was following her called in and asked what he should do, so I put him on the train. Plain clothes. Discreet. It was at an off-peak hour so they had to change trains at Southeast. She got off. So he did. Then she got on the connecting train and he followed her in, but just as the doors closed she got out. She must have known we were tailing her.'

'Correction. She must have known that *someone* was tailing her,' Jacobus said.

'Had she checked out of the motel?' Nathaniel asked.

'No. Her belongings – which weren't much – were still there. And she had paid up in advance, so it looks like she was ready to hightail it on a moment's notice. The car's still at the train station.'

'When did she take off?' Jacobus asked, even though he knew the answer.

'Last evening.'

'A little after seven?'

'Yes. How did you know?'

'Because that's when the news about Falcone was on the TV.'

THIRTY

Jacobus never thought he would miss having a telephone. He had given Forsythe his number, which was now defunct, but he didn't have hers. Now she was at large and, if she had been hoping to contact him, there was no way for her to do it. For a change, he wanted to contact her. She knew something about Falcone that was enough to keep her on the run, but which also prevented her from going to the police. For some reason she had picked him, and him alone, to be her conduit, but now the lifeline had become frayed. He was tired of the game, but feared that if he stopped playing, there would be nothing left to his existence.

'Can you pick a lock?' Jacobus asked Benson.

'What kind?'

'Car door.'

'Yes, I can do that.'

'Drive me to Wassaic. I'll need sandwiches and coffee. A lot of coffee. Maybe in that fancy Thermos of yours. And one other thing. You said that Borlotti's bank account was all in order?'

'Yes. Why?'

'Because if he was involved in what I think he was involved in, there's a lot more of it stashed away somewhere.'

'Maybe it's cash in another safe, like the two-hundred-thirty-thousand we found.'

'No, not cash. Hefty checks from insurance companies.'

'OK. We'll keep digging.'

Yumi and Nathaniel were pleased to see Jacobus begin to rally, but much to their dismay he insisted on being left alone in the back seat of Minerva Forsythe's car in the Wassaic train station parking lot. Many of the cars that were in long-term parking had snow drifting up their sides, their windshields covered over. Forsythe's, at least, had been parked there less than a day and hadn't yet been transformed into a walk-in freezer. Yes, it was cold, but Jacobus was well-bundled and had what he needed to stay warm enough. The cold reminded him he was still alive, for what that was worth. He discovered a pipe, tobacco, and matches in Forsythe's glove compartment, and after considering the pros and the cons of indulging himself, gave in to the pros. He had time on his hands to think. Particularly to think about Minerva Forsythe, a subject that for the past few days he had shoved to the back of his mind.

Though he didn't expect her to return until evening rush hour, when it would be dark and crowded, he also hadn't wanted to risk the possibility of missing her. He had memorized the train schedule that Benson recited to him, so whenever a train pulled into the station, which wasn't very often during the afternoon, he knew what time it was. And whenever he heard commuters' footsteps come close to the car he slunk down in the backseat, though he imagined that after an hour or two his breath would have condensed and frozen on the windows, making it difficult to see inside anyway.

Shortly after the four twenty-four train left the station, the wind picked up and snow and ice began pelting the windshield. Then the wind seemed to die down, but the sound of each arriving train engine became progressively more muffled, the toot of its horn more forlorn. Jacobus realized the car was being blanketed with snow. By the time the seven thirteen arrived from Grand Central Station, it was two hours past sunset and the cold was getting severe. The feeling in his fingers and toes began to escape him, and his thought processes started to slow. Passengers spewed out of the train, their hurried, snow-cushioned footsteps barely audible. Car doors quickly opened and shut. Engines wheezed into life. Cars drove off.

All was quiet again. Maybe she wouldn't show up at all and he would freeze to death. He would hardly feel anything. He had enjoyed the pipe. But then, finally, he heard footsteps approach the car – the footsteps for which he had been waiting for hours but now almost begrudged. Piles of arm-shoveled snow thudded on to the ground. Ice was scraped from the windshield. The lock clicked and the frozen door yanked ajar on the third attempt.

'Only a few minutes late,' Jacobus said.

'Jesus Christ!'

She slammed the door closed and began to run off. Jacobus waited. He knew she would come back, and she did.

'You startled me,' she said.

'Tit for tat, but it was the only way to find you I could think of. You did a good job eluding the cops. Getting off at Southeast and then taking a train back up here.'

Jacobus wheezed out a laugh.

'The police? I didn't know it was them. I was afraid it was someone else. I tried calling you, but your phone's been out of order.'

'Long story.'

'Why did you wait here instead of at the motel?' she asked.

'Two reasons. First, you'd already paid up at the motel so you didn't need to go back. But since you hadn't paid for the car yet, at some point you'd need to return it so that they won't report you to your credit card company and start tracing your purchases. I didn't think you'd care for that.'

'And second?'

'If I was wrong, you'd still need to come here to pick up the car to get to the motel.'

'You're very astute, Mr Jacobus. That's why I need you. Maybe you can tell me why the police were following me.'

'We've learned a lot more about Borlotti,' he said. 'Thought you'd like to know.'

Whether it was the talking or just having another warm body in the car, Jacobus felt himself beginning to function again.

'After having given my associate, Mr Williams, the cold shoulder, various insurance agencies, including Concordia, your employer, were much more forthcoming when approached by law enforcement authorities at Mr Williams's behest. So were Borlotti's customers, who became very accommodating when asked to turn over all the documents – certificates, appraisals, bills, invoices, insurance claims – that were submitted by Borlotti and his customers over the past decade. And believe me there were lots of them. In consultation with one of the world's most foremost violin experts Mr Williams came up with a very interesting scenario. It's no surprise you were caught up in Borlotti's nefarious net.'

'I'm fascinated. And what have you learned?'

'Amadeo Borlotti started out small, with inflated repair bills. I knew that, myself, because his buddy, Jimmy Ubriaco, told us so, and various insurance claims and customers corroborated that. But when Borlotti saw how he could manipulate the system, he thought, "Hey, this isn't a bad idea!" and started to inflate bills even more. But not *all* bills. Only the ones that were submitted to insurance companies. The others, he continued to charge very little because it seems he had a gentle and generous soul.'

'It's not really a crime to overcharge a little when billing insurance,' Forsythe said. 'It's done all the time. We even account for that in our projections. Hardly anything to blackmail someone over.'

'Did I say anything about blackmail? I don't recall saying anything about blackmail. But you're right. It's not a big deal in and of itself. But it gave gentle, generous Amadeo – who it turns out was also crafty Amadeo – some bigger ideas. He started to file claims for repairs he never even made, giving a small part of the insurance reimbursement as a credit to customers, which kept them very happy. And very quiet.

'That's what started Borlotti on a more precipitous path. Why overcharge just on repairs, he wondered? Why not on the violins themselves? For example: When someone walked into Ye Olde Violin Shoppe wanting to place a violin on consignment, Borlotti would give it a very low appraisal. He would spin his handy Rolodex and sell it to a customer for just a little bit more than the low appraisal, which would be just enough to satisfy the ignorant schnook who put it on consignment. Then Borlotti and Mr Rolodex would sell it at its real market value and share the handsome profit. That is not unheard of in the violin business.

'And, you see, the reverse worked for Borlotti also! He would buy a cheap instrument for a little bit *more* than it was worth, making the seller happy. Then he would write up an extremely bloated appraisal for it, sell it at slightly *less* than that to another unsuspecting schnook who walked away thinking he'd gotten the deal of the century, while Borlotti pocketed a handsome piece of change.

'But, you know, it's not such an easy thing to sell a violin. One doesn't always have the patience. In cahoots with one customer, Borlotti sold him an inexpensive, no-name, old Italian instrument, but drastically overvalued it in his appraisal. A year later, wouldn't you know, the owner then "accidentally drove over it" and filed an insurance claim! They split the reimbursement for the repair, and they also collected on the depreciated value of the bogus violin, the total of which was far greater than the schlock they began with.'

'Why, this is terrible!' Forsythe said. 'I could give you a seminar on diminished value clauses in insurance policies, but it would be too boring for anyone outside the industry. To think this was going on under my nose! I had no idea.'

'Go figure. Borlotti was very careful, always just under the radar.'

'I'm stunned!' Forsythe said.

'I thought you'd be,' Jacobus said, 'But, as they say on the late-night infomercials, there's more! Out here in the boondocks, good violins don't come into a shop everyday or even every week. Months might go by before a decent violin passed through the hallowed doors of Ye Olde Violin Shoppe. This is where Borlotti started to get really ingenious. Amadeo would buy cheap fiddles from the kind of people who read the *Shopper's Guide*, the kind who find a violin in the attic that once belonged to Grampy Jones and think that a hundred dollars for a beat-up violin is a goldmine, or from antique dealers who couldn't be bothered with the vagaries of the violin business. Borlotti would then doll up the violins using parts from more valuable violins, or maybe even replicate those parts himself. And then, claiming they were good, old fiddles, he would sell them for a lot more than they were worth.

'With success upon success, Borlotti's creativity expanded exponentially. Why even troll for the random fiddle to float by? Borlotti started making "old" violins entirely from scratch! He began to have vintage wood smuggled to him by his loving family in Italy, and from that made remarkably authentic-looking violins. He wrote up just as convincing fake documents, supposedly signed by eminent violin dealers, all of whom are conveniently deceased.

'And, don't turn your dial yet, there's even more! This guy's ingenuity knew no bounds. Knowing that if some enterprising owner might trace the documents all the way back to the original dealer – an unlikely but unsettling possibility – Borlotti found actual old documents for actual old violins. He then forged copies of the documents, with their detailed description of the instruments and all the precise measurements, and custom-made violins to fit the descriptions! Generous, gentle, crafty Amadeo became super Amadeo!'

'If he was so amazing,' Forsythe asked, 'why didn't he just sell his violins as his own?'

'You know the business, Ms Forsythe. You can guess. What could an elderly, unknown shlump of a tradesman get for one of his own instruments? Twenty, twenty-five thousand? But for a Scarampella? A Vuillaume? A hundred-thousand, easy.'

'Still. Why would he do something, so, so . . . dishonest?'

'That's the sad part, Minerva. He did it for love.'

'Love?'

'Yes, something that might be hard for people like you and me to fathom. Amadeo Borlotti fell head-over-heels for a skanky little lass in Saratoga, much younger than him. And she loved him back, too, in her own way. I think partly she loved him because she couldn't imagine anyone ever loving her. I think he felt the same way about himself. Amorous Amadeo wrote her love letters every day. The problem was, she has a problem. A big problem. Drug addiction. Borlotti couldn't stand seeing her suffer, so rather than confront it, he fed it. She took his money and his gifts and spent it all on drugs, and he kept rewarding her. It's easy for us to say this was not a healthy relationship, but it is what it is.'

'How tragic!'

'Tragic, indeed. Tragic, indeed. But getting back to the subject at hand, according to Concordia's records, you managed to acquire a pretty decent old fiddle on the cheap, yourself.'

'Yes, that's right,' Forsythe said. 'The violin I told you about. A nice violin whose maker was unknown. It had a Stradivarius label, just like thousands of others that were made by other makers trying to profit off the Stradivari name. It had been stolen from one of our clients. We promptly reimbursed him in full. When it was recovered after five years, which often doesn't happen, we offered it back to the client for the same amount we had given him. It would have been a good deal for him because of course the violin had appreciated over those five years. But he turned it down. He had moved on in life and didn't want to have anything more to do with violins. So the insurance company became the defacto owner. They put it on the market for a year with no takers. So I bought it. All on the up and up.'

'And you took it to Borlotti for an appraisal.'

'Yes. And to my amazement he said it was a Stradivarius. I've already told you the rest. Once I had the certificate, I found a buyer for the violin, a businessman who buys art and instruments solely for investment. Who cares nothing about aesthetics or culture but who trusted me. If I had only known what Borlotti was up to! It was despicable!'

Jacobus admired the way Forsythe spat out 'despicable.'

'Yes, it was,' Jacobus said. 'And maybe Borlotti got what he deserved. But still . . .' Jacobus let the unfinished thought linger.

'What?' Forsythe asked.

'All those years, Borlotti was very, very careful. Pushing the limits but never exceeding them. Then, to write a bogus certificate for a Strad? He might as well have shouted out, "Come get me!" I wonder what made him do that.'

'Maybe his girlfriend's expenses. Maybe she got into some bigtime trouble. What did you say her name was?'

'I didn't. It's Maggette. Dahlia Maggette. I suppose you're right. That must have been it.'

Jacobus opened the car door to get out.

'Don't you need a ride?' Forsythe asked. 'Can I drive you home?'

'Nah,' Jacobus lied. 'I'm taking the next train into the city.'

'Just one question, then. How did you know my train was late?'

'It's Metro North. Some things are predictable.'

He closed the door behind him. Forsythe drove off into the night. Jacobus stood alone in the parking lot. Waiting. Suddenly colder again, he hugged himself and stamped his feet. Another car drove up and Jacobus got in. He disconnected the microphone from his coat and handed it to Lieutenant Brooks.

'Good job, Mr Jacobus. You think she's lying?'

'Through the teeth.'

'And why is that? She sounds pretty convincing to me.'

'Because she's still got two million and Borlotti's still dead.'

'Any ideas how we're going to prove she was blackmailing him?'

'Easy. Find who arranged Borlotti's murder. He'll be happy to tell us.'

THIRTY-ONE

Pizza and news awaited Jacobus when he rejoined Nathaniel at the makeshift office in Miller's basement. The thought of the former almost made Jacobus sick to his stomach, but the latter, an update from Bertoldo in Italy, provided adequate compensation.

The dutiful lover had decided to bypass the Carabinieri as an unnecessary impediment to carrying out Yumi's request. Instead, he approached Ansaldo Vassari directly, asking him to go back to Rome to obtain a copy of the paperwork for the string bass case from the cargo clerk at Fiumicino Airport. But Vassari replied that he would rather be crucified and hanged by the balls than have to go back to Rome, so Bertoldo hung the *Chiuso* sign on the front door of his shop and took a day off from violin making. He drove to Fiumicino alone and found the cargo clerk for whom Vassari had provided a location and description. A modest bribe with the extra cash he had brought along for the purpose led to an introduction to the head of the freight crew. That gentleman, who also responded to financial incentive, showed Bertoldo a copy of the carnet for the bass case.

'What exactly is a carnet?' Yumi asked Nathaniel.

'It's like a passport, except it's for merchandise and not people, for the temporary importation of goods. It's so the shipper doesn't have to pay a lot of fees and taxes.'

'But when Falcone shipped it, he intended it to be permanent,' Jacobus argued. 'At least as far as Borlotti was concerned.'

'True, but if customs thought it was only going to be temporary, there would be fewer questions asked,' Nathaniel said.

'They told Marcello that Ubriaco's case was shipped by a small company named Prime Transport,' Yumi said.

'I checked them out,' Nathaniel added. 'They mostly ship internationally.'

'They and a hundred others, I'd wager,' Jacobus replied. 'I'm not impressed.'

'But there is one detail I discovered that might impress you more. They also do domestic trucking here in the US.'

Jacobus's ears perked up. The truck outside Borlotti's house!

'You think there might be a connection between Falcone and this Prime Transport?' Jacobus asked.

'Why don't we ask the experts?' Yumi suggested.

Jacobus called Lieutenant Brooks.

'My God!' Brooks said. 'Do you have any idea who owns Prime Transport?'

'Donald Trump?'

'Vincenzo Primo!'

'Is that worse than Donald Trump?'

'Primo is an ape in an Armani suit with a five o'clock shadow by lunchtime. His organization in Boston makes the Mafia look like the Boy Scouts. Even Whitey Bulger skipped town when Primo thought Bulger was honing in on his territory.'

'How did he get to be mister big shot?' Jacobus asked. 'It doesn't sound like it was from studying the violin.'

'Vince Primo started out as a trucker who tried making an extra buck as a middleweight, figuring his street fighting would serve him well in the ring. He didn't win many fights, but either because his brain was so small or his skull was so thick, he never got knocked down, either, which is why his nose is flatter than Kansas.

'His specialty outside the ring was intimidation, and pretty soon his handlers became his handlees. He cast his stooges in his own image, and pretty soon he was fixing fights and fixing his trucking competition . . . for good.

'These days, any stone you turn over in Boston, first the worms crawl out, then Primo's shadow. His gang has controlled the Wonderland dog track in Revere for ten years. Between you and me, Mr Jacobus, there are men in my own department from whom I keep my own counsel. And you know the Big Dig?'

'Only by the gridlock that Benson and I got stuck in.'

'That's the one. The original estimate was under three billion dollars. Now it's over twenty billion. Guess whose trucks are hauling the cement and the stone and the concrete and the tarmac? Vincenzo Primo's. And you know why? Vince Primo's got something on everyone in the State House. They're scared to death of him.

'We've put some of Primo's stooges away over the years, and we've had a tap on his personal phone and on the Prime Transport phone for months.'

'Is that legal?' Jacobus asked, but that was not his primary interest.

'We made it legal,' Brooks said. 'But he figured out a way to block it and we've been coming up with blanks. If he's the one who hired Falcone to get rid of Borlotti . . . Mr Jacobus, I'd give my right arm to lock these guys up and throw away the key.'

'Then I hope you're a lefty,' Jacobus said. 'We could be going down a totally wrong road here, so don't get too carried away. Maybe there's a connection between this guy, Primo, and Falcone. Maybe not. But what would Primo have to do with Borlotti? It doesn't make any sense. At least not yet. Any word on Frau Falcone, by the way?'

'We've got the current location of her and her kids nailed down, but no sign of Frankie.'

'Yeah? Where are they?'

'You really want to know?'

'Why the hell else would I ask? Small talk isn't my—'

'Pirates of the Caribbean.'

'What's that?'

'A ghost ship of singing cutthroats. Disneyland.'

'Disneyland, huh? Maybe you'd have more luck finding him at A Small World.'

THIRTY-TWO

Tuesday, January 10

Jacobus had some unfinished, unpleasant business to attend to in Saratoga. Yumi drove and dropped him off in front of Sloppy Joe's. Yumi wanted to go in with him but he refused.

Jacobus returned to the car after only a minute.

'Doesn't work here anymore,' he said. 'Got fired. They didn't say why, but I can imagine.'

Next they tried Nasty Brews, but she didn't work there, either.

'They said to try Bangs For The Bucks.'

'What's that? A hunting supply store or a brothel?' Yumi asked.

'They said it's a hair salon.'

When they entered Bangs For The Bucks, the receptionist curtly said to Yumi, 'Sorry, we don't take walk-ins.'

Jacobus said, 'It's not for her, it's for me.'

'What do you need?'

'I want to have my back shaved.'

When he explained their true reason for their presence, the relieved receptionist was happy to tell them what they wanted to know. Dahlia Maggette had interviewed for a job there but they had chosen not to hire her because they heard she had stolen from the cash register at Sloppy Joe's. With a frown in her voice, she told them they could try a massage parlor near the racetrack called Hot To Trot.

'Yeah, Dahlia works here,' the Hot To Trot attendant said, 'but her shift's not until tonight. You guys want a couple's massage? Forty bucks for an hour, fifty for ninety minutes. Tips at your discretion.'

'I'll give you a tip,' Jacobus said and was about to tell him where he could put his hot stones but was prevented by Yumi's restraining hand.

'We really do need to find her,' she said to the attendant. 'Do you know where we might be able to?'

'There's a homeless shelter on Walworth. Sometimes she hangs out there.'

A block from the shelter, Yumi spotted Dahlia from the car and pulled up alongside her. Jacobus rolled down his window and called to her.

'I don't have his money,' Maggette said. 'I can't give it back.'

'That's not what we're here for,' he said. 'Get in,' said Jacobus.

They found a small park nearby. Like everything else, it was covered with snow. Maybe in the summer, with kids running around, it was a nice park. Jacobus told Yumi to wait in the car.

There were worse things in life than death and Jacobus didn't have that hard a time telling Maggette that Borlotti was dead. He sensed that she suspected it, anyway, after his previous meeting with her. What her response was, he couldn't tell, because she didn't say a word.

What he had a harder time telling her was that Borlotti's love letters, which she had entrusted to him, with their flowing poetry and elegant handwriting, had gone up in flames with the rest of his house. Those letters were meaningful to Jacobus because he had hoped to prove from them – by means of their ink, paper, and handwriting – that Borlotti had forged the violin labels and certificates. But he knew they were meaningful to Maggette in other ways, and he regretted their loss.

'Can I go now?' she said.

'Yes, but before you do, I want to know something. Borlotti knew you were an addict, didn't he?'

'You sure are subtle, aren't you?'

'You want me to be subtle?'

'No. Why bother? Yes, he knew. I told him I was.'

'And he still gave you the money because he loved you.' It was an observation, not a question.

'He said he trusted me no matter what. What a fool. This fucking world.'

Jacobus wanted to say, *Hey, sweetheart, I'm homeless just like you are. My family was gassed in World War II, a slimy Russian violinist tried to boff me when I was a kid, and I went blind the day I was supposed to embark on an illustrious career. So if you want to blame the world for being a victim, find someone else.* But instead – he didn't know why – he put his arm around her shoulder and said, 'If you decide you want some help, let me know.'

Since he didn't have a phone anymore, Jacobus searched his pockets and gave her one of Nathaniel's business cards. He left Dahlia Maggette standing in the snow and got into Yumi's car.

'I saw you put your arm around Dahlia,' Yumi said. 'That was a nice thing for you to do.'

'Eh?' Jacobus said. 'Commiserating loves company.'

THIRTY-THREE

Wednesday, January 11

Nathaniel handed his phone to Jacobus.

'We've got a situation, sir,' Frank Case, the on-duty officer, said to Jacobus, interrupting his breakfast. He had progressed to being able to tolerate a boiled egg. 'She's making a lot of noise. Says you're a friend of hers. We can release her into your custody, but frankly, I wouldn't do it if I were you.'

Two hours later, Jacobus and Yumi were back in Saratoga Springs, at the police department.

'She popped another lady real good,' Officer Case said. 'Gave her a fat lip.'

'What's she charged with?'

'Nada. The other lady declined to press charges, though if she had, your friend could have been in some serious trouble. I've seen girl fights before, but your friend has a right cross that Sugar Ray would envy.'

'Leonard or Robinson?'

'Either.'

'How come the other lady didn't press charges?'

'She said it was just a misunderstanding and took off before I could even get her name. So I didn't file a report, but I didn't feel I could let your friend just walk away.'

Dahlia Maggette didn't even look at them when she was let out of the holding room, nor did she say anything until they found a seat at Nasty Brews. Almost noon, there was already an undercurrent of conversation unfit for public consumption. A monotone, pulsating beat throbbed to a stream of rambling obscenities by a wannabe rap sensation on the bar's speakers. They ordered three coffees.

'Tell me about it,' Jacobus said.

'Why?'

'You called *me*, honey. I didn't come all this way just to take the salubrious waters.'

'So someone got in my face. I don't like it when someone gets in my face.'

'What was her name?'

'She didn't say.'

'Was she smoking a pipe?'

'Not for long.'

Jacobus had made a mistake when he mentioned Dahlia's name and whereabouts to Minerva Forsythe, and regretted it. It couldn't have been easy for her to find Maggette, and he didn't understand what Forsythe would want from her, except their common interest in Borlotti.

'What did she want?' he asked Maggette.

'My letters from Borlotti. I told her, "Who the hell are you? My letters are none of your damn business," but she kept bugging me. I told her even if I had them I'd never give them to her. She said, "what do you mean 'if you had them'?" I said, "Don't you understand English?" and turned my back on her and started walking away.'

'So why did you hit her?'

'She wouldn't take no for an answer. She grabbed me from behind and opened her purse and said, "Oh, so you want money? Here's money." And threw it on the ground. "You want more?" She threw some more down. She thinks because she's rich and soooo sophisticated she can treat people like trash.

'I told her to take her money back. There was no way she was getting any letters. So she shoved me. Now, you can say whatever you want to me. I've heard it all. But no one touches me without my say so. No one. That's when I hit her. Have to hand it to her, though. I thought I'd knocked her out cold, but she didn't even go down.'

'And that's when the cops came?'

'Yeah. I was hoping they'd lock me up for a few years.'

'Why?'

'Free room and board. But she just walked away. I shouted at her that the letters were burned and she got her fat lip for nothing.'

'So what are you going to do now?'

'Nothing. I'll survive.'

Much to Jacobus's surprise, an offer to take her in was on his lips, but then he realized that, like Dahlia, he too was homeless.

They left her at the bar. When they were back in the car, Yumi dialed Lieutenant Brooks's number. Jacobus gave him a summary of the altercation between Dahlia Maggette and Minerva Forsythe.

'You know where Forsythe is now?' Jacobus asked.

'No. We can't keep someone on her twenty-four-seven.'

'How about the other lady?'

'Maggette?'

'I damn well know where Maggette is,' Jacobus said. 'I'm talking about Falcone's wife, who you seem to think is going to lead us to her beloved.'

'For your information, Nadine Falcone has deposited her children with some relatives in Venice Beach and has checked into a rather posh country inn in Napa. And guess what? She booked a room with two queen-size beds.'

'Damn. I was hoping for one king.'

'Our plan was to move in once Falcone arrived.'

'*Was?*'

'That plan might be moot. We've finally caught a break, Mr Jacobus. Frankie Falcone called us.'

'He got you an extra queen bed?'

'Falcone wants to turn state's evidence. He's afraid that his employer is going to kill him.'

'Primo?'

'We don't know that.'

'What *do* you know?'

'Falcone's holed up somewhere. We don't know where. Apparently his employer doesn't either. Falcone believes he's somewhere where no one will find him. He went into hiding when he heard on the news we were on his tail. But his wound is worse than he thought. He said when he unwrapped the bandage the wound "was dripping stuff and he almost puked." He called his employer to come get him out of a jam because he was running out of food and water, but his employer was standoffish.'

'Gee, no honor among thieves?' Jacobus remarked. 'What's the world coming to?'

'Falcone made the mistake of asking his employer why he had been worried about "a small-time hick punk like Borlotti." Clearly, that was not the right question to ask. His employer responded that if word got out that he got swindled by a small-time hick punk and got away with it, he'd be a dead man. I tend to agree with that assessment, knowing the world those types dwell in.

'Falcone's employer then allegedly threatened him. He said, according to Falcone, "That's why I hired you. To get rid of the problem so nobody would even know it was a problem. And now the whole fucking world knows it." He also lambasted Falcone about screwing up with "that blind prick" – not *my* words, Mr Jacobus. And not coming through on the other part of his original assignment, which involved a woman cheating him out of millions.'

'What woman?'

'Could be Forsythe. Could also be Maggette. Could be someone we don't know.'

'Falcone doesn't sound like the kind to spook easily,' Jacobus said. 'And what you've told me so far doesn't sound like much of a threat.'

'Falcone didn't think so either. Until his employer inquired a little too matter-of-factly where he was hiding out. That's when Falcone started to have some misgivings.'

'And you tend to agree with that assessment also?'

'I do.'

'Does Falcone's sudden change of heart amount to a confession?' Jacobus asked.

'Not quite. But if we can get our hands on him, offer him protection, I think we'll get it.'

'You mean we have to keep the crud who burned my house down alive?'

'I'm afraid so,' Brooks said. 'Long enough to put him in prison, anyway.'

Jacobus was hardly assuaged.

'So is his boss this guy Primo or not?' Jacobus asked. 'And where is Falcone?'

'Those are his bargaining chips and he won't tell us either of those things until we grant him immunity. Of course we won't do that, but we're negotiating.'

Brooks once again told Jacobus how much his assistance meant to him.

'OK, Brooks,' Jacobus replied. 'Knock off the bullshit. What do you want me to do now?'

Brooks asked Jacobus to make a trip to Berkshire Bliss Holiday Cottages and see if there was any sign of Forsythe there.

'Later,' Jacobus said. 'Right now I'm ready to plotz.'

Yumi and Jacobus returned to Miller's house, where Martha's special family recipe meatloaf for dinner awaited them. Two bites were as much as Jacobus could stomach. Putting his head under the cold tap did more to resuscitate him.

'You must be exhausted,' Miller said to Jacobus.

'You ever play Schubert's Ninth Symphony?'

'No. Why?'

'Because *that's* exhaustion.'

Miller took a turn being Jacobus's chauffeur on the drive to Berkshire Bliss. There was no response when they knocked on the door of the room Minerva Forsythe had rented. They roused the on-duty manager, half-asleep watching *Bowling for Dollars*, and had him unlock the room. The only trace that Minerva Forsythe had ever been there were vestiges of perfume and pipe tobacco in the air.

'Might as well head back home,' Miller said. 'I could use a Jack Daniels about now.'

Though Jacobus was frustrated, he could not disagree. It was the first time since his house had burned down that he was even tempted by alcohol. He considered that a positive development.

As they drove north on Route 23, light snow started to fall. A car slipped in behind them. Miller made a quick decision to detour on to Route 41. The other car stayed behind them, remaining three car lengths behind.

'I think someone's following us,' he said.

'Who is it?' Jacobus asked.

'Can't tell.'

Jacobus, impatient after the long day, asked, 'Why the hell not?'

'Well, Jake,' Miller responded, no less tired, 'it could be because it's night-time. It could be because it's snowing. It could be because he's got his brights shining in my rearview mirror, and it could even be because he's staying too far back. Take your pick. Any more questions?'

'Sorry. I've forgotten about those things.'

Jacobus thought about who might be following them and, considering the worst of the possibilities, thought it advisable to stop only where they wouldn't be alone.

'What's playing at the Mahaiwe tonight?' he asked.

'Some folk music, I think,' Miller said.

'Folk music, huh? I don't know.'

'That's where we're going.'

Miller, who had repaired leaks and installed toilets in every nook and cranny of the Berkshires, knew all the back roads by heart and wended his way up to Great Barrington. The car, which continued to follow them until they parked in a brightly lit spot in front of the Mahaiwe Theater, maintained its ominous distance.

Jacobus and Miller bought tickets and hurried into the old restored theater and found a seat in the middle of the audience. The show was a retrospective of the life of Woody Guthrie presented by his almost-as-illustrious son, Arlo, whose spiritual retreat was just a few miles away on Van Deusenville Road.

While Arlo whipped the crowd into a joyful anti-establishment frenzy, Jacobus kept his ears open for anything incongruous.

The audience watched film clips of Woody singing 'Dust Bowl Refugee' and the unfamiliar 'I Ain't Got No Home.'

'I ain't got no home. I'm just a-roamin' 'round, Just a wandrin' worker, I go from town to town. And the police make it hard

wherever I may go, And I ain't got no home in this world anymore.'

Jacobus didn't think it was a subject worth singing about.

The audience joined Woody on the screen with 'Red River Valley' and was just starting to clap rhythmically along with the big finale, 'This Land Is Your Land,' when Jacobus felt a tap on his shoulder. He inhaled the perfume and exhaled with relief. It wasn't someone out to kill him. At least he didn't think so.

'How's your lip?' Jacobus asked.

'Where can we go?' Minerva Forsythe replied.

'What's wrong? You don't like folk music?' Jacobus replied.

'We need to talk. I want to help.'

A voice from behind them asked them to pipe down.

'Follow us,' Jacobus said. 'It's not far.'

They got back in their car. Jacobus told Miller where to go. Forsythe followed them as they backtracked south on Route 23. The snow started to come down more heavily and Miller drove slowly.

They arrived at their destination. The smell of wet ashes, now almost imperceptible, hung in the air. That was all that remained of Borlotti's home. Getting out of Miller's truck, Jacobus asked him to wait there and with his cane followed the now-familiar icy path to the ruins. Cottony flakes of snow melted on his face. They felt good and he didn't wipe them off.

'I thought you'd want to see for yourself, honey,' Jacobus said as Forsythe's footsteps approached. 'I don't imagine there's much left. But you get the picture.'

'Why did you bring us here?' Forsythe asked. 'It's cold out.'

'Context. For what you're about to tell me.'

'As I said, I want to help.'

'You mean, now that you've gathered that Borlotti's potentially incriminating letters have gone up in smoke, you want to be of service in exchange for protection.'

'What do you mean?'

'You've been giving me a song and dance about being an innocent victim of Borlotti writing a certificate for a violin, falsely claiming it was a Stradivari.'

'That's exactly what he did.'

'Not exactly, Ms Forsythe. Not exactly. He did indeed write that certificate, but it wasn't so he could get an easy quarter million. It was because you were blackmailing him.'

'That's absurd.'

'I'll bet at first Borlotti absolutely refused to write that certificate, and that's when you told him you knew exactly what he had been up to for all these years, with the fraudulent insurance claims and the forged documents and phony instruments. You threatened to expose him. He knew he'd have no choice. If Borlotti didn't write the certificate, not only would he lose his reputation, he would be locked up for a very long time. He wouldn't be the first violin dealer who ended up like that. You forced him to write that certificate and then you gave him enough of a piece of the action to shut him up.'

He paused, expecting Forsythe to protest. She didn't. In the silence he was struck by peacefulness of the night.

'Between a rock and a hard place,' Jacobus continued, 'Borlotti caved in and accepted your hush money. He wrote the certificate that would ultimately become his own death warrant. And you know what galled him the most, Ms Forsythe?'

'I have no idea.'

'The story you told me was that the violin you purchased, and that you said Borlotti insisted was a Strad, had previously been attributed to an unknown maker. Well, it may have been an unknown maker to the world. It might even have been an unknown maker to you. At first. But Borlotti knew who made that violin. Because it was Borlotti, himself, who had made it! Wasn't it?'

'How would I know?'

'Because Concordia had been insuring it when it was stolen. You told me that. Yes, Borlotti made that violin with his own crafty little hands and his precious old Italian wood. So it must have twisted him in knots to write that phony certificate. Meanwhile, you disappeared into the ether, or at least that's what your plan was.'

'Why would I do that?'

'Greed, honey. Two-million dollars worth.'

'I had no reason to believe Borlotti wasn't an honest, reputable workman,' Forsythe said.

'That, in two words, madam, is B.S.'

'That's offensive. I don't know what you're talking about.'

'Really! Well, I'll spell it out for you, then. You, Ms Self-Proclaimed Insurance Expert, knew very well what was going on with Borlotti. How could you not have? You were his agent for all those years. Who better than Minerva Forsythe, who filled the coffers of Concordia Insurance better than anyone else in the firm, to keep a wary eye on

the company's fortunes? You kept tabs for years on the larceny Borlotti
was up to, and you bided your time, waiting for the right moment
when he was in too deep to get himself out. You knew and you let
it happen. It had been going on for about six years. Right?'

'How do you know that?'

'Because that's when he fell head over heels with his sweetheart,
Dahlia Maggette, and started providing her with a lifestyle to which
she tragically became all too accustomed. Why didn't you ever tell
your employers that Borlotti was defrauding the company?' Jacobus
asked. 'Isn't there some kind of ethical obligation to be honest? Or
is that not part of the job description.'

Forsythe laughed.

'You've heard of the glass ceiling?' she said. 'Concordia's was
made out of lead. I worked for those pompous asses for seventeen
years. I delivered them the most lucrative accounts, the highest
premiums, the fewest claim payouts. And while every pimply
Wharton and Amherst do-nothing moved up the ladder to respect-
ability, what did I get in return? A thousand-dollar Christmas bonus,
a pinch on the ass and a grab on my boob. How nice. Yes, *I* saw
what was going on with Borlotti. They didn't. But that doesn't mean
I blackmailed him.'

'Maybe it wasn't you who set up the system,' Jacobus said, 'but
you used it. When you bought that violin from Concordia, you saw
a chance to strike it rich. You went to Borlotti and threatened to
expose his misdeeds unless he forged a Stradivarius certificate for
the violin. He knew he would go to jail for a long time for what
he had done. But that wasn't the worst of it for him. If he went to
jail, he wouldn't be able to care for his sweetheart. He couldn't
bear the thought of that, and when you offered him the quarter
million in hush money, that tipped the balance. He got out his
fountain pen and ink and old paper and wrote away. Were you
standing over his shoulder, drooling over every word?'

'I never saw him write any certificate.'

'But he knew, as you should have also, that it's one thing to write
false documents for run-of-the-mill violins. It's another thing to
write one claiming a violin is a Strad. But greed blinded you. You
sold the violin, convincing the buyer – let's call him Mr Chump
– that he was getting a great deal. Showed him some appraisals for
other Strads that cost three and four million. But Borlotti knew that
Mr Chump would eventually find out. And when Mr Chump did

find out he got very angry, because two-and-a-half million dollars is a lot to fork over when it's based on misplaced trust. He must have felt humiliated and downright vengeful.

'And, that's why Borlotti called me on Christmas Eve. He knew his deception had been discovered and he was in danger. How he found out, we may never know. Could have been he got a phone call. Could have been he saw Falcone cruising his neighborhood. But he knew he was in trouble. And I could have helped him. I could have helped him, but didn't.'

Jacobus drew circles on the ice with the point of his cane. Not that he was going anywhere. With a pencil he wouldn't be able to know if he'd completed a turn, but with the etching in the ice he could feel when he came full circle. That pleased him. He thought about Borlotti – his ruined house and ruined life. And his own.

'When you heard about the arson and Borlotti's disappearance, you figured you might be next, even though you'd try to pin the blame on Borlotti. But then a chilling thought entered your analytic head. Maybe before they killed Borlotti they got him to confess to everything.

'Then I made the unfortunate slip of mentioning to you his letters to Dahlia Maggette. You worried he might have unburdened himself to her and that they'd incriminate you. You were probably getting pretty paranoid at this point, and I can't say I blame you. Hell, that explains why you broke into my house. To try to find out if we had anything that would tie you to Borlotti. So you tried to get those letters back. Once you realized they'd gone up in smoke, here you are Miss Innocent again. "I want to help." Yes, Borlotti was going to confess everything to me and try to make a clean break of it. He really was a good man who had taken a wrong turn – lots of wrong turns – but he was not an evil person.

'You, on the other hand? Where were you? Nowhere to be found. After you paid off Borlotti, you thought you were free and clear. But then something happened. Borlotti's house burned to the ground.'

'I had nothing to do with that!' Forsythe said.

'That's the *only* thing you had nothing to do with. After all, why pay Borlotti off and then kill him and leave the money? No. Doesn't make sense. But why would Mr Chump go after Borlotti first? Borlotti, who was otherwise unknown to him, and, as far as Mr Chump knew, had no association with the violin other than having written the certificate? Maybe because someone told Mr Chump the violin was really made by bogus Amadeo and didn't take kindly to the fact that he'd been swindled. I think it was you who sold out Borlotti in order to save your own skin. But Mr Chump is still not happy because he's still out two-and-a-half million, and I don't think he will be happy until he gets it back. Do you? No, you didn't burn Borlotti's house down. But you went into hiding, letting Borlotti take the fall. You might as well have killed him yourself.'

'Why do you persist in thinking I had anything to do with this?'

Jacobus was tiring of the cat-and-mouse game, and he assumed Miller was running out of patience waiting in the car.

'In life, as in music, timing is everything. The first time you called me, after the arson, you were scared. The second time, after Borlotti's murder, you were more scared. Now, just after the presumed perpetrator of the first two crimes is exposed in the news, what do you know? Here we are again. You know who Falcone is working for, and you know that you're next on the list. So who is it, Ms Forsythe? This is your last, best chance to redeem yourself.'

'This is all fantasy!' Forsythe said.

'Fantasy! Well, I'm freezing my ass off. I'm going to bed.'

Jacobus, poking his cane into the new snow, made his way back to Miller's car. He recalled the lyrics to one of the Guthrie songs he had heard at the Mahaiwe, from a song called the 'Massacre of 1913,' if he remembered correctly. It wasn't Schubert, but it fit the occasion: *'The piano played a slow funeral tune, And the town was lit up by a cold Christmas moon. The parents they cried and the miners they moaned, 'See what your greed for money has done.'*

Nathaniel's excitement was so infectious when Jacobus and Miller returned that Trotsky was spinning in circles like a pup.

'Jake, I think I've found out something interesting,' he said.

'Mind if I thaw out first?'

'How many years'll that take?'

'Too many, I hope.'

Jacobus removed his coat and sweaters, found the easy chair, which had become his seat of choice in Miller's house, and collapsed into it.

'So, what's your news? Someone going to kill us?'

'Probably. But that's not the news. I was thinking, when you ship something valuable, like an instrument, you can't be too careful insuring it, like Dedubian said. But when you go to the post office, or FedEx, or UPS, or any shipper, they ask if you want to insure it. Right?'

'So you think Falcone insured Borlotti's body in case it got damaged?'

'No, but I thought that Prime Transport would need to have an insurance company on retainer.'

'You think a front for a crime organization needs insurance?'

'If only to give the appearance of legitimacy.'

'And?'

'They do. And guess who their insurance company is?'

'Concordia?'

'And guess who their agent is?'

THIRTY-FOUR

Thursday, January 12

'I need to go to Great Barrington,' Jacobus said to no one in particular.

'At eight a.m.?' Nathaniel asked, pouring the coffee.

'What do you need?' Yumi asked. 'I'll go there for you.'

'You can't. I want to be alone. Like Garbo. Too many people around here. I'm suffocating.'

Miller had to go there, anyway, to get some outdoor cleaning supplies at Mist For The Grill, so he offered to take Jacobus.

'Where do you want me to drop you off?' he asked when they got into the heart of town.

'Where are we?' Jacobus asked.

'Corner of Main and Pleasant.'

'Right here.'

'Is there a particular store you're going to?'

'I'm getting off here.'

'Suit yourself.'

They arranged to meet at the same place in a half hour. If it was snowing, which was in the forecast, they would meet at Cuppa Cabana.

After he was certain Miller drove away, Jacobus took his time walking two blocks south, gingerly crossing at the crosswalk and praying there were no New Yorkers who would ignore the Stop For Pedestrians sign. He walked two stores north and entered Fly By Night. He had hoped he'd be the only customer there, but he found two others already in line who were returning Christmas presents that were not to their liking. As he waited, he heard another customer enter and get in line behind him. Jacobus wanted to be alone when he spoke to Simon so he told that person to go ahead of him.

'Are you sure?' the woman asked. 'I have to return all these things.'

'Why don't you just burn them?' Jacobus asked.

The woman wasn't sure whether Jacobus was joking, nor was Jacobus, but he gestured for her to move up and she didn't argue.

It was finally his turn.

'Morning, Mr Jacobus,' Simon said. 'Another cold one.'

'You still do Western Union?' Jacobus asked.

'Well, yeah. Today. But maybe not tomorrow.'

'What do you mean?'

'They're becoming dinosaurs real fast. With faxes and email and cellular phones, pretty soon telegrams will be extinct.'

'No way,' Jacobus said, but the news made him happy.

Miller returned Jacobus home and went off to work. Though it wasn't even ten o'clock, Jacobus was tired and in need of solitude. The efforts of the past week, since his house burned down, had caught up with him. He told Nathaniel, Yumi, and Martha Miller he didn't want to be disturbed and went to his room. There he sat in quiet contemplation, waiting.

'What time is it?' he asked when Yumi shook him.

'About six.'

'a.m. or p.m.?'

'p.m. Why don't you come down? I don't want Roy and Nathaniel to eat all your dinner.'

Jacobus made his way to the kitchen with difficulty. His friends tried not to make a big deal out of his frailty and the conversation continued as if he had been there the whole time. Martha made lasagna, which Jacobus would have normally enjoyed, but he could hardly get a bite down. When Yumi said that he should eat more because he needed to keep up his strength, he snapped unfairly at her, but then mumbled something that might have sounded like an apology.

Martha asked Jacobus if he wanted some tea. Before he could think of a polite way of refusing, the phone rang. Martha answered it and quickly put it down.

'It was Sigurd Benson. He said to turn on the Channel 4 news.'

'. . . Yes, Bob. So, about an hour ago the police discovered Falcone's body in the family's yacht, Torch Song, which docked in the marina you can see right here behind me, only blocks from his home on Revere's Wharf in Boston's North End. He was found holding a handgun and had a single bullet to the head, fired at point blank range. Falcone had long been suspected of being part of a local arson for hire ring but had never been arrested.'

'Do we know what kind of gun it was, Andrea?'

'I'm told that it was a Wesson Model Ten revolver, Bob.'

'Andrea, after Channel 4 News 4U broke the story of the nationwide manhunt for Falcone, which literally had been turning up blanks, how did the police know where to find him, literally in his own backyard?'

'Yes, Bob. Absolutely. So, the police were called by a local resident, Iphigenia Martinuzzi—'

'Try saying that name five times fast!'

'You said it! Mrs. Mar-tin-uz-zi heard what she described as "a loud popping sound" and called the police, because – and listen to this, Bob – because she said "it was the right thing to do."'

'Mrs. Martinuzzi, or however you pronounce it, is a true hero. Isn't she?'

'She certainly is, Bob.'

'Andrea, have the police suggested any motive?'

'Right, Bob. So, Lieutenant Russell Brooks, head of the Greater Boston Arson Taskforce, or G-BAT, told Channel 4 News 4U that no possibility is being ruled out but that everything points to suicide. Whatever the result of the investigation, Bob, it is a sudden and stunning ending to a manhunt that had stymied law enforcement agencies around the country.'

'We understand Falcone left a wife and four children.'

'Yes, Bob. That's right. The family is on its way back from vacationing in California. So far they have declined to make a statement and have requested privacy. But according to friends, the Falcones are devout Catholics and may well be troubled by the fact that Francis Falcone died by his own hand. There's a funeral service planned at Our Lady of Mercy in the North End on Sunday.'

'We'll have more on this breaking story as it develops. Live from Revere's Wharf, this is Andrea Montcrief for Channel 4 News 4U. Back to you, Bob.'

'Speaking of boating, the weather this weekend—'

Miller turned the television off. They sat in silence. Falcone, dead!

'Get me Brooks's business card,' Jacobus demanded. 'Get me a phone. I'm calling that son of a bitch. Now.'

'Brooks speaking.'

'Suicide? You're an even bigger idiot than I thought you were.'

'Hello, Mr Jacobus. I never said it was suicide.'

'Were you not on the TV news just now?'

'Yes. And?' Brooks replied calmly.

'And what did the reporter say?'

'That everything points to suicide.' Brooks said. 'That's accurate. Everything does point to suicide. That's what it was made to look like. But, like you, I don't buy it a bit. I strongly believe it was a gangland execution to shut him up because Vince Primo knows we're getting close. Would you have liked me to advertise that theory, Mr Jacobus?'

'I guess you're not as big an idiot as I thought.'

'Thank you. For now, my main concern is that you, your friends, and everyone else surrounding this case are all in danger until we apprehend Falcone's killer. Whoever had the ability to get to Falcone is truly a dangerous man.

When Jacobus hung up, he said to his friends, 'Smart guy, that Brooks.'

THIRTY-FIVE

An hour later Brooks was back on the phone.

'My men are reporting that Minerva Forsythe is heading east on the Mass Pike, going well above the speed limit. I suspect she might be thinking of getting to Logan and taking a flight somewhere far away.'

Jacobus could understand why she might be doing that. It wasn't just the law she would be trying to escape.

'When do you plan to stop her for speeding?' Jacobus asked.

'There's a rest stop a few miles from her current location. I can have the trooper steer her there and detain her.'

'Arresting her?'

'Benson thinks I should. The Boy Scout in him. And we probably could, but I nixed it, much to his dismay. Primo's the grand prize, so I'd rather keep her on a loose rein and use her as bait.'

'I'll overlook your mixed metaphor, Brooks, but if I leave the house now, can you keep her entertained until I get to the rest stop?'

'I think we can do that, but hasn't it been an awfully long day for you?'

'Actually, I feel like it's just getting started.'

'All right. We'll wait.'

'Thanks. And one more thing.'

'Yes?'

'Order me a cheeseburger. I'm suddenly feeling better.'

Jacobus and Minerva Forsythe sat in a booth by themselves near the window of the fast food court. Brooks had excused the state trooper who had escorted Forsythe to the rest stop and was sitting with Roy Miller far away by the condiments. The only other person in the area was a janitor sweeping the floor.

Jacobus took a bite out of his cheeseburger and invited Forsythe to help herself to his fries. She declined.

'Brooks says he thinks you might have been trying to ditch it out of Dodge.'

'That's preposterous.'

'Does the name Vincenzo Primo ring a bell, Minerva?'

Jacobus heard the ends of the metal legs of her plastic chair scrape the floor, as if she was backing out. At first he thought she was going to make a dash for it, which would have been stupid. But Minerva Forsythe wasn't a stupid woman. She was backing away from the name. The name Vincenzo Primo.

'I think I might have heard that name, but I can't quite place it.'

'I can understand how you'd want to block it out, so let me refresh your memory,' Jacobus said. 'Mr Williams has discovered that your multifaceted expertise in the fascinating world of insurance extended beyond musical instruments, Minerva. You also oversaw corporate accounts, including shipping companies. I find that very interesting.'

'There's nothing all that interesting about it.'

'Oh, I beg to differ! Not the least of which is that one of your corporate clients happened to be Prime Transport, the owner of which is the gentleman in question. Vincenzo Primo. Prime Transport coincidentally was the company through which Frances Falcone shipped dead Amadeo to Italy in a bass case. Do you perceive a common thread here? I do. And I think it's time you stopped playing the naive innocent. It doesn't really become you.'

Jacobus sucked on his chocolate shake, but the icy stuff got stuck in the straw. He pulled the straw out of the plastic cup, sucked on it from the other end, and replaced it back in the cup. For the first time since his house burned down he was enjoying life. He almost felt like a kid again.

'Just what is it you want me to tell you, Mr Jacobus? That I sold a violin I knew to be a fake to Vince Primo?'

'For starters.'

'All right. I'll admit it. I sold the violin to Primo. And I'm scared to death of him.'

'You didn't think Primo would eventually figure things out?'

'Primo's an ape. He knows nothing about instruments. He knows nothing about art. To him it's just another commodity. Pork belly futures. Buy and sell. I don't know what tipped him off. I thought he'd just put it in his vault and let it sit there and appreciate in value.'

'Why would you think that?'

'Primo liked me. Because I had made him a lot of money as his insurance agent and because he liked showing me off to his pals. We'd go to a cocktail party and he'd say, "I'd like you to meet my lady insurance agent." He thought it was funny.'

'You were sleeping with him?'

'So what? I considered it part of my job. You may think that was immoral, mercenary or just basically disgusting, but I don't care. I had seen everything Borlotti had been doing under the radar. Everything. He was making money hand over fist, and let me remind you it was illegal. And no one had spotted it except me. I figured it was my turn.'

'Well, I hate to tell you, honey, that your risk assessment objectivity was clearly out of whack. You should've known you were playing with fire. You can talk all you want about Primo in love and Borlotti's chicanery, but there was only one thing that caused all of this. Greed. Your greed.'

'Call it what you will. Yes, I wanted to make money. But I swear that it was Borlotti who swindled us both. And you can't prove otherwise.'

'You don't think? Well, I see it a little differently. You figured that once you knew Borlotti was dead you could make up any cockamamie "Borlotti cheated me" tale you wanted and who could say otherwise? Right? But there's one other person who knows the truth, isn't there?'

'Who?'

'Vince Primo, Mr Chump himself. Hell hath no fury like a mob boss scammed. When Primo's lawyers finagle a plea deal in return for telling the DA who it was that swindled him in the first place, a swindle that led to two arsons and two murders, we'll hear his side of the story. Don't you suppose Primo might try to pin it on you? Don't you suppose he might tell them you tried to convince him that it was all Borlotti's fault only after he found out the violin was a fake. Don't you suppose he'll point out that you have two-and-a-half million dollars and he has nothing? We don't really know what he'll say, do we? But we do know he'll want to kill two birds with one stone, don't you think?'

'What two birds?'

'Reduce his own sentence and increase yours. Let me remind you, Vince Primo has never spent a day in prison. That's pretty good for an ape. He must have very convincing lawyers. I don't give you much of a chance against them.

'If, on the other hand, you were magnanimous enough to turn state's evidence in return for a lighter sentence, our good Lieutenant Brooks could put Primo in the slammer for as long as he's been drooling to, and you'd feel much safer for a long time. Win-win, don't you think?'

Forsythe hesitated.

'Tell them that I'm trying to help solve Borlotti's murder,' she said. 'Tell them I'll help them nail Primo. Tell them I want to cooperate.'

'And in return?'

'I want immunity. And protection.'

'Let me tell you a little story, honey,' Jacobus said. 'Once upon a time there was a construction worker. On Monday he opens his lunch box and in it is a peanut butter sandwich. He looks around at the rest of the crew and he sees roast beef, cold cuts, pastrami, you name it. Tuesday, same thing. Peanut butter sandwich and everyone else has something better. This goes on for a whole week. Finally on Friday he says, "Damnit! Why do I always have to have this crappy sandwich for lunch?" To which another worker says, "Quit bitching. If you don't like it, tell your wife to make you something else." To which our hero says, "My wife? I make my own lunch." So Ms Forsythe, I say to you, you have made your own peanut butter sandwich, and if you think I'm going to protect you after you threw Borlotti under the bus, you don't know the first thing about me.'

'Let me think about it,' she said.

'Good. You do that. That risk-benefit stuff really works, doesn't it? In the meantime there's just have one small item to take care of.'

'What's that?'

'Nab Vincenzo Primo. And you're going to help us.'

Jacobus beckoned Brooks and Miller over to their table, and within a half hour they had reached an informal agreement to go easy on Forsythe in return for her cooperation to apprehend Primo.

'So far, so good,' Brooks said. 'Now we go after Primo. That's going to be the hard part.'

'Actually,' said Jacobus, who already had the scheme outlined in his head, 'it may be easier done than said.'

THIRTY-SIX

Friday, January 13

'Yeah?' Primo asked over the phone. His voice was dismissive.

'My name is Hitomi Sato.'

'A Jap?'

'I represent a consortium of Tokyo businessmen.'

'So what?'

'The consortium is interested in diversifying its investments. One area of investment they seek to expand is in art and musical instruments. A small part of their overall portfolio, of course. No more than one-hundred-million American dollars at this point.'

'What do you want from me?'

'It has come to our attention that you own a Stradivarius violin and might be interested in selling it.'

'How would your consortium know that?'

'We have been contacted by a woman named Minerva Forsythe. Is that name familiar to you?'

'It might be. What did she say about it?'

'She said that the violin was genuine and in excellent condition. That is our primary concern. Is her opinion trustworthy?'

There was a pause.

'It could be.'

'She said you might be willing to sell it for two million dollars.'

'Three.'

'I am authorized to spend two. I will need to report back to my supervisor for authorization to spend more.'

'You do that.'

'Of course, we will have to inspect the violin first.'

'Whatever.'

'Shall we set up an appointment, then?'

'How do I know this isn't a scam?'

'Like you, the businessmen I represent prefer to remain out of the public eye. If we decide to buy the violin we will pay you on the spot, in cash. If that is not acceptable, we need not discuss anything further.'

'I want names.'

'I am sorry to have troubled you. Thank you for your time.'

Again, there was silence.

'All right. Just be sure to bring the money. You better not be jerkin' me around.'

'Would tomorrow morning be acceptable? Nine o'clock?'

'I'll be here. I hear you Japs are the punctual type.'

'We don't wish to waste anyone's valuable time.'

'Virtuoso performance, Yumi,' Jacobus said, after she hung up.

'Piece of cake. Good thing you also taught me how to improvise.'

'What if he had insisted on who your supervisor was?'

'I would have given him your phone number.'

'It's out of order.'

'Exactly.'

When Boris Dedubian arrived from New York City, they had a quick lunch, then spent the rest of the day rehearsing and reviewing the details.

THIRTY-SEVEN

Saturday, January 14

F oot-high plowed snow had turned black and icy along the curbs. Snow that had gone unplowed formed a slippery slurry on the street and sidewalks, so there were few cars and even fewer pedestrians. Jacobus and Nathaniel, along with Lieutenant Brooks and Minerva Forsythe, sat in the refitted cargo area of a white, mildly dented van with a faded Kendall and Sons Heating logo on its exterior. Another van, inside of which was a squadron of heavily armed, uniformed G-BAT agents, idled at the corner. Across the street was the nondescript, cinderblock office of Prime Transport, located on an industrial side street in East Boston, spitting distance from Logan Airport.

Jacobus had never been to East Boston before.

'What's it like?' he asked Brooks.

'You know how they call Boston the Athens of America?'

'Yeah.'

'East Boston is the other part.'

A chauffeured, black Mercedes limousine pulled up in front of Prime Transport, from which Yumi and Boris Dedubian emerged. Dedubian, tall and regal, wore his usual custom-tailored Savile Row suit and silk tie. Yumi had bought a black, wool business suit for the occasion that was tight enough and short enough to show off all the important curves, but severe enough to show that she meant business. Crossing the street, her black patent leather high heels made exclamation points in the slush.

They walked up four icy steps and rang the doorbell. Boris Dedubian carried an empty violin case, ostensibly intended for the violin whose purchase they were about to negotiate. Embedded within the case's handle was the audio connection to the van. Yumi carried an attaché case, filled with the cash Forsythe had surrendered to Lieutenant Brooks as the downpayment for her redemption.

Jacobus's stomach tightened when he heard Yumi and Dedubian buzzed in. Before entering, Yumi was to bend down to wipe the slush off her high heel, and while doing so, surreptitiously insert an unnoticeable shim into the doorjamb. It was all Jacobus's plan, and even though everyone had gone along with it, now he was beginning to regret being so vengeful that he was being fast and easy with his friends' lives. Brooks had warned them that Primo would use his physical presence to intimidate – his square-shouldered, linebacker build; his hairy, powerful hands; his square, protruding chin. He would be in your face and challenge you to back away, and if you did, the game was over.

Yumi's voice, tinny and distant through the audio link, interrupted his thoughts. It was too late to go back.

'I am Hitomi Sato,' she said. 'May I present my business card.'

Yumi had designed a traditional card, Japanese on one side, English on the other, very formal and official looking. With Nathaniel playing the part of Primo, they had practiced the traditional Japanese method of exchanging *meishi*, a much more ritualized and meaningful ceremony for the Japanese than for Westerners. Yumi held the card in both hands, English side up with the text facing Nathaniel. They had gone through every possible scenario, from Primo being impressed to Primo calling in his henchmen. It wasn't that Yumi didn't know the ritual. It was to get the butterflies out. To make sure her hands didn't shake and her voice didn't quaver. The preparation had had all the intensity of a dress rehearsal for a Carnegie Hall debut. And since Yumi, the violinist, had experienced that, Jacobus concluded she would also survive this ordeal.

There was silence in the office of Prime Transport. Presumably Primo was examining the business card. A light, flapping sound through the wire caught Jacobus's attention.

'What's that?'

'They're being patted down,' Brooks said. 'His men are checking for weapons and bugs.'

'Who's he?' Primo finally said with undisguised suspicion and menace.

'May I present Mr Boris Dedubian?' Yumi replied, unperturbed. 'He is a highly respected violin expert and will inspect the violin. Here are his credentials. His phone number is on the cover letter in case you would like to call his office.'

'You didn't say anything about bringing a so-called expert,' Primo said.

Jacobus, in the van, held his breath. Nathaniel began to say something, but Jacobus put his index finger to his lips, intent on hearing the words they had practiced.

'Surely you wouldn't purchase merchandise of any kind without being entirely certain what you are buying,' Yumi said. 'We feel the same way. As your President Reagan recently stated, "Trust, but verify." If you are confident the violin is authentic, this will be a mere formality. You have nothing to be worried about.'

'Like hell I don't!' Primo barked. 'I know what you're trying to do. You're just trying to Jew down the price. Get the hell out of here.'

'I'm sorry we have wasted your time,' Yumi said. 'We wish you success selling your violin. Elsewhere.'

With that, Jacobus heard Yumi and Dedubian turn to leave. This was the crucial moment. Jacobus had forewarned her that as much as Primo wanted his two-and-a-half million, he would believe the deal was for real only when he was convinced she would walk away from it.

Dedubian's involvement had been crucial. Jacobus had not believed Forsythe's contention that the reason Primo hadn't insured his violin was out of concern for personal privacy. And clearly, with the deaths of Borlotti and Falcone, and with Forsythe's efforts to stay clear of him, no conclusion could be reached other than that Primo had somehow discovered the violin was a fake. Jacobus had needed to find out how.

Dedubian had called his colleagues worldwide. He was well aware that violin dealers have not shown themselves averse to occasionally denigrating a rival's opinion about a certain violin in order to achieve a competitive edge, even though a violin dealer's reputation could be ruined by a single mistaken opinion of an instrument. But when a multi-million-dollar scandal is afoot, dealers circle their wagons. Word spreads through the grapevine quickly and accurately.

In this case it hadn't. No one had heard of Borlotti, ironically, until his disappearance was in the news. They knew nothing of his violins, including a fake Stradivarius. Dedubian had to dig deeply into his network to unearth the crucial information.

Dedubian learned that Primo had quietly taken the violin to Taylor Bradford, a well-known violin dealer in Boston, for an insurance appraisal. Clearly, Forsythe had not been convincing enough to dissuade him from seeking insurance. Primo's choice of Bradford had nothing to do with his Boston proximity but everything to do with family relations. Bradford's brother-in-law, Kevin Connolly, was the Speaker in the Massachusetts House of Representatives.

Bradford examined the violin and determined it was not original. Primo was not happy to hear this and showed him the certificate.

'Yes,' Bradford said. 'The certificate may be original, but so what? Borlotti is a nobody. You would need someone with an international reputation to corroborate it, so in itself it's not worth anything. In any event, even if the certificate is original, the violin is not. In my opinion.'

After that, Primo swore Bradford to secrecy, which he was able to do because Primo threatened to expose certain idiosyncrasies in the state budget having to do with Connolly's district if the violin's uncertain origin became public knowledge. But the strength of the violin fraternity was too strong. Trading future favors, Dedubian prevailed in overcoming Bradford's fears. Bradford had sworn Dedubian to secrecy, which lasted as long as it took to call Jacobus. The only critical thing for Jacobus was that Primo, who made no further attempts to insure the violin, knew it was a fake.

Jacobus heard Primo's office door open through the audio feed. One more step and Yumi and Dedubian would be out. It would be over and they would have to go back to square one.

'I tell you what?' Primo said. 'Have your Mr Doobie here take a look. If he says it's for real I get my three million. If he says it isn't, he still writes a letter saying that it is and I let the two of you walk out of here intact. That's the deal.'

'If Mr Dedubian says the violin is authentic,' Yumi said without hesitation, 'we will pay you an amount with which you will be totally satisfied. I can't speak for Mr Dedubian more than that.'

'What does Doobie have to say?' Primo asked.

'Your concerns are probably irrelevant,' Dedubian said. His tone, usually so suave and genteel, was stiff and less assured than Yumi's. To Jacobus, the words sounded memorized rather than responsive to the moment. *Wouldn't have made a great violinist*, he thought. He hoped Primo would be so intent on getting his money that he'd overlook Dedubian's unconvincing performance. He fretted that Dedubian wouldn't warm to the task. There was a long way to go. 'We have no reason to believe it is not a Stradivarius,' Dedubian continued, 'so why don't we just take a look at it first?'

'All right. Let's get this over with.'

The hollow, wooden ring of a violin landing on a desk or table echoed through the wire and made Jacobus cringe. Forsythe had told the truth about one thing. Primo truly had no idea how to handle valuable instruments and he probably didn't know the difference between Mozart and Manilow. But then Jacobus reminded himself that the violin was not a Stradivarius, but a fake. Just like the set-up he had devised.

As Jacobus had instructed, Dedubian took his sweet time. He gave Primo a primer in violin history and how to spot forgeries, just as he had given to Jacobus in New York. *Make him sweat*, Jacobus had said. *The more impatient you make him, the more you make him want that money, the less he'll be aware of the trap he's in.* So Primo learned more than he bargained for regarding every aspect of the age-old debate about the secret of Stradivari's varnish – 'some even think there is urine in it' – the differences between his Long Pattern and Golden Period, and all those great musicians who absent-mindedly left their precious Strads in taxis or on top of cars.

Jacobus, in the van, said to Nathaniel, 'All this crap about violins and not a word about the sound of them.'

'You're thinking like a musician, Jake,' Nathaniel responded. Even though they were in a soundproof van, he still whispered. 'With these fiddles you have to think like a collector or investor. The important things are name, authenticity, and condition. Sound is almost irrelevant. You have to channel your inner stockbroker.'

'Thank you for making my life meaningless.'

'Miss Sato,' Dedubian finally said, 'I find there is some difficulty with this violin. It clearly is the work of a fine maker, has wood from the period, and has the earmarks of an authentic Stradivarius.'

'What's your problem then?' Primo interrupted belligerently.

'You see, with such a famous maker we have accounted for all the extant violins. We know where all of Stradivari's violins are. He made hundreds, but we know them all. Who owns them. Who is trying to sell them. What museums they are in. The label in this one says 1708, but we know all the violins he made that year. To suddenly see a new Stradivari out of the blue is . . . Well, to say the least, it is unexpected. In all honesty, Miss Sato, I don't know what you should report to your superiors.'

'You want to see a certificate?' Primo shouted. 'I've got a certificate!'

'Certainly,' Dedubian replied. 'That would be very helpful.'

A desk drawer opened and slammed shut.

'Here,' Primo said. 'Take a good look.'

Dedubian took a very long look, though from his conversation with Bradford he already knew what he was going to see. Now he was playing his part like Laurence Olivier, though decades of practice in his profession made that habitual.

'This is a very authentic-looking document,' Dedubian said at last.

'I told you,' Primo said.

'However, the author of it – this Amadeo Borlotti – is not someone very highly respected in his field. He may indeed be right about the violin, but to be sure we would need to see its provenance – older documents by well-known luthiers or at least previous owners – to corroborate Mr Borlotti's opinion. So, in effect, what I am saying, and I'm sorry to say it, is that this document, however accurate and however well-intended, is essentially worthless.'

That was the cue for Lieutenant Brooks and Minerva Forsythe to slip out of the van. The agents from the other van emerged behind them. Under Brooks's strict orders, Jacobus and Nathaniel had to sit tight. If there was going to be any violence, Brooks argued, he didn't want to have to be responsible for their lives as well.

'I've had enough of your bullshit,' Primo said, almost cutting Dedubian off. 'Foreplay's over. Take it or leave it. I want three million.'

'I will have to consult my superiors,' Yumi said.

'No consulting,' Primo said. 'You buy it right now for two-and-a-half or it's off the market. Final offer.'

Yumi hesitated.

'Considering the uncertainty about the violin, I will take upon myself the risk of paying you two million. No more. Even this could put my future with the consortium in serious jeopardy.'

'If you don't buy it, it could put your future in jeopardy, period. Two-and-a-half.'

'That is not possible.'

The silence lasted forever. Jacobus had instructed Yumi that when they approached the endgame there would inevitably be an uncomfortable silence. Under no circumstances should she be the one to break it. If she did, at best the price would be higher. At worst, Primo would smell a set-up. But now Jacobus thought he might have overstated the case. He was certain Primo was about to walk away from the bargaining table.

'Hey, don't you Japs buy your sushi with yen?' Primo asked.

'What is your point, Mr Primo?'

'The value of the yen to the dollar changes everyday. Give me the two-and-a-half and wait until the yen gets stronger. Then you can sell the violin for more dollars on top of the appreciation.'

'You make a valid point in principle, Mr Primo, but to hope for a twenty-five percent surge in Japanese currency against the dollar would be a foolish investment strategy. That could take years, if ever.'

'All right, then. Two-and-a-quarter. That's it. Take it or leave it.'

'Actually, Mr Primo, I'm going to make you a final, generous offer. One million dollars. Take it or leave it.'

'What did I just hear you say?'

'I said one million dollars, Mr Primo. Take it or leave it.'

'I don't know what the hell—'

Jacobus held his breath.

'It has come to our attention that you engaged a gentleman by the name of Francis Falcone to burn down the house of, and then to murder Amadeo Borlotti, the very same violinmaker who wrote the certificate for your violin. You then ordered the execution of Mr Falcone. If you decline our generous offer of one million dollars, this is information that would be valuable to the authorities. Worth more, perhaps, than an investment in a bogus violin.'

'What is this? A frame-up? You got nothing on me!'

'You think not? After killing Mr Borlotti, Mr Falcone hid the body in a string bass case, which he then transported in a Prime Transport delivery truck to Logan Airport. There it was loaded on to a Prime Transport cargo plane and shipped to Cassalbuttano, Italy.'

'I don't know anything about any Mr Baloney Borlotti or any Mr Fucking Falcone.'

'You have no recollection of a phone conversation initiated by Mr Falcone to you shortly before his tragic demise? You were the only one who could have known he was hiding in his yacht, Torch Song. We can play a recording of that conversation to refresh your memory if you request—'

'Get the hell out of here!'

'We can share this recording with the police, or we can give you a million dollars for the violin and hand that recording over to you as a sign of good faith. It is your choice.'

He heard the clasps of the attaché case snap open.

'There is the recording. There is the money. Please count it, Mr Primo,' Yumi said. 'If you agree to our terms, it will be yours.'

Jacobus held his breath.

'OK. Just take the fucking violin and get the fuck out of here,' Primo said.

In tandem, Jacobus heard Dedubian close the violin case and Primo close the attaché case. With its click, Brooks burst through the office door, followed by the heavy tread of armed G-BAT agents.

'What the hell?' Primo screamed.

'Get your hands up!' Brooks ordered. 'All of you.'

'You're under arrest, Primo,' Brooks said, 'for the murders of Amadeo Borlotti and Francis Falcone. Not to mention the million-dollar fraud you just transacted.'

'Like hell I did!'

'Like hell you did!' said Minerva Forsythe, entering the office. 'And I'll testify to it!'

'You! You bitch! I'll kill you!'

Jacobus heard shouts and a scuffle and he feared the worst, but Primo and his outnumbered guards were subdued without a shot being fired. He heard Brooks read Primo his Miranda rights and then the wire went silent. Nathaniel helped Jacobus out of the back of the van.

The police escorted Primo into a patrol car, but Jacobus waited at a different one. He met Minerva Forsythe before she was placed in it, to be driven to the DA's office where she and her newly retained lawyer would continue to negotiate her plea deal. The two-million-two-hundred-fifty-thousand dollars she had voluntarily relinquished had already helped her cause. At least as far as the law was concerned.

'Now I have two fat lips, Mr Jacobus,' she said.

'Must make it difficult to smoke a pipe.'

'I hope they'll give me credit for taking my lumps.'

'There's a story,' Jacobus said, 'that after a recital by the great violinist Jascha Heifetz, an admirer went to congratulate him backstage. "Oh, Mr Heifetz," she said, "Your violin" – which happened to be a Stradivarius – "sounded so wonderful." Heifetz held the violin to his ear and responded by saying, "That's funny. I don't hear *anything*."'

'I don't understand what that has to do with anything.'

'I'm not surprised. The moral of the story, honey, is that if people like you realized that it's the music that's important, not the violin it's played on, our dear Mr Borlotti might still be alive today.'

THIRTY-EIGHT

I t wasn't the Last Supper. Jesus and the apostles had gone the way of Vivaldi and Corelli when Jacobus's house burned down. This puzzle was of the nearby bucolic Tanglewood Music Festival grounds in summer. Like its predecessor it was also five hundred pieces, so Jacobus, intent on fitting the last pieces of the Last Supper into place, pretended that it was.

Yumi baked a victory chocolate cake for dinner. As she sliced it – small portions for her and Jacobus, a quarter of the cake for Nathaniel – she said, 'In a way, I feel sorry for those people – Primo, Falcone, Forsythe, even Borlotti. They never heard the music in the violins. They only saw money.'

Maybe it's better to be blind, Jacobus thought.

'The crooks got their just desserts,' Nathaniel said, adding a third scoop of Rocky Road to his plate. 'Francis Falcone's dead. Vince Primo's going to be put away for a long time. Minerva Forsythe will be working on a plea deal for the foreseeable future.'

'Wasn't Minerva the Roman goddess of wisdom?' Yumi asked.

'The cunning Miss Calculation didn't learn much from her namesake, did she?' Jacobus said.

'And didn't Smetana compose an opera called *The Cunning Little Vixen*?' Nathaniel asked.

'Yeah, and Forsythe was both. Do you have any more dumb questions or are you going to let me finish this puzzle?'

'I don't know if this comes under that category,' Yumi said, 'but if Minerva Forsythe was so petrified of Primo, why did she go to you? Why didn't she go to the police in the first place?'

'She hoped the cops would catch Falcone or Primo and never even get wind of her. That way she could keep her two million dollars. But even her larceny was small potatoes compared to Primo's very large potatoes. Since he was responsible for hiring Falcone to commit arson and to murder Borlotti—'

'And probably a lot of other people—'

'It would then have been his word against hers,' Nathaniel said. 'And she's a real pro at putting on the innocence act. They wouldn't have believed that a seasoned thug like Primo could have been set up by sweet Minerva Forsythe.'

'She probably had her fingers crossed they'd kill him before he could talk,' Jacobus said. 'Ah! Problem solved.' Jacobus was referring not to the Forsythe saga, but to finding that there was only one more puzzle piece.

'That was so nice of Boris to help us!' Yumi said. 'He was risking his life!'

'He said he was happy to do his part to help keep predators out of the violin business,' Nathaniel responded.

'Other than himself,' Jacobus chuckled.

'What really scared me for a minute,' Yumi said, 'was that Boris was almost fooled about the violin!'

'What do you mean?' Jacobus asked.

'When he was telling Primo about how to spot a fake, he said' – and here Yumi imitated Dedubian's carefully cultivated European accent – '"It is easy enough to make the outside of a violin look old, but one of the telltale signs for a fake is the absence of dust on the inside." But when he looked inside Primo's instrument his face turned white.

'Later, Boris told me that it was very old dust. Borlotti must have brushed the dust and loose glue from a different violin, then applied it to all the wood of the fake Strad. He even blew it on to all the blocks and bass bar before he glued them so every part of it looked old. I can't imagine what would have happened if Boris had said the violin was a Strad!'

Yumi began to laugh.

'He seemed so scared to be in the same room with Primo,' she said. 'I was dying to hold his hand to reassure him, but I couldn't. That wouldn't have been an appropriate thing for "Hitomi Sato" to do.'

'I was worried when you told Primo that white lie about having a recording of the phone conversation,' Nathaniel said.

'Well, we did know from Falcone there was a conversation,' Yumi said, 'and we did know what it was about. And with everything being bugged and tapped and wired it seemed like something Primo would believe. When he saw the cassette sitting there next to the money in the briefcase his eyes almost bulged out of his head!'

'All's well that ends well,' Jacobus said, more intent on finishing his puzzle than hearing the whole post mortem.

He held the last puzzle piece in his right hand. As he felt with his left for the space in which to insert it the front door of Roy Miller's house opened. In burst Trotsky, as always irrepressibly delighted with everything. His claws were unable to gain traction on the tile floor. He spun a hundred-eighty degrees and careened into the table on which the puzzle sat, knocking it over and sending every piece flying, except the one that was still held high aloft in Jacobus's right hand.

Trotsky, sensing his offense, rolled over on to his back and wagged the stump of his tail in pitiable contrition. Yumi, afraid for the dog's imminent demise, said, 'Don't worry, Jake. I'll put it all back together.' Nathaniel said, 'That dog's in deeper doo-doo than Primo.' But while they anticipated Jacobus's explosion, he continued to hold the piece above his head like a statue, remaining unexpectedly and unaccountably silent.

'The last piece! I've been missing the last piece!' he finally said.

'It's in your hand, Jake,' Nathaniel said. 'Are you feeling all right?'

'Call the high school!' Jacobus said. 'Get me the office!'

'It's Saturday night, Jake,' Nathaniel said. 'They won't be open. What's the story?'

'Ubriaco! He never exactly said he was fired. He said "laid off" and "redundant." Maybe he quit *before* they decided to discontinue the school orchestra. We need to pay Jimmy a visit. And shovel that puzzle back in the box. I have a little gift for our friend.'

Yumi tested the speed limit on Route 41, keeping her eye out for black ice, and took the back road around Great Barrington, bypassing the traffic on Main Street.

'He's leaving,' Yumi shouted, as they pulled up in front of his house. 'With a U-Haul.'

'Block it,' Jacobus said.

He heard Ubriaco sit on his horn to get them to move. Yumi began to get out of the car.

'No!' Jacobus said. 'We wait in here until he gets out of his. Otherwise, he might just run your car over.'

'But why?'

'You'll see.'

Ubriaco finally silenced his horn. Jacobus heard him get out of his car.

'Nathaniel and I are getting out,' Jacobus said to Yumi. 'You stay in the car to cut off any escape route.'

'Mr Jacobus, Mr Williams,' Ubriaco said. 'To what do I owe the displeasure this time? First you try to run me out of town, and now you won't let me leave.'

'Going somewhere?' Jacobus asked.

'You better believe I am! Sunny California, here I come!'

'We've got a little bon voyage present for you. You might be going away for a long time.'

'A present?'

'Shall we go inside?'

'Why the hell not? It's cleared out, but at least we won't freeze our asses off.'

Jacobus signaled to Yumi to join them. Once inside Ubriaco's house, they stood in the empty space that used to be the living room. Ubriaco turned up the thermostat but then remembered that the utilities had been disconnected. Yumi handed Jacobus the jigsaw puzzle, who in turn presented it to Ubriaco.

'Ah, Tanglewood!' he said. 'That'll be a nice remembrance. Thanks.'

'Have you ever thought of yourself as a pomegranate in Jesus's face?' Jacobus asked.

'Can't say that ever occurred to me. Interesting concept, though. Why?'

'The last piece of the puzzle. Even though it fits, it's in the wrong place. Something a blind man might screw up . . . with a jigsaw puzzle.'

'You're a man of many riddles, Jacobus.'

'It's just that when your friend, Amadeo, called me on Christmas Eve I haven't been able to stop wondering, why call *me*? He hardly even knew who I was. I got to thinking, if you and he were so close why didn't he call *you* to tell you what his troubles were?'

'Yeah, that's been bugging me, too,' Ubriaco said. 'To tell you the truth, I felt a little deflated by that. Jealous, really. I suppose he just didn't want to burden me. Or he didn't want me to know he hadn't been on the up-and-up all these years. Geez, can you believe what he was into? I still have a hard time with that,' Ubriaco sighed. 'But I guess we'll never know, will we?'

'But we do know. Don't we, Jimmy?'

'Is this another riddle?'

'Not any more. The real reason he called me and not you is that there was no need to call you. You knew everything that was going on with Borlotti for the simple reason that you were part of it. A big part. Borlotti called me because he wanted to tell me about what *both* of you had been up to. That's the last piece of the puzzle, Jimmy.'

'You've got a great imagination, Mr Jacobus. And like I said when we first met, I've got a lot of sympathy for the disabled, so I won't take any of this personally. But now I gotta go, so if the young lady could move her car—'

'E-string tuners and fountain pen nibs and ten thousand dollars,' Jacobus said. 'What do those things have in common?'

'Is this one of those Mensa riddles?' Ubriaco asked. 'I'm still working on Jesus's pomegranate face.'

'None of those three things that should have been in Borlotti's house were there. If the tuners weren't there, that meant the violins had to have been removed before the fire.'

'That gangster, Falcone, stole them.'

'That's what I thought at first, too. With the delivery truck, and the tracks in the snow. It fit. But what didn't fit was that neither Falcone nor Primo knew anything about violins and cared even less. It probably would have given them extra pleasure to see them used as kindling. It had to have been someone else.

'Borlotti knew something terrible was bound to happen, that it was just a matter of time, so he thought about what precautions he could take. Sure, he had a security system, but even those are fallible, especially here in the Berkshires. What would have made more sense for true security than to give the violins to a trusted friend, a *paisano*, until the smoke cleared? And for doing him such an invaluable service, Borlotti took ten thousand bucks out of his personal till and gave it to you.

'Except the smoke only got a lot thicker when Borlotti's house got torched and he was murdered. And so you not only pocketed the money, you kept the violins, assuming the owners and insurers would think they had burned in the fire. You showed up at the police station the next morning, rending your vestments and gnashing your teeth. Poor, heartbroken Jimmy! It was a swell smokescreen.

'The missing nibs were a variation on the same theme as the tuners. If Borlotti were the forger, there would have been metal nibs, even if most of the other paraphernalia a forger would need – the paper, the ink, the glue, the pens – would have been incinerated. What threw me off were Borlotti's love letters and what Yumi told me about his flowing, old-fashioned handwriting. He had all the same earmarks as the forger of the certificates and labels inside the fiddles, so I assumed he was the one. But I was wrong. Though you can't believe much of what Minerva Forsythe ever said, she denied ever seeing Borlotti himself write a certificate. And I couldn't understand that when she coerced Borlotti into writing a certificate for her fake Strad he didn't forge an antique Wurlitzer or Francais one, which would have been convincing, but did it in his own name. It was because he *couldn't* forge it. What nailed it for me was that Benson never made any mention of nibs after they sifted through the remains of Borlotti's house. Unlikely as it seems, the true and simple reason for his flowery penmanship was he thought doing things the old-fashioned way was romantic and proper and would win over the heart of his beloved. Go figure! So it was a joint operation all along, eh, Jimmy? He made the fake fiddles. You made the fake documents.'

'You have no way of proving any of that.'

'Sure we do. Just open the U-Haul.'

'Why should I?'

'Because if you don't, we'll just have to wait here blocking your driveway until Benson and the rest of the Egremont Falls police department get here. And it's so damn cold. Don't you agree?'

No one spoke. Jacobus had said all he needed to and was disinclined to break the silence. In fact, he quite enjoyed it.

'What a night that was,' Ubriaco said, 'the night poor Amadeo died! Christmas Eve, of all nights,' Ubriaco said. '*Mi amico. Mi fratello*! It seems like a lifetime ago. He called me to his house because he was afraid they were after him. "Come to *my* house," I said, and I meant it. But he said, no, they would find him there anyway and then it would be the end of both of us. "Take the violins, though," he insisted. "Protect them, and if anything happens to me, give them back to the owners."

'So I hid them for safe-keeping. Who knew that bastard, Falcone, would burn down his house and everything in it? And then afterwards? Sure, I could have returned the violins, but Amadeo never got around to telling me who the owners were, so how was I supposed to find out? I'm no mind reader. Besides, which of the violins were really what Amadeo said they were? Most of them were secondhand fiddles that he'd doctored up or made himself. I only put the finishing touches on them by printing the fake labels and writing the phony certificates. So if the owners ever made insurance claims they'd end up getting a lot more than what the instruments were worth. Hey, that makes me sort of a Robin Hood, doesn't it?

'Boy, did I put my time in with those certificates! Not once were they ever questioned!'

'How did you get into forgery?' Nathaniel asked, out of professional curiosity.

'The Mormons.'

'I could have sworn you were a Catholic boy,' Jacobus said.

'It was that guy out in Utah, Mark Hoffman.'

'Who forged Mormon nineteenth-century religious documents a few years ago and sold them for a king's ransom to church officials,' Nathaniel replied. 'They actually consulted me, the FBI, and just about every other law enforcement agency about Hoffman. When he realized he was under suspicion, his paranoia took over and he blew up several people. Now he's doing life, all because the crackle pattern of the ink he used went the wrong way.'

'You blow up anyone lately, Jimmy?' Jacobus asked.

'So I learned my trade from Hoffman,' Ubriaco said. 'But, believe me, I would never kill anyone for any reason whatsoever. I confess, all the materials are in the U-Haul: old paper, old ink, old glue, old pens, you name it.'

'And the fiddles?'

'And the fiddles.'

'Which you were going to peddle in California,' Jacobus said, 'where you wouldn't have to worry about someone saying, "Hey, doesn't that violin belong to Joe Shmo?" Because all you need to do is replace the current fake label with another of your choosing, and then write out a new certificate to go with it that will look identical to any of the big, old reputable violin houses.'

'Yeah. I've got that all down pat,' Ubriaco said. 'But the main thing I learned from Hoffman's story is that it's not just the perfect forgery that convinces them. It's that if a buyer wants to believe something bad enough, he'll be convinced by anything. If you tell someone who really, really wants a Testore that a piece of crap fiddle is a Testore, you can give them a document written by a six-year-old and he'll believe it. It's the greed in people, I guess.

'But you know what the sad part is? Poor old Amadeo's violins were not crap. They were pretty good. Damn good. Made from that old wood. You can't forge that, now, can you? I wish I could've gotten that old wood from Amadeo's basement, but hey, you can't have everything.

'You know, it's kind of funny. When I started to back out of my driveway, I see your girl's shiny, red Camaro pulling up. I'm thinking, a prospective homebuyer! With a car like that someone's got a few bucks to throw around, right? I say to myself, not the best timing in the world, but what the hell? Maybe it's my lucky day and I can sell my house. What's another five minutes? Now I'm thinking five years. So, tell me, what do I do now, Jacobus?'

'When Benson gets here,' Jacobus said, 'throw yourself upon his mercy and tell him what you just told us. The truth. All of it. But don't mention we had to squeeze your balls to get it out of you.'

'I think I'll do just that, Jacobus. Meanwhile, while we wait, you want to help me with this jigsaw?'

THIRTY-NINE

Sunday, January 15

Jacobus, Nathaniel, and Yumi stood huddled at the empty place where his house once stood. It was a cold day, but the sun, rising above leafless trees over the frozen Williams River, warmed Jacobus's cheeks, and he supposed that felt good. Bare branches rattled against each other like bones. Melting snow seeped up through the soles of his shoes. He ignored Trotsky, whose barking beseeched them to play, and the thud of the dog's bulk as it landed on its back, rolling in the snow. Whatever conversation Yumi and Nathaniel were having was distant and Jacobus paid no attention. He felt no compunction to move from the spot. He could stay there for another minute or for the rest of his life. It didn't really matter. He felt neither happiness nor sadness. He felt nothing much at all.

He didn't move when Roy Miller's truck drove up, arriving with Sigurd Benson.

'Martha's made coffee for everyone back at the house,' Miller told them.

Benson reported that Jimmy Ubriaco's Barrington Savings safe deposit box had been flush with cash.

'His mountebank account,' Jacobus muttered.

'He came totally clean to me,' Benson said, whose swagger made it apparent he thought Ubriaco's flood of confession had been uncorked by his crack interrogation methods.

'His box had the ten thousand dollars that Borlotti had given him for safekeeping the violins and a heck of a lot more from their years of collaboration.'

'That's a surprise,' Jacobus said without surprise.

'It also contained Amadeo Borlotti's will, which appointed his friend, Jimmy Ubriaco, as his executor. Ubriaco swore the will was not a forgery.'

'You believe it?'

'Yes, I do. Because there was very little in it for him. Almost everything Borlotti owned, including the two-hundred-thirty-thousand dollars in his home safe, the insurance reimbursement from his destroyed home and business, and the money in the safety deposit box was left for Dahlia Maggette. But I do have some serious concerns as to whom the rightful owners of all those assets were.'

Jacobus silently vowed to make sure she got all of it. What she decided to do with the money was up to her.

'The violins, of course, will be returned to their rightful owners,' Benson continued, but Jacobus wasn't listening anymore.

'That'll be a relief to the insurance companies,' Nathaniel said. 'Some of those owners, though, are going to be pretty ambivalent when they learn that instead of possessing valuable old violins they're proud owners of a new Borlotti.'

'And how are things working out for your new house?' Benson asked Jacobus.

'Eh?'

'Tell him, Jake!' Nathaniel said. 'If you won't, I will. The insurance company didn't share our high opinion of his house's value no matter how much I argued with them. But after I inventoried all the contents, including his violin and hundreds of one-of-a-kind musical scores, recordings, memorabilia—'

'That we euphemistically used to call "his stuff," ' Yumi inserted.

'The overall payoff will be enough to build and furnish a better house than Jake ever had.'

'You kept documentation for all that?' Benson asked Jacobus.

'Ask Nathaniel,' Jacobus said.

'Between you and me,' Nathaniel continued, 'I took a page out of Jimmy Ubriaco's book and made a catalogue ex post facto. Dates and everything. The insurance company still needed some arm-twisting so I told them that if they didn't honor Jake's policy, it wouldn't look too good for them in the news that they threw an old blind man out on the street who had just put Vince Primo behind bars.'

'Isn't that sweet?' Jacobus asked. As much as he appreciated what Nathaniel had done, a new house would never restore his peace of mind. In a way, being out on the street would have afforded him more comfort. He almost longed for it. Starting over again was almost more of a burden than he could hope to endure. He could just stand on this spot until he was covered by snow and he wouldn't have minded.

'Don't forget to come to the house,' Miller said. He and Benson got into the truck.

'Come on, Jake,' Yumi said, with more enthusiasm than seemed warranted. 'A little hot coffee will do you good.'

She, Nathaniel, and Jacobus got into her Camaro and followed the truck to the Millers'. Martha had hot coffee and pastries waiting for them.

'What do you say we play some music for everyone?' Yumi said to Nathaniel when everyone was settled. 'I think we should celebrate Jake's new house with a little concert!'

Nathaniel heartily agreed, but Jacobus, who would never recover from the loss of his violin and could not bear being a mere listener, said, 'You go ahead. I think I'll just go to my room.'

There was a knock at Miller's door.

'Lieutenant Brooks!' Miller said. 'What a surprise! Come on in!'

'I can't stay long. I just wanted to drop a little something off for Mr Jacobus.'

Jacobus was in no mood for festivities. The last thing he wanted was a slice of Bundt cake or a new clock radio to celebrate his brand new house. He got up to leave, but Yumi almost tackled him to prevent him. He heard a box opening.

'I thought you might be able to use this,' Brooks said.

Jacobus felt Brooks place something in his hand. It fit with the familiarity of a painting returned to its impression on the wall where it had hung for fifty years. It was the neck of a violin.

'What the hell?' he asked.

'Mr Jacobus, congratulations! You're the proud owner of a new

Stradivarius! And I do mean new. We don't need it as evidence anymore and I figured it should have a good home.'

Jacobus played a few tentative notes on the violin made by Amadeo Borlotti. A sweet sound. Not like his old friend, his Gagliano. But sweet. And it would get better. Over time.

'And I just happened to bring the Corelli trios!' Yumi said.

'What do you say, Jake?' Nathaniel asked.

'You still know how to play the cello?' he responded.

From time to time Jacobus's memory betrayed him, and with the new violin he didn't play as well in tune, but they performed for the Millers, Benson, and Brooks for almost an hour, until Jacobus became too fatigued. With the evening nearing its end, Yumi announced she was returning to Italy 'to try out some new violins that Marcello wants me to play.' She would drive Nathaniel back to New York with her the next morning. Though Jacobus felt the emptiness of their imminent absence from his life, the promise of his new violin helped fill the void. He shook Brooks's hand and thanked him for it.

'No. It's me who should be thanking you,' Brooks said. 'Without your help I don't think we'd ever have cornered Primo. But, you know, one thing I'll always wonder about is how Primo figured out Falcone was hiding in his yacht. We thought the wife would lead us to him, but she was a decoy the whole time.'

'Yeah. Pirates of the Caribbean.' Jacobus faked a laugh. 'Wild goose chase.' He'd had enough of the conversation and wanted to get away.

'Someone must have tipped Primo off,' Brooks said.

'Really? Didn't you say Falcone asked him for help?'

'Yes, but he never told Primo where he was. And we had Primo's phone tapped. It's not foolproof, and I suppose someone could have given Primo a message in person. Maybe a letter, but who writes letters these days, right?'

'Telegram.'

Brooks laughed off that notion. Jacobus laughed along with him.

'We'll never know,' Brooks said.

'No, I guess you never will.'

AUTHOR'S NOTE

For the concertgoer, the world of classical music is a swirl of white tie and tails, elegant flourish, and ineffable beauty. What goes on backstage, though, can be, and often is, a cultural Dorian Gray. Just as Mozart's *Don Giovanni* shows us the ugly underbelly lurking behind the gay frivolity of eighteenth-century mores, the Daniel Jacobus mystery series holds a mirror to the glittery façade of the concert world, taking the reader deep into its murky recesses, where greed, ambition, and power supersede notions of collegial creation and artistic perfection.

Playing With Fire, the fifth book of the series, delves into the multi-million-dollar sleight-of-hand of violin dealing: forged instruments, counterfeit documents, manipulated valuations, and insurance fraud. In real life, countless unsuspecting and trusting musicians have been burned by devious dealers. In *Playing With Fire*, that figure of speech becomes more than a metaphor.

Not everyone in the violin and insurance fields is a scoundrel. Quite the contrary. Without an abundance of honest brokers, acquiring and maintaining valuable violins would be chaos for professional musicians. As with fine art, every violin is different. Unlike fine art, those differences among violins, even over almost five centuries of the instrument's existence, can be extraordinarily subtle. Any layperson can tell the difference between a Rembrandt and a Picasso. They might have a harder time between an Amati and a Vuillaume. And when attribution is not convincingly documented, and when experts learn more and more about certain makers and change their opinions, even honest brokers are bound to be second-guessed. For example, I've been the proud owner of a fine nineteenth-century Parisian violin bow since the late 1960s. Over the years, some of the most reputable bow experts in the world have identified its maker as Pierre Simon, Dominique Peccatte, and most recently Dominique's brother, Francois Peccatte, all of whom worked together in the same shop. Who knows what the verdict will be ten or twenty years from now? Of course, I have a certain rooting interest who the maker is, as it changes the market value by tens of thousands of dollars. For a violin bow! Thus enters the temptation for shady dealing.

Here's a true story from the dark side, which provided some of the background for *Playing With Fire*. It's compiled from 2012 news articles in *The Washington Post, Business Insider, Der Spiegel*, and Huffpost Arts & Culture:

On Friday, November 9, 2012, Dietmar Machold, described alternately as the violin-dealing world's Bernie Madoff and Jay Gatsby, was sentenced by Vienna's Criminal Court to six years in prison. It was four years less than the maximum he could have received, but the judge took Machold's partial confession and acceptance of responsibility for losses estimated at two hundred million dollars into consideration.

At its peak, Machold's empire had offices in Vienna, Berlin, Bremen, Zurich, New York, Chicago, Tokyo, and Seoul, where he bought and sold eighteenth-century string instruments valued at millions of dollars made by the likes of Stradivari and Guarneri. With the profits of his wheeling and dealing he maintained a lifestyle for which the word lavish would be an understatement. Ultimately, though, when he was finally caught it was determined the empire could more accurately have been described as a house of cards. Major banks had loaned him millions of dollars of credit, astoundingly, for violins they never even saw. Some of those instruments Machold did not actually own, or had appraised himself, or had allegedly forged certificates of provenance for, or had promised a single instrument to multiple banks for multiple loans, or were fakes, or never even existed. But because Machold, who lived in a fourteenth-century castle and drove a yellow Rolls Royce, was a charming and persuasive gentleman who lived the high life and clicked champagne glasses with the upper crust, he was taken at his word by those who should have known better.

Jet-setting Dietmar Machold, who escaped detection for so long by flying above the radar, ultimately paid the price for his crimes with prison time and public scorn. 'You played high and lost big,' Judge Claudia Moravec-Loidolt said to Machold when she handed down her sentence.

Amadeo Borlotti, in *Playing With Fire*, took the opposite tack, remaining *under* the radar, away from the limelight. A seemingly humble practitioner of his craft, Borlotti preferred the quiet life in the country. He even found love at an advanced age. But his larceny, which began as a typographical error in a bill for a violin repair, grew like a malignant tumor. In the end he became a helpless captive of his past indiscretions and was consumed by it.

ACKNOWLEDGEMENTS

Among the many good guys are several who were extremely generous with their time in helping me prepare the material for this book. Terry Borman, who made a wonderful violin for me in 1992, provided me with explosive insider information about flammable fluids in a violin shop and also offered some creative possibilities of what might lead a violinmaker into temptation. Timothy Stephenson, who lives up the block from me in Salt Lake City and who made me a fabulous copy of my Peccatte bow, gave me a detailed tour of his shop, including his store of aging, valuable wood, and gave me a seminar about his tools and supplies. Michael Selman, a fellow violin student at Yale and now an internationally renowned violin expert, provided an insider's look on high-level commerce in the violin world. Peter Prier, founder of the internationally famed Violin Making School of America in Salt Lake City, let me pick his brain while he did an amazing restoration of my 1785 Joseph Gagliano in 2014. Sadly, it was to be his last project, as he passed away in June of 2015. I think he would have been tickled to know that my character, Boris Dedubian, is partly based upon him.

For decades I have insured all of my instruments with Anderson Musical Instrument Insurance Solutions, LLC. I've known Peter Anderson, the company's Managing Member, from the early days of his practice. Peter was gracious enough to provide me with the ins and outs of that complex field. (Not that I understand all of it even now.) What happens financially when the status of a precious instrument is in limbo? At what point do we decide a violin has gone from lost to stolen? How is its value determined after it has been damaged and repaired? Which experts do we believe? What kind of corroboration is necessary? There is a very large gray area where the insurance and violin fields overlap, and it is only rarely black and white.

These days, traveling with instruments, especially on international flights, can be an unintentional and dispiriting adventure. Airlines have become fussy, and at times capricious, in deciding what they'll allow to be carried on. Instruments that are checked are sometimes damaged, usually inadvertently. Customs agents around the world have been known to confiscate million-dollar violins based upon arcane regulations, but which in reality seems little more than a whim. And most recently, the totally justifiable ban on commerce involving elephant ivory has made traveling with string instrument bows – many of which older ones have a fraction of an ounce of ivory at the tip – an absolute bureaucratic nightmare. John Demick, stage manager of the Boston Symphony and the guy in charge of shipping the musicians' instruments when the orchestra goes on tour, gave me the lowdown on the ever-changing sea of red tape and managed to keep a smile on his face the whole time. Well, almost the whole time. Paul Liddiard, who manages Mail Express in Salt Lake City and is the world's fastest package taper, took time out of his busy day to give me a tutorial on the art of shipping parcels from the U.S. abroad.

For all things Italian in *Playing With Fire*, a hearty *grazie mille* to my dear friend and colleague, Sergio Pallottelli, a fine musician with equally excellent culinary skills, with whom I've collaborated on many an enjoyable *concerto* and *cena*. Speaking of concertos, thanks to David Cowley, principal oboist of the BBC National Orchestra of Wales, for permission to share our translation of Vivaldi's sonnets for *The Four Seasons*. Over the course of the Jacobus series, the character Roy Miller has played a role. So thank you to my pals Joe Roy and his wife, Anne, for being such significant role models in *Playing With Fire*. Finally, because I was totally ignorant of how fires are fought in rural areas I turned to my friend, Jim Hallock. Jim, who plows my driveway in winter, cuts down my trees in summer, and is a former member of the vaunted West Stockbridge Fire Department in Massachusetts, was kind enough to explain in patient detail how the firemen extinguish a fire where there are no hydrants. Hopefully, I'll never have to call upon his firefighting skills.